THE ULTIMATE SACRIFICE 5

Anthony Fields

Lock Down Publications and Ca$h
Presents
The Ultimate Sacrifice 5
A Novel by *Anthony Fields*

Lock Down Publications
P.O. Box 944
Stockbridge, Ga 30281

Visit our website @
www.lockdownpublications.com

Lock Down Publications
Like our page on Facebook: Lock Down Publications @
www.facebook.com/lockdownpublications.ldp
Cover design and layout by: **Dynasty Cover Me**
Book interior design by: **Shawn Walker**

Stay Connected with Us!

Text **LOCKDOWN** to 22828 to stay up-to-date with
new releases, sneak peaks, contests and more...
Thank you.

Submission Guideline.

Submit the first three chapters of your completed manuscript to ldpsubmissions@gmail.com, subject line: Your book's title. The manuscript must be in a .doc file and sent as an attachment. Document should be in Times New Roman, double spaced and in size 12 font. Also, provide your synopsis and full contact information. If sending multiple submissions, they must each be in a separate email.

Have a story but no way to send it electronically? You can still submit to LDP/Ca$h Presents. Send in the first three chapters, written or typed, of your completed manuscript to:

LDP: Submissions Dept
P.O. Box 944
Stockbridge, Ga 30281

DO NOT send original manuscript. Must be a duplicate.

Provide your synopsis and a cover letter containing your full contact information.

Thanks for considering LDP and Ca$h Presents.

Anthony Fields

CHAPTER 1
MARNIE

CLICK...CLICK...CLICK...CLICK...

I squeezed my eyes shut tighter with every click of the gun, with every squeeze of the trigger. But why was I still able to squeeze? My pulling the trigger should've been over with the first explosion. The first time the firing pin shammed against the bullet in the chamber. I should've been dead three squeezes ago. But yet I wasn't. I opened my eyes and the brightness of the light bulb in the closet assaulted my irises. I looked at the gun quizzically. What had gone wrong? I was supposed to be dead. My body sprawled out on the floor, a pool of blood congealing by my head. I was supposed to feel no pain, but my death would be messy. I was supposed to be reunited with Khadafi on death's journey through the afterlife. I saw nothing visibly wrong with the Ruger nine millimeter so I put it back up to my temple and squeezed the trigger. *Click...Click...*

"Shit!" I muttered and ejected the clip out of the gun. As soon as I pulled the clip out, I could feel its lightness and I knew immediately that it was empty. But how could it be empty? I'd loaded it myself the last time I'd held it in my palm. Khadafi had had to come into her closet drawer and removed the bullets from the gun. Tha was the only explanation for why the clip was empty. But when had he done it and why? I turned to the dresser and rummaged through all the drawers in search of bullets. After not finding any, I went to Khadafi's walk-in closet to search for the small instruments of death. There were no bullets there either.

"Where can they be?" I asked aloud and scratched my head. My eyes scanned the entire room before a small voice in my head said, 'the basement...check the basement'. I darted down the stairs to the basement. I went through all the bags and boxes until I found several boxes of bullets. Bullets for guns of all calibers. Grabbing a box of nine millimeter bullets, I walked briskly back upstairs to my destiny and my date with death. As I methodically loaded 10 bullets into the clip, I invited the darkness and the quiet that death would bring. Out of all the 10 bullets, only one would be needed to send me on my way. A noise in the house caught my attention, but I passed it off as nothing. To my left, my pain stood leaning on the wall. Watching me. Waiting. I heard another noise, but again ignored it. Explained it away as frayed nerves. I gathered my wits, steadied my hand, and apologized again to my unborn child. My guiltless fetus growing in my belly. It would never see the light because the darkness beckoned.

"Khadafi is dead…"

I raised the gun and decided to put it in my mouth. There was no surviving that. I hooked my index finger around the gun's trigger. Tears fell down my cheeks. I heard something…

"MARNIE! N-O-O-O-O!"

Before I could seal the deal, my hand and the gun was yanked out of my mouth. Then the gun was wrestled away from me. Everything happened so fast, but the next thing I knew I was on the closet floor looking up into the face of my mother.

"What the fuck was you about to do? Huh?" My mother questioned. On her face was a hurt and wounded look that I'd never seen before. Tears fell down her cheeks. "Answer me, gawddammit! What was you about to do? Kill yourself?"

My lips moved but no words came out of my mouth. I couldn't speak. I didn't have the courage to tell my mother the truth. Suddenly, I was a child afraid of getting a beating for acting out in school.

"You selfish, stupid ass bitch!" My mother exploded. "You wanna die?"

My eyes watched as my mother's hand that held the gun in it, came up and was aimed directly at me.

"You wanna die? Kill yourself about that nothing ass nigga? I should kill you myself. You selfish muthafucka. I can't believe your stupid ass. You got a beautiful two year old daughter that loves you and needs you and this is what you wanna do to her? Fuck the rest of her life up having to grow up knowing that her weak ass mother killed herself? Because her father got shot? Bitch, you really are crazy, huh? Answer me! Sitting there looking all stupid and shit. Like the cat ate your tongue. You wanna kill yourself?"

"Yes!" I muttered and then covered my face in shame.

My mother stooped low and smacked at my hands that covered my face.

"What did you say? I couldn't hear you. Say it again. Say it again. Uncover your demon face and look at me. At least be woman enough to do that. You was just woman enough to stick a muthafucking loaded gun in your fuckin' mouth, be woman enough to face your mother." I kept my face covered. "You got an eight week old baby growing inside you. Does that mean anything to you? Huh? You inconsiderate, selfish ass heifer. I should smack your stupid ass with this gun. Take it and beat your stupid ass to death. But that's probably what you want, so I won't."

I couldn't face my mother, but her every word penetrated my heart.

"What if I wouldn't have come back here? What if I hadn't left Dada's bag over there by the bed? I would have lost my only child. Killed by her own hand. Did you ever stop to think about me? Huh? What about me, Marnie?"

All I could do was cry. Hard and loud. Each word stabbing me in the heart. Killing me softly. I wished now more than ever that the gun would have been loaded the first time I pulled the trigger. I wouldn't have to listen to my mother's words, feel her pain.

"You have no right! No fuckin' right to kill yourself. You didn't create yourself. You didn't give birth to yourself. You didn't carry yourself for nine months. Or change your own diapers. You didn't nurse yourself when you got sick. You didn't take care of yourself as a child. You didn't work to jobs to feed and clothed you and make sure that you had toys and shit.

"I did. I did all that shit for you. I gave up a lot of my dreams, my goals, my life to be there with and for you. When your father left us, I was devastated, Marnie! I was beside myself with grief and despair. I was fucked up mentally for a long time, but I never put no muthafuckin' gun in my mouth. Why? Because of you. I couldn't leave you by yourself. As sure as my name is Tawana Curry, I've had it rough.

"There's a lot of shit that you don't know. Things that I had to do to be able to take care of you, fucked up shit. But I did it and never complained. Did I? Did you ever hear me complain while I was raising you? I have loved you, Marnie, since the first time I felt you move inside my stomach. And you know that.

"So, how could you decide to kill yourself and take yourself away from me? From your daughter? And here I was thinking I raised a thorough bitch. One who could stand the test of time and never fold under any type of pressure. But I was wrong. I birthed a muthafuckin' sucka. A punk bitch. A selfish ass coward that can't live without her man. Tryna kill yourself about some dick..."

"He was more than that to me!" I screamed in my own defense.

"Oh, so now you can speak? After all I've said, you speak up to defend who you feel for that nothing ass thug? The same nigga that you inherited from your childhood friend after she died?"

"I can't help the way I feel. The way I've always felt. I love him!"

"Says that stupid bitch that tried to eat a bullet because the nigga got shot or might be headed back to prison. Like your life is over because of that. You can't possibly be that weak."

My mother still spoke of Khadafi as if he was still alive. There was no way that he could go back to prison from the grave. She didn't know. Then it started to make sense to me. If my mother would've known that Khadafi was dead, she would understand my heartache, my pain. My suicidal need for peace. "Khadafi's dead, Ma!"

"Dead?" she repeated. "When did he die?"

"When I got to the scene of the shooting, he was dead."

"And who told you that?"

"One of the cops at the scene. A black detective. He told me that Khadafi was dead. I fainted right there on the spot. When I woke up I was in the back of an ambulance. Then I came home and…I can't live without him, Ma. And if that makes me a coward, then so be it. I'm weak…for him."

"Aww, baby." My mother said as I felt her arms wrap around me. Her face pressed up against mine and I could feel her tears on me. "If you have to, you can live without him. And you will. You have to believe that. We gotta get you some help baby. Some professional help. I know a woman, a therapist named Sandra Sturgil…"

"I'm not crazy, Ma. I'm just head over heels in love with Khadafi. Nobody can help me. Unless they can bring him back from the dead."

"Marnie, baby, listen to me. Khadafi isn't dead."

An uncontrollable rage swept over me from out of nowhere. I wrestled myself out of my mother's embrace. I shot straight to my feet, eyes filled with tears. "Get off of me! How could you say that? How could you deny what I told you? What I know is the truth?"

Tawana Curry stood up then. "Whoever told you that Khadafi was dead…"

"What do you mean whoever told me…I told you who told me. The detective, the black detective, the one the regular cops called over to talk to me. He said he wasn't supposed to tell me because I wasn't next of kin…"

"I don't care who told you what. The detective was mistake. I have the news app on my phone and I started watching it the moment I got here to watch Dada. I checked it after I dropped Dada off to Wanda. And then again right before I walked in here minutes ago. Nothing's changed. Nobody died. I didn't for sure if the man who was in the gunfight with the police officer was Khadafi, but I know that neither man died. The news would've announced it if somebody died. The last thing it said was that both men suffered serious gunshot wounds and were rushed to local hospitals clinging to their lives. If that was Khadafi that got shot out there, he's still alive."

My mind had already received, processed, and accepted Khadafi's demise. To listen to my mother was only to invite false hope into my world along with deeper pain and hurt. It was easier to just deny the possibility of Khadafi being alive. "Khadafi's dead, Ma. The news is mistaken."

My mother wiped tears from her eyes. "Well, there's only one way to find out for your sake, I pray that I'm right. But no matter what we find out, you gotta get some help. All of this suicide shit, that ain't us, baby. Curry women are strong, black bitches. I don't know where you got that punk shit from. Had to be your father's side of the family."

"Ma, can you just leave that part alone for right now?"

"Okay. Okay, but real talk, Marnie, that shit wasn't cool. So as of right now, I'm not leaving your side for nothing. If Khadafi did die...God forbid...you gonna have to kill yourself over my dead body. Then Wanda can bury the both of us. Cause you ain't leaving here without me. And another thing, you ain't getting this stupid ass gun back, so don't even ask for it."

CHAPTER 2
DETECTIVE COREY WINSLOW

"What the hell happened out there?" Captain Greg Dunlap asked.

I was at P.G. Community Hospital talking to Rio Jefferson when the Captain walked up.

Rio finished the coffee in his cup before he responded to the captain. "All I know is that there was a shooting. I was called to the scene by one of the P.G. cops that knew me and Moe. I talked to Moe earlier today. I joked with him about what happened last night at the car lot on New York Avenue and the fact that he was in the dog house. He asked me about the case that Khadafi caught out Maryland, the domestic case. I gave him the run down on that.

"He asked me if I could get a copy of the 304 report and I told him that I could and I would get it to him. I asked him why he wanted it and he told me that he was following a hunch. We joked about his hunches and that people lost their jobs because of them. I told Moe, I'd get back at him and that's the last time we spoke. In light of all that's happened, knowing Moe like I do, he wanted the address of the residence that Khadafi was in the night he was arrested on the domestic beef."

"That's the house on Montrose Avenue?" I asked Rio.

Rio shook his head. "That residence was in Tacoma Park. But once the cop involved shooting hit the wire, Marjorie Duval, she works in ViCop, called me and told me that it might be Moe. She said that Moe called her and asked her for an address for Mary Henderson, that's Khadafi's aunt. She looked it up and gave it to him. The address she gave him was the one for the house on Montrose Avenue."

"That gung ho, stupid fuck..." Captain Dunlap uttered. "I should've left his ass on the couch at home. If he dies, it's my fault."

"Naw, Cap if Moe dies, it's Khadafi's fault." Rio stated emphatically. "He was off the force, I brought him back. If he makes it through this...he'll be kicked off the force this time and won't be coming back. Fuckin' Moe Tolliver, always hot dogging and lone

13

wolfing. I told his ass about that shit. Now look at him. The end run is gonna be hard to get around. He went across state lines to confront a criminal, that he had no warrant to arrest. He fucked up. We fucked up. The maneater is gonna eat our dicks for this shit." Captain Dunlap ran the palm of his hand down the length of his face. "Have you heard anything about his condition, Rio?"

"He's still in surgery, Captain. That's all I know."

"And what about Fuller? Is that piece of shit dead?"

"I wish that I could tell you he is, but I can't. Last I heard, he was taken to Medstar Montgomery and is in surgery, too. He had two guns. He shot Moe five times. Twice in the chest."

"He wasn't wearing a vest?" I asked.

"Yeah, he was wearing a vest, but the bastard Khadafi had a .45 ACP loaded with black talon rounds. They went through the vest like he wasn't wearing one."

"How the hell would he get access to Black Talons? They're only sold to law enforcement." Captain Dunlap queried.

Rio shrugged his shoulders. "Beats me. Either Khadafi has a connection on the force or he got em on the black market."

"Have you talked to anyone in Moe's family?"

"His girlfriend Dollicia." Rio retorted. "She's at a Realtor's Convention in San Diego, but she's catching the next bird back here tonight."

"Okay, good. Winslow, I want you to stay here and keep me posted on Moe's condition. As soon as he's out of surgery, I wanna know about it, okay."

I nodded my head, "I got you, Captain."

"Rio, you get to Montgomery Medstar and check on Khadafi. Tell the folks out Maryland, who exactly they're dealing with. Ask them if we could get access to them guns Khadafi had to cross check them with our ballistics to see if either weapon was used in a homicide in D.C. If he makes it out of surgery, I wanna know as soon as he does, do you hear me?" Rio nodded. "In the meantime I gotta see what we have to charge Khadafi with. And call Ann Sloan to try

14

and figure out how bad the blowback on this things is gonna be. You've both got my cell phone number. Use it."

I stood in my spot and watched the Captain leave. Then I turned to go to the cafeteria. Rio Jefferson headed for the exit. I called out to him stopping him in his tracks. "Hey, who in the hell is the Maneater that's gonna ear our dicks?" I asked.

Rio smiled, "The Maneater is the Chief of Police Kathy Lorey. You gotta watch her, bro, Cap's right, she'll eat you alive and spit you out. Call me when Moe's outta surgery, okay!"

"I got you, dawg. I got you."

Anthony Fields

CHAPTER 3
MARNIE

"The boyfriend of a Hagerstown woman has been charged with murder in the death of her eight year old daughter, who police say was tied up and beaten for eating cupcakes without permission. Police say that Leroy Williams, 27, beat Katrina Gardner on March 3rd after the girl's uncle, Andrew Bynum, 24, tied her to a kitchen table leg. Katrina's mother, Iris Gardner, later told police that she was at work at a local retail store during the attack and had left her daughter in the care of the two men. Katrina later died at a nearby hospital. The girl's mother and uncle have also been charged with murder and child abuse in connection with her deaths...

In other news, a decorated D.C. homicide detective is still fighting for his life at an area hospital after what Maryland authorities are calling an old West styled gunfight in Upper Marlboro, today. A thirty-one year old D.C. man is also fighting for his life in the case. Authorities have just released the identities of both men. The D.C. homicide detective has been identified as Detective Maurice Tolliver. The forty-two year old decorated detective has been at the Metropolitan Police force for over twenty-one years.

The Southeast man involved in the shooting has been identified as Luther Fuller. Mr. Fuller has an extensive history of committing violent crimes in the District and the surrounding areas. Nothing has been confirmed, but sources close to the scene tell us that the homicide detective worked a case last year that Luther Fuller was acquitted of in Superior Court. Sources also tell us that Luther Fuller is believed to be responsible for over twenty murders in the District. Authorities believe that the detective was attempting to arrest Fuller prior to the gun battle that ensued. Stay tuned to Eyewitness News Seven for more coverage on this still developing story."

I channel surfed for a while to see if any other news broadcasts were covering the story about Khadafi. They wasn't, so I clicked the T.V. off and just stared in space. Hope crept into my soul,

17

strengthening me as my spirits soared. My mother was right. The news said that Khadafi was alive, but fighting for his life. A smile crept across my face. "That's right, baby. Fight!" I stood up with the remote in my hand and danced around the living room. Something inside of me made do the Nae Nae.

"Marnie!" my mother cried out to me.

With the cordless house phone glued to her ear, my mother sat on a stool by the kitchen counter. She waved me over. She shushed me with one finger to her lips. "I'm taking notes ma'am, can you repeat that for me please?" My mother hit the speaker button on the phone.

"...A gunshot wound patient was brought in by ambulance. His wounds called for immediate surgery. He was taken to OR 4 and operated on, is still being operated on. As far as I know, the man is still in surgery."

"Thank you, Nurse Thomas, I appreciate the update."

"You're welcomed, Special Agent Curry. Anytime. Bye." The line went dead.

"*Special Agent Curry?*" I asked.

Sitting the cordless down on the counter, my mother looked at me and smiled. "You don't think they give that information to just anybody do you? Of course not, so I had to become Special Agent Tawana Curry, FBI liaison to the P.G. Police Department. I said it on the fly and she went for it, so...now do you believe me?"

I couldn't believe the turn of events. Two hours ago I thought Khadafi was dead. Two hours and one minute ago I had the barrel of a gun stuffed in my mouth ready to end my life. Now, I knew different. He was alive and I was alive because of reason known only to him, Khadafi took the bullets out of my gun. Without even knowing it, he had saved my life. I thought about everything in its entirety and just started laughing. I didn't even know what was funny. I just laughed, hard.

My laughter was infectious because my mother started laughing, too. "You are losing your damn mind. Why the hell are you laughing?"

I shrugged my shoulders and kept laughing.

"That nigga's dick is dangerous as shit. Got you in here acting crazy as hell. I need to find me some dick like that, that causes temporary insanity and schizophrenia. When your goofy, lunchin, ass get finish laughing, we're calling my friend Sandra the therapist and making an appointment for you to see her. We gotta figure this suicide shit out. I never want you to do no shit like that again. But before we do that, call your aunt Wanda and check on Dada and then tell her that we need her prayer circle to pray for Khadafi."

As quickly as it started, my laughter subsided. "I'm sorry, Ma. For everything. I love you!"

"I love you, too, baby. More than you will ever know. Get yourself together, so that we can get down to that hospital. But on the way, I need to make a stop."

"Make a stop where?"

"I need to stop by the nearest bridge, so that I can throw this damn gun in the water."

***

At the hospital, I just hovered around the lobby while my mother took charge. After a while, she walked up to me and said, "I just talked to the head nurse at the nurse's station…"

"It's the same nurse that you talked on the phone?"

"Naw, that's a different one there now. Her name is Jeffries. Anyway, she says that Khadafi is still in surgery and all we can do is wait."

And that's what we did, we waited. About forty minutes later, I saw a tired looking, short white doctor come into the room and walk up to a couple uniformed officers congregated there. They talked for about ten minutes as I tried to read the doctor's lips, and read his body language. I wondered if he was the doctor who'd operated on Khadafi. He had to be my mind said, if he was talking to the police.

"Ma, I think that's the doctor over there that operated on

Khadafi. The one talking to the police."

"You might be right, baby. Let me go and holla at that nurse again."

I watched my mother talking to the nurse and then she walked over to the doctor. They both looked in my direction. My mother waved me over.

"The quick response of the ambulance saved his life. He took a bullet to the shoulder. It damaged his rotary cuff, chipped some bone and then exited out of the back of the shoulder blade. One of the bullets ripped through his stomach causing severe damage to his small intestines and spleen. The spleen had to be removed. I was able to see that the small intestine had been damaged before..."

"He was stabbed repeatedly in the stomach years ago. He wore a colostomy bag for over a year." I interjected and said.

"We were able to repair most of the damage. The good thing about the small intestine is that we didn't have to remove any of it and it heals quickly. The bullet that he took to the chest did the most damage. It was precariously close to his heart. We had to fight to repair the left ventricle and valve near the myocardium. We had to do a transfusion because he'd lost a lot of blood. The last bullet that he took went into his pelvis and exited a testicle.

"What lasting effects that may have, we just aren't sure, but we worked hard and long and we were able to get him through the roughest moments. He's not completely out of the woods yet and the next 72 hours should let us know how he'll recover. Shortly, he will be moved to a private recovery room where I'm told he'll be under police guard. It will be weeks before he can receive visitors. I have to get going. You ladies have a good night."

"Thank you so much, doctor." I told the man. After he walked away, I lowered my head and said, "Thank you God. Thank you. Thank you."

"So what do we do now, girlfriend?" My mother asked.

I was just about to respond when I looked up and saw a familiar face. The detective that told me that Khadafi was dead earlier that day was over by the nurse's station talking to the uniformed cops.

20

"Ma, see the dude over there talking to the cops?"

"The one with the Helly Hansen coat on?"

"Yeah, him. That's the black detective that I told you about."

"The one that told you Khadafi was dead?"

"Yeah." I replied and got extremely upset. "Wait right here, I wanna have a word with the brotha."

I walked over to the trio of cops and waited until a break in their conversation came. Then I tapped the detective. "Excuse me, we met earlier today. On Montrose Avenue..."

The detective looked me up and down, then said, "I remember you. What can I do for you?"

"You lied to me earlier today and I wanna know why?"

"Oh...okay, you're Khadafi's girlfriend, right? Well, your boyfriend has killed more people than Ebola and you have the audacity to question me. Well since you asked, I'll tell you why I told you he was dead. That is the lie that you're referring to right? Me telling you Khadafi was dead?"

"That's right."

"I told you that because I hope that I could speak his death into existence. I thought that if I kept saying it, it would really happen. I prayed that it happened. But my prayers weren't answered and I couldn't speak his death into existence. I guess that means I won't be putting any money in the church's collection plate this Sunday. You win, I lose. Congratulations."

"I don't need your congratulations. And I don't care..."

"You're going to need something or someone, Ms. Curry. You are Monica Curry, right? Khadafi's girlfriend?"

"That would be me." I responded sassily.

"Well, you're gonna need a lot more than congratulations to help his ass this time. If he does survive this, he's going to prison forever. So, then again, you didn't win, because you'll never get to be with him again as a free man. I'm see to that."

"Yeah, whatever. Do what you gotta do. Have a nice day."

"And you do the same."

As I walked back over to my mother, my cell phone vibrated. I thought it might be my aunt Wanda, but it wasn't. It was a jail cell. After listening to the recording I pressed the five. "Hello!"

"Marnie, it's me, Bay One. What's going on with Khadafi?"

CHAPTER 4
BAY ONE

"Marnie, it's me, Bay One. What's going on with Khadafi? I just saw the news and they talking about a gunfight, and all this wild shit. Is baby boy, alright?"

"Hey, Bay. I'm at the hospital right now. We just talked to the doctor and he said that Khadafi was shot four times and he's in bad shape, but he's expected to fully recover. They way he'll be under a police guard or some shit and he won't be able to have visitors for weeks. Overall, I'm just glad that he's still here, Bay. I couldn't imagine my life without him."

"I feel you, boo. No bullshit. I'm still tryna find my way in the dark. My daughter was my light, you know? Esha, was my whole world and I'm lost without her here with me. So believe me when I say that I feel you."

"Bay, I always felt like Esha took sides in the beef with me and Kemie. That's why I didn't come around as much. But, I loved her, Bay. I loved Esha with all my heart and I miss her crazy ass. Believe it or not, I miss all my girls. I miss Dawn, Reesie, and Esha, a lot."

"You, too, huh. Every day I think about them. Kemie, too though. Girlfriend was crazy ass hell, too, but I loved her and I miss them all. Bean, Omar, Devon, Dean, Wayne-Wayne, Marquette. And now my nigga is all fucked up in the hospital. I can't take no more death, Marnie. I'ma lose it if Khadafi dies. Real talk. I'ma be a bitch's worst nightmare, in here. Somebody better pray for me."

"My baby is not gonna die, Bay. He's superman. He told me that once, you know. Do you need me to do anything for you? What's up?"

"I'm good, boo. Your man came to see me about a month ago and gave me the kiss of life, so I'm gucci. You just make sure you keep in touch and let me know what's up with my nigga. You hear me?"

"I hear you, Bay. And I got you. You know that."

"A'ight, boo. I'ma get off this jack. You be good and get some rest. I heard that you're pregnant again. Is that true?"

"It is. I'm two months pregnant."

"That's what's up. Give everybody my love. I'm out."

"Okay, Bay. Bye. I love you!"

"Love you, too, baby. Bye."

I ended the call with Marnie and replaced the receiver onto its hook. I sat at the table by the phone and thought about my situation. Especially after seeing the news broadcast. The detective that Khadafi banged it out with was the same detective who was the only witness against me in T.J.'s murder. With him incapacitated or even dead, there would be nobody to testify against me. So instead of sticking a cop to ten years. I could go for a trial and probably beat he charges. The wheels in my head started spinning ninety miles going north...

"The D.C. Homicide detective has been identified as Maurice Tolliver."

I thought back to the day I met the detective...

T.J. was in a crowd of dudes, standing in one of the courts in Capers projects. He was my target, my focus. I crept through the cuts between the buildings until I came out into the open behind the gathered crowd. I sprinted up to TJ and shot him three times. His body dropped immediately. Covering the extra ground in seconds, I was now up on him with my gun aimed at his head. Then I heard a voice scream, "Freeze! Police!" The lone figure walked slowly in my direction. I glanced in his direction momentarily.

"Put the gun down!" the cop yelled. "Drop it. Don't make me shoot you. Don't do it, Bay One." And I'm thinking to myself, "How does this cop know my name? Then the cop says, "He's not worth it. He's not worth you doing life in prison. Drop the gun, Bay One. Do it now! Drop the gun and it's over."

Time seem to pass in zero seconds. My heart was broken about my daughter and my vengeance hungered for blood. T.J.'s blood. And he lay wounded at my feet. I couldn't stop halfway through total annihilation. He could recover and seek his revenge out against me. I had to kill him.

"He killed my daughter. I was on the phone with her when he came in the house. I don't know why, but he killed my baby and I gotta make it right."

"Bay One, please..." the cop pleaded, but his pleas fell on deaf ears. "Put the gun down. Let the courts do their job..."

I pulled the trigger eight more times. With every bullet that entered his head I felt vindicated. I shot T.J. for myself, for Esha, for Dawn, for Tereasa, and the other people that he was rumored to have killed. The gun clicking on an empty clip, I dropped to my knees and put my hands behind my head.

"Now it's over." I mumbled to myself.

As the cop, cuffed me, he said, "You just did the world a favor. Don't ever forget that."

At the homicide division on Pennsylvania Avenue, I learned that that cops name was Maurice Tolliver. He told me that he had come there to the hood that day to arrest T.J. for Esha's murder. But it wasn't any jail in T.J.s future. Only cold earth and the darkness of death.

***

"That bitch Tika is wild as shit. She be telling on muthafuckas for nothing. What could she be benefiting? The broke bitch ain't got shit." Latonya Venable said as she blew weed smoke out of her nose. "She think ain't nobody hip to her hot ass, but I am. I'm hip to her."

I was laying on the floor with my feet under the side of the desk doing sit-ups while listening to my girls complain about the head detail chick named Mytika.

"I know that bitch fucked up. All up in here tryna jump on a bitch's case. I don't say shit to her ass." Thursday Jones commented. "She hang out in the police office all day. Ain't no telling what she telling them people."

"Tonya pass the muthafuckin' weed, bitch. With your deep throatin', deep lung ass." Tameka Murphy joked. She got the weed blunt and hit it deeply.

"Damn Linda Lovelace! And you calling me deep throat." Tonya said and everybody laughed. "Fuck Tika, dawg. That bitch been here for six years. Who the fuck does all their time in a detention center? Bitches leaving for the feds every other day around here, but not her. That bitch been the police if you ask me."

"I know one thing. This weed is like that."

Everybody cracked up laughing at Tameka's comment. But I kept doing sit-ups, silent the whole time, wondering if Mytika was the culprit responsible for the C.O.'s constant shaking my cell down for drugs. It was no secret to any of the women in the unit at CTF that I was the main supplier of drugs. The more I thought about it, Tika became the perfect candidate to be our rat.

"Bay, you gon hit the weed?" Thursday asked after pulling on it.

"Naw, I'm good. Pass it to Glo. She's over there in her own little world."

Gloria Dunbar was petite and beautiful, but she was also dangerous. Her murder game was well known to all the people in D.C. She reminded me of the bitch Angel El-Amir that was murdering shit years ago I the city. She accepted the outstretched blunt from Thursday and exhaled it three times, then exhaled. She blew weed smoke in the air, then she started to sing…

"…you said that memories never die/ just fill your head with why/ then you're caught living a lie again/ you said that, all he ever said was that he loved me today/ but then he's gone again and I was wrong again/ you think it's easier/ easy like that/ just when I wasn't finished/ you were gone like that/ can't you hear me crying/ cause I need you back/ I'm slowly dying/ cause I need you back/ but you're gone and never coming back/ gone and not coming back/ he's never coming back…"

When Gloria sang, it was from deep within her. Her voice was melodic and angelic. Sounds emanated from inside her and rose to her mouth. As she belted out the lyrics to Melanie Fiona's song, she made you feel every word. Everybody was dead quiet, listening to Gloria.

"Should've known/ the long kiss goodbye/ would bring sadness in my life/ wearing this disguise again/ I wish that you would've said or lied to me instead/ like a bullet to my head..."

I stopped my sit-ups and laid down on the blanket on the floor. I had no other choice but to listen to Gloria sing. But my mind wasn't on a man, my mind was on my daughter. Esha was gone and never coming back. Tears formed in my eyes and threatened to fall, but I wiped them away.

"Now, what was y'all bitches saying before my song came on?" Gloria asked.

"We were telling Bay how we think Tika is the rat that's getting our cells shook down."

"I'm sick of that bitch." Gloria ranted. "Bitches in here smoking and chilling tryna escape the reality of this fucked up spot, waiting to get sentenced to football numbers and this bitch wanna put the police on a muthafucka for that. I'ma kill that bitch. That's it. Fuck it."

The only person in the cell that knew that Gloria was serious was me. From one killer to another, I could see the look in her eyes. The conversation changed to another and then before we knew it, it was court time. As the other girls left the cell, I grabbed Gloria and told her that I needed to holla at her.

"Listen, I told Gloria once everybody had left. "I'ma kill Tika."

"What? Bay, why would you do that? I'ma get her her ass. I'm just waiting for the right time."

I shook my head. "Not gon happen. You already facing the death penalty out Virginia. I can't let you go out like that. I'ma take this one for the team."

"But why? When you can potentially get out after trial?"

"What can I say? I'm bored. Plus I'm sick of that bitch Tika myself."

"But how... how do you plan on doing it without getting caught"

"You just fall back and let me handle this. See you in the morning."

***

In order to kill a rat, you have to set a trap. I know that Mytika loved whatever drugs she could get her hands on. And raw dope was the one thing that I had plenty of thanks to Khadafi. For the next couple of days, I spoon fed Tika stepped on heroin. I cut it with coffee creamer and vitamins. Since both of us was on pussy and dope made Tika horny.

I had to put my disgust to the side and take one for the team. I never used dope while with Tika, just smoked weed. After eating her pussy a few times, I had the bitch geeking for more tongue and even more dope. Then early one morning on a weekend, I was in the cell fucking Tika with a makeshift dildo that I made. She had already cum twice and was high as a kite of the dope.

"I wanna do something different, Tika." I said in mid stroke.

"Oooh shit...you hit my spot. Like what?"

"I wanna choke you as I fuck you. One of my bitches did me before and the orgasm I had was some galactic, other world, shit. Ain't nothing like it. You gotta try it, Tika. I'm telling you."

"I don't know about all that freak shit, Bay."

"You scared to cum hard as hell?" I asked.

"Fuck no. I would love that shit." Tika retarted.

"Let's do it, then. Right now. First I'ma do you and then you can do it to me. I been wanting to see what this dick feels like anyway."

"I thought you was all the way butch."

"Usually, I am. But every now and then I feel like a nut."

"Almond Joys got nuts, Mounds don't."

"What?"

"That was a commercial back in the day. Lighten up."

28

"You with the rough fuck or what?"

"Come on. I'ma try sexual. I'll try anything once."

"That's my bitch." I told Tika as I raised up and took off my T-shirt. I ripped it into strips and then plaited it.

"This shit better be like you said it was, Bay. I wanna cum super hard and it better feel good."

"Oh, baby, you gon love it to death. You ready?"

Tika wiggled her naked ass in the air. "As I'll ever be. Get to it."

I laid on top of Tika and pushed the fake dick inside her. Then I put the braided shirt around her neck and held each end in one hand. Every time I gyrated the dick inside her pussy. I tightened my grip on the braided shirt. Tika's body moved beneath me like a stripper on a lap. I smiled as I tightened the cloth.

"Damn, Bay this shit feels bomb as fuck!"

I tightened the braided strips.

Suddenly, Tika's words cut off in her throat. She tried to say something but she couldn't.

I stopped grinding into her and used all my strength to choke the life out of Tika. She bucked underneath me and struggled to free herself from my death grip on the braided cloth. But I was too strong. Too determined to kill. Mytika Lemons days as a rat were over. I closed my eyes and pulled. And pulled and tightened. Even as Tika's movements ceased all together, I kept choking her ass. Then I started grinding the fake dick back inside of her.

In death, Tika's pussy had tightened up. I knew because it was harder and harder for me to thrust in and out. As quickly as it came, my black rage left. I raised up and made sure that Tika wasn't breathing. She wasn't. I cleaned up the cell to cover all traces of me being there. I put on my uniform shirt and hoped that my titties didn't bounce too much with a T-shirt on underneath. I dressed Tika and turned her over as if she was sleeping. Then I quietly left the cell.

CHAPTER 5

"Nicole, what's up homegirl?"

"Antonio, hey, boy you must be a mind reader."

"Why you say that?" Ameen asked.

"Because I was just reminding myself to call you and give you the latest news about your wife."

Ameen's hopes soared. "You found something?"

"My friend out Quentico called about a half an hour ago and told me that so far he's found about five different hits on your wife's name. The debit card that she's using is under Shawnay Dickerson and not Felder like you said."

"I figured that she'd revert back to her maiden name, but not so soon. What did he find? Where is she?"

"Before I tell you that, let me say this. I am really sorry about what happened to your daughter. I remember when she was little and you use to have her around the Park. And even though, you haven't told me everything, I can pretty much guess why your wife left you. I grew up with your crazy ass and I witnessed your last demonstration that sent you to prison for all them years, so I knew that all the recent murders in the city have something to do with your daughter. And that's just the investigator in me talking, so pay me no mind.

"Just wanted to get that off my chest. Back to the wife, who is one lucky woman if you ask me, one of the hits on the card was at a Chick-Fil-A in Suffolk Virginia. The next one was at a gas station in Richmond, she spent close to a hundred dollars on gas, so she's driving either a large van or a big SUV. There was a small purchase at a Target in Wellon North Carolina. Then another at South of the Border. The last hit was at a Waffle House in Columbia South Carolina..."

"My kids love waffles." Ameen muttered.

"What did you say?"

"Nothing. Go ahead with what you was saying."

"She hasn't used that card since, but when she does, he'll call me. He told me that a map would show that she's headed in one direction. She's definitely headed South, he says. Everywhere she stopped is right of I-95 South."

"That's good to know. Thanks a lot, Nic."

"Antonio, you know that I have always had a thing for your fine ass. I'd do anything for you with emphasis on anything. All you have to do is ask."

"You sure wasn't saying all that while I was in prison." Ameen said.

"I couldn't say it. I work for the city, you know I can't do no jails."

"I can dig it. It's all good. Don't even trip. I appreciate you though."

Ameen disconnected the call just in time for him to see Furquan headed for the door.

"I'm about to bounce, ock, you got everything else right?" Furquan asked.

"Yeah, I'm good. I got everything else, you go ahead and do you. Insha' Allah. I'll see you tomorrow."

Furquan El-Amin stopped in front of the exit door and said, "Ameen I hate to see you so down, ock. You go ahead and leave and let me close up the store."

"Naw, ock. I'm good. Wallahi. I'm messed up in the head a little, but I'm good."

"Just hate seeing you like this. Every day when I walk through the door, I pray that I see the old Ameen. May Allah give your heart some peace."

Ameen appreciated the kind gesture that the young Muslim was giving, but he knew that there wasn't peace for his heart to have. His daughter was murdered and his family was gone. "I'm good, ock. I just gotta find a way to deal with my reality right now."

"After all difficulty comes ease. The Quran tells us that."

"I hear you, ock, but you don't have a clue as to what ease is for me. I need to find my family and I need my daughter back, can the Quran tell me how to do that?"

"Astaghfiruallah, ock. I know you're hurting, but you gotta resist the whispers of the Shaitan. No matter how rough it gets and you're right, I have no clue about what you are going through, but still hold fast to the rope of Allah. And die not except in a state of Islam." With that said, Furquan turned and walked out the door.

Ameen thought about Furquan's words as he walked through the store and refolded clothes that had been taken off the shelves.

"Go through what I just went through for the last few months and then come and preach to me." Ameen said to himself, dismissing all thoughts of ayats from the Quran.

He knew how dangerously, close his soul was to the hellfire, but at the moment, he just didn't care. With the death of his daughter, his faith had been shaken to the core. He found himself questioning his beliefs more and more every day. No matter how hard Ameen tried to make sense of his situation, he couldn't. He had committed sins against humanity and he was alive, yet his daughter had committed no sins and yet she was dead.

Where was the fairness and equality in that, he asked himself every day. Then he became frustrated when no answers would come. Guns jammed, bullets missed their marks. People got shot multiple times every day and still survived. Why couldn't Kenya have been one of those stories?

Ameen let his thoughts go back to what Nicole had said on the phone. Apparently, Shawnay was in South Carolina or somewhere near there. Why had she chosen South as her desired path to disappear? And where exactly was she headed. Ameen remembered the night that he first discovered the house empty. He remembered the rage he felt. The vow that he made to find Shawnay and kill her. But as time went on, and days became a blur, he realized that Shawnay wasn't to blame for what happened.

He was. Her finding out about all the people he was killing in the streets, was his fault for not hiding his nefarious activities from her better. He'd inadvertently left the mask and black clothes in the basement by the washer. Shawnay had had every right to be afraid. Afraid for her safety as well as the kids. Her leaving was justified in his eyes. The rage he felt at first turned into acceptance and empathy. Ameen accepted why she'd left, but he couldn't accept the fact that he'd never see Shawnay or his children again.

To accept that would be to accept death. All that would be missing is dirt to cover his face. No matter how long the quest took, Ameen promised himself that he would never stop looking for his family. He had to find Shawnay and tell her that it was over and that she had won. Their enemies were dead and their lives could go on. They could start over again. Ameen believed that with all his heart. Now all he had to do was find his wife and convince her that what they had is worth saving. He hoped that it wasn't too late.

CHAPTER 6
SHAWNAY

Standing beside the bed, I stared down at my son's sleeping face. He laid on his side and snored a little. A smile crossed my face as I imagined the dreams of a three-year-old. I bent down and planted three soft kisses on his face just as I did every night since he was born. Kashon was a great kid. Born out of betrayal and lust, but nurtured in nothing but love. Every fiber of my being was connected to the little boy with ruddy brown curls and freckles, given to him by his father.

Whenever I stared at Kashon, I had to shake images of me and Khadafi out of my head. All of the steamy, passionate nights and days we'd spent together which eventually produced my son. My baby. My future. I looked across the hotel room and spotted my thirteen-year-old daughter Asia totally absorbed on her cell phone, texting and surfing the internet. Her sweatpants lay in a heep at her feet with her socks and tennis shoes.

"Asia, get your clothes up off the floor and go take your shower, so that I can get in the bathroom next."

"Okay, Ma. Just let me finish this…"

"Now, Asia!" I said sternly.

"Okay, okay." Asia replied, gathered her clothes and disappeared into the bathroom.

"Bring the cellphone back out here, Asia. Now!"

My daughter appeared with a shy smile on her face. "Dag, Ma, you gotta miss something sometimes." She tossed her phone onto the other bed and went back into the bathroom.

I walked around the room picking up Kashon's things wondering how life would turn out for us. My impromptu move was well thought out, but hastily executed. I thought about all of my family's belongings that I'd taken and put into storage. At some point I'd have to return to Arlington to recover those things and that's what I dreaded the most. Antonio was Arlington.

The man that I loved more than my own breath. The man that was no good for me and my children. The man that loved us with all his heart. The man that I was on the run from. I thought about my decision to leave Antonio and knew that I had made the right one. It hurt like hell to be away from my husband every day. my soul felt his absence.

But my motherly instincts were in survival mode. I had to protect my children. The ones that I had left. I had already failed in protecting my oldest daughter. Visions of Kenya brought pain to my heart and tears to my eyes as always. Men are not the only ones who cry in the dark. Women do too, so I let my tears fall unabated. I missed my daughter like hell. I still couldn't believe that she was really dead.

I sat on the bed that my son slept in and listened to the shower water running in the bathroom. And I let my tears fall. I thought about Kenya and the events that lead to her death. I thought about Antonio and all the people that he'd killed to avenge her death. I thought about all the innocent people and all the heartbroken parents. Then I thought about the night I told Antonio that I'd leave if he didn't stop killing people. He thought I was joking. I wasn't. I could still see Antonio as he embraced Khadafi at the car lot.

That in itself told me a lot. I knew at that exact moment that I had to leave. If I didn't leave in the next day or so, I knew that I never would. So I made my plans and the next day I implemented them. I sold my car back to the dealer and got a check from them. I quit my job at the hospital, then went home with a rented Chevy Surburban and loaded it up with the things that I wanted to keep for me, Asia, and Kay Kay.

I drove that stuff to a storage unit in nearby Alexandria and left it. I picked up the kids, hit the highway, and never looked back. I heard the water shut off in the bathroom and quickly wiped my face and eyes I was still getting myself together when my daughter appeared too quickly. She looked at me and then looked away. I wondered exactly what part of my pain had she witnessed. Asia dressed briskly in pajamas and then walked over and sat beside me.

"Ma, what happened at home? Why are we here and where are we going? Why isn't Daddy with us? Did we leave because of what happened to Kenya? When are we going back home? Why can't I answer my phone when Daddy calls me? And why are you trying to pretend like you don't cry whenever you think me and Kay Kay are not looking." Asia asked at a rapid fire pace.

"Damn. Did you breathe at all just now? In between questions?"

"Ma, please, just answer the questions."

I turned away from my precarious teenage daughter and wondered just how much to tell her. Did I tell her the truth? Or fabricate something? How did a mother look her thirteen-year old child in the face and tell her that her father was a serial killer? How was I supposed to explain things to her so that she'd understand?

"There are a lot of things that I can't say, won't say. You'll understand better when you get older and have children of your own. Your father and I had a disagreement and I needed to leave. I needed to get you and Kay Kay away from the D.C. area before I lose another child. And baby, that would kill me for sure if something happened to you or your brother. Your father doesn't understand my reasons for wanting to leave but one day, he will.

"He'll see that the decisions I made are for the best. Best for me, you and Kay Kay. Your father is my husband, will always be my husband, and I love him to death, but I had to leave him behind. He has his store to run and other stuff that he wants to do. Did us leaving have something to do with what happened to Kenya? Not directly, but it's all related. We need a new start, somewhere different, where our grief isn't a constant reminder that Kenya's gone and we're still here.

"When are we going back to Arlington? Maybe never baby. If you decide to go back there as an adult, I can't stop you, but I may never go back there. The DMV holds too many painful memories for me. But nothing's etched in stone, you know. I might change my mind one day. And right now your father is looking for us. I didn't tell him where we were going because then I didn't even know. I just prayed and picked a direction to drive in. The South won.

37

"My plan is for us to drive far away until I feel like I've gotten enough miles between us and D.C. If you answer your phone and tell Daddy where we are, I will only head in another direction, so I'm asking you not answer his call. Just trust your mother for now and everything will be okay. In time you'll be able to talk to your father all you want. The rest, baby, will work itself out in due time. I just need you to do what I say and help me with Kay Kay.

"I know this abrupt move will be hard on you for a while. You'll miss school and all of your friends. But believe me, Asia, it's for the best right now. In a few months, you'll be fourteen-years-old with more responsibility. I need you to think like a fourteen-year-old and trust me. Do you trust me?"

Tears formed in Asia's eyes and fell down her pretty face. She looked just like Antonio and her hurt expression crushed me on the inside. She nodded her head. "I trust you, Ma."

I reached out and wiped tears from my daughter's eyes, oblivious to my own. "See, this is why I cry when I think that you and Kay Kay are not looking. Seeing you cry right now is breaking my heart. We are gonna be alright. I love you baby!"

"I love you, too, Ma. I love you, too!"

Eight Months Later...

Anthony Fields

CHAPTER 7
KHADAFI

"Trespassing is a crime, ain't it detective"

"Put your guns down, Khadafi."

"What about stalking? That's definitely a federal offense. How long have you been out here waiting for me? Or did you follow me here?"

"Doesn't matter, Khadafi. In a few minutes, this place is gonna be crawling with cops. If they see you with them guns pointed at me...you know what can happen. We all know how trigger happy P.G. County Police can be. Put your guns down and let's talk this thing out."

"Talk it out? It's a little too late for that. You're outta your jurisdiction. You're behind my people's house without permission, all alone and you're threatening me. What's there to talk, about?"

"Don't be stupid, Khadafi. Put the guns down."

"Last time I checked, cop. I never gave you permission to call me Khadafi. We ain't friends, so it's Mr. Fuller to you."

"Whatever you say. Just put the guns down before you make us both do something that we don't wanna do. Nobody has to die here today."

"Why not? It's a little cold, but the sun is shining. It's a beautiful day to die. But the thing is, I don't plan on being the one that dies today. You put your gun down and I promise I'll let you live. You walk away. I walk away and we do this another day. Nobody will ever know. How 'bout that, cuz?"

"I'm not gonna be able to do that, big guy. At the end of the day, I'll know that I walked away and I'd never be able to live with myself. You've killed too many people and it has to stop. Here. Now. You have to be stopped."

"And you plan on doing that, how?"

"By taking you in. By any means necessary on the kidnapping charge."

"There's no way in the world that I'ma let you arrest me. You must be putting gun powder in your coffee in the mornings, if you think I'ma lay down like that. I'm never going back to prison. Besides, I play the odds and at the moment, the odds are in my favor. You got one gun. I got two. Do the math. Then be smart and walk away."

"I already told you I can't do that and why. I need you to drop the guns and get down on your knees. Then lace your fingers together behind your head. I..."

"You must be crazy, cuz."

"I've been told that a time or two. C'mon, Khadafi, let it go. You don't want shooting a cop on your record. Do you? Do the right thing and drop the guns. Think about your little girl."

"Fuck you, cuz. How 'bout that. You don't know me or nothing about me. Let's see what's written in the stars for us, cop."

"Khadafi! Don't do it! Don't make me..."

"Bis''millah..."

Gunshots rang out, and then I opened my eyes to discover that I was in a cell. The same cell that I'd been in since being brought to Seven Lock Detention Center. Light from the lamps attached to the wall outside my window shone into the cell. I laid in the bed like I did every night after reliving the day that I thought that I would surely die. It was befitting of a gangsta to go out in a hail of bullets. Taking a cop with me was the ultimate prize. But again, I had survived. Battered and wounded, but never broke all the way. Alive, but back in the very place that I vowed to never return to. I thought about what I'd told the cop before I blazed my guns...

"Let's see what's written in the stars for us..."

I guess being back in jail was what was written in the stars for me. Because dying wasn't for some reason, known only to the creator. I was still alive. I'd taken for bullets and survived.

"You're a very lucky man." One doctor had said to me.

"God was not ready for you, yet." The hospital chaplain told me.

"From what I hear around here. Somebody up there is watching over you." The nurse that took care of me daily remarked one day as she bathed me.

After that day, I asked myself almost daily could it be true? Was there really someone in the spirit world protecting me from the Grim Reaper? It had to be some truth to it I concluded after a while. Otherwise how could I explain escaping deaths clutches so many times? The I lived my life, death was my constant companion. I lived with its breath, breathing on my back at every turn and corner, but yet it had failed to wring my life from my body.

"Somebody up there is watching over you."

I thought about my mother. She'd been dead since I was seven-years old. Was she the powerful spirit watching over me? Shielding me from death? Getting out of the bunk, I walked over to the mirror mounted on the wall. I was the man in the mirror. He was the only person that I couldn't hide from. I had to face myself every time I looked in the mirror. Everything about me was the same, but upon closer inspection, a lot about me was different. In the four months that I'd been in the detention center, I'd let my beard grow out.

My reddish, brown beard made me resemble Denzel Washington when he played Malcolm X in the movie. My eyes were brown, but they were so cold that they appeared ice blue. My hair was cut close to the scalp. Moving my shirt a little I saw the scar that the bullet in my shoulder left. I took the T-shirt off and stared at my body from the waist up. My scarred body told a story of the last few years that my mouth couldn't. It told of violence and near death experiences repeatedly.

My scars spoke of hurt, pain, betrayal, loyalty, and revenge. My scars spoke of being stabbed, being jumped and stomped, they spoke of being shot four times. My scars spoke of bruises that had healed, they spoke of blood that had been spilled. I looked in the mirror and let my fingers trace every scar on my body, remembering. I remembered the scar on my arm that the closet door's jagged edge put there as I hastily ran into it and hid while my mother was being killed by two men. There were scars on my back that I couldn't see, but the one on my neck I could. I stood in front of the mirror and remembered the day I sat in my Range Rover on MLK Avenue at a stoplight.

I remembered the dude with the choppa under a towel that let off maybe fifty rounds into my truck as I dove for cover. My scar intersected on my body. The old ones with the new ones. The new scar on my stomach ran over one of the ones Ameen put there when he stabbed me in Beaumont, Texas. A rec cage at the prison there was supposed to be where I lost my life. But again, I survived. Eight direct stab wounds to my stomach and chest couldn't kill me, didn't kill me. Neither could feet and fist when Lil' Cee and the bald head, black nigga jumped me and stomped me out at the all-white party in the Omni Shoreham Hotel one night.

I killed the bald headed nigga in the parking lot but Lil Cee got away. I had small scars that gave birth to small scratches still visible on me. Ones that were put there because I had to run through a plate glass window that had been shot out by bullets. I slipped on the broken glass and had to dig sherds out of my hands, arms, and legs. It seemed like everywhere I went somebody wanted my head, my blood to spill. I thought about the blood that Devon spilled of mine. After shooting me in the back and leg, he stood over me and kicked me several times. All the while, I laid on that ground on 3rd St. in Southwest and waited to die.

I knew that eventually his foot would be replaced by full metal jackets, but I was wrong. Devon thought I was dying already, because he started talking instead of killing. Then he wanted to look in my face, he said, to make sure I died. But that was a bad mistake on his part. I had my gun in my hand and when I turned over, I shot him. Stood up and killed him. My life saved by a bulletproof vest. In the mirror, I glanced to my left and let my right hand run over the two scars there. The two, two inch scars were as deep as they were long. The incident at D.C. jail came to mind.

Ameen was on a writ fighting his case and I was there after my shootout with TJ lead me on a high speed chase, where I had to run my car off a bridge to get rid of the guns inside it. Ameen pulled a

44

classic trick on me. He got me called out to the chapel while he waited for me under the escalator. I remembered our knife fight in the hallway. I ended up stabbed in the shoulder twice, once in my firearm and slashed across the cheek. I traced the scar on my cheek as if to touch it was affirmation that it happened. Finally I stepped away from the mirror and put my shirt back on.

My life was an open book and I was tired of reading it. At the bunk, I reached beneath the bed and pulled out a bundle of letters. The majority of the letters were from Marnie, but a few were from Erykah. She still belonged to my man Mousey, but she wanted me to know that I had put my mark on that pussy and that if I ever shined again, I could get it, whenever, wherever, however. I by-passed the letters from my homegirls Kesha and Bay One and stopped at the latest one I'd gotten from Marnie. I reached inside the envelope and pulled out the pictures, about twenty in all. I held the pictures of my one month old son, Khamani in my hand and stared at them.

The little dude was gorgeous. The spitting image of his mother, only with brownish, red curly hair. My son was a representation of everything good and wholesome in a crazy world. My heart warmed considerably every time I saw him, his tiny hands, his eyes, his tiny feet, and his smile. Marnie's smile. In one picture, my daughter almost three years old, held my son. Khadajah and Khamani, mini manifestations of me.

I loved them both with all my heart and soul. Looking at both of my children made my heart yearn for the oldest one. Kashon. Something tightened in my chest and felt like an unseen hand had squeezed the arteries leading to the hard pound heart muscle. It had been eight months since the shootout and my last near death experience. I hadn't heard from Ameen not one time. I wondered if Shawnay had come back to him or if she knew my predicament. Probably not.

I put aside thoughts of Shawnay like I always did and focused on the women that I loved and the one who loved me back. Marnie. Putting the pictures of my kids back in the envelope, I kept the ones in hand of Marnie. One month after having my son, Marnie's body looked incredible. I juggled picture after picture of her in different positions, dressed in nothing but a see through tank top and matching thong panties. My eyes focused on Marnie's pretty feet, her toes the color of ripe oranges. Her fingernails the same color.

Her stomach was flat and unblemished. Her ass still phat and juicy looking. I stared at Marnie's pussy print and as always my dick got hard. I laid the pictures on the bed where the most light from the window could illuminate them so that I could see them clear. I lined Marnie's pictures up side by side and saw her on our bed on all fours as she looked back over her shoulder. I saw her standing, but bent over the bed. In one picture she lay on the bed, spread eagle with her fingers in her panties.

My eyes scanned every photo as my mind remembered all the times, I'd fucked Marnie in those positions. Then like a real locked up nigga, I pulled my dick out of the slit in my boxers and stroked it. I scanned the pictures and stroked. Stroked and scanned. In my head, I could hear the passionate sounds that Marnie made when she had that dick in her. Then as quickly as it started, it was over fast. I bust a nut all over my fist and the concrete floor.

***

The next morning as soon as I came out of the cell, the nurse rolled a medicine cart into the pod. The African nurse was pretty as hell with a nice body and all the niggas in the unit knew it. So, all the weird niggas came out the woodwork. The perverts, the gunners, the niggas who would rape a bitch. I'd been in prison all my life and knew that some men got off by doing a rack of freak shit, but I vowed to myself that if any dude on the pod ever pulled out his dick while I was around, that I was gonna kill him.

"Fuller!" The nurse called out. "Luther Fuller!"

I walked up to the nurse's cart and flashed my wristband that had a picture of me on it, my name and my Maryland DOC number on it.

"Here's your diazepam, sir. Your lutel butins, and your blood thinners."

I popped the blood thinner in my mouth, but cuffed the other two pills and walked away. The other meds were just muscle relaxers and a pain pill. I flushed them down the toilet in my cell and then went to the phone mounted on the wall by the T.V. room. I dialed Marnie's cell phone number.

She answered on the second ring. "Hey, baby!"

"What's up, cuz? How you doing?"

"I'm good. On my way to see my doctor. Dada and Mani are with my mother. How you doing?"

"I'm good. You know me. Suppose to see my lawyer in a day or two. Did you give him that money yet?"

"Naw, because you told me not to pay it out of what I have. You told me to get the money from Pee-Wee and I haven't caught him yet. What you want me to do?"

"I got more than enough money at my aunt's house, but I want Pee-Wee to pay that. That nigga making money off my shit and he need to do that. I couldn't catch him neither, but I'm not gonna think bad thoughts. That's my man, he'll play fair and pay the lawyer. Just keep calling him."

"I got you, baby. Anything else?"

"Yeah. What color panties are you wearing?"

CHAPTER 8
MARNIE

"What color are my panties? Uh...they are..." I had to undo my pants to look and see. "black. Black with lace butterflies all over them."

"Is that pussy wet?"

"It's always wet and you know that."

"Rub that clit for me, Marnie."

"Bay, are you crazy? How I'ma do that while I'm driving?"

"Well, stop driving then. Find somewhere to pull over for a minute."

"Khadafi, I just told your ass that I'm on my way to see my doctor."

"So, what. You can be a few minutes late. What are you driving?"

"I'm driving the Escalade. Why?" I asked.

"Do you remember back when I first copped that Escalade?"

Khadafi thought he was being slick, but I knew exactly where he was headed. "I do."

"You remember what we did in the Escalade the day I copped it?"

"The same thing we did in your first Range Rover, the second one, and the Infinite truck."

Khadafi laughed, then said, "I remember the day I first picked you up in the Escalade. You had on some tight ass jeans and that hitting ass BeBe shirt with the black Gucci tennis shoes. I remember how you couldn't wait for me to stop the truck, so you climbed onto your knees and leaned over into my seat. You pulled my..."

"Dick out and sucked it while you drove the truck." I said nostalgically. "I remember that day. Let me pull this truck over before I get I a wreck." I pulled off of 16th Street onto Meridian Hill Road. I parked the truck and then said into the phone. "Okay, finish what you was saying."

"I wasn't saying shit. You was. I started it and you took over. You wearing pants?"

"I better be. It's winter time out here."

"Well, unbutton your pants. As a matter of fact, take them pants off." Khadafi demanded.

"These windows ain't tinted and I'm right by Howard University's dorm…"

"I don't care. Take 'em off."

Furtively I scanned the street I was on and saw that the majority of the pedestrian traffic was on 16th and not Meridian. "Hold on. I'm taking them off." I lifted my body and wiggled out of my Rock and Republic jeans, after kicking off my boots. Then I removed my panties. "They're off."

"What color are them toes?"

"They are candy apple red, but I still got my socks on."

"That's cool. Where are your panties at?"

"On the floorboard by my pants."

"Lift one of your legs up and put your fingers in that wet pussy."

I closed my eyes and did whatever Khadafi said.

"Now play with that pussy while you listen to me. I wanna hear you cum…Right there in that truck you in right now, I sat where you're sitting and looked down at your head bobbing up and down in my lap. Your mouth felt so good on my dick, Marnie…damn, your head was bomb as shit. Your tongue was so wet and your lips so damn pretty. I had to pull over and let you do you. I remember how your hand gripped this dick as you stroked it as you sucked it. My dick is rock hard right now…"

Listening to Khadafi narrate the story as I remembered it myself, made me extremely horny and my pussy super wet. My juices coated my fingers and ran down my pussy to my ass and pooled on the seat. "Oooh shit…I'm wet as shit, baby…the seat is wet already."

"That's right, baby, wet that seat up like you use to do. I wish that I could see it and taste it."

"Oooh…ooh I wish you could, too. Umm…I'm wet as shit…"

"I pulled over on 60th Street by Eastern Avenue, you remember that?"

My fingers had a mind of their own now and positioned in and out of me at a fast pace as I massaged my spot in me. "Uh huh...I remember I sucked your dick right there. I loved sucking your dick. It tasted so good, Khadafi, damn!"

"Then we crawled into the backseat and I took off your jeans. I wanted that pussy so bad that I just pulled your panties to the side..."

"Oooh...shit...shit...you gon' make me..."

"I put your feet on my shoulders and slid that dick in you deep."

"Too deep. It was in me too deep like that."

"You like it, though. Your pussy was so tight and good. Wet and tight and warm. "I didn't care who saw us, I was gonna fuck that pussy until you came on my dick. Cum on my dick for me, Marnie. Cum for me. Squirt for me. Squirt that cum all over them seats like you used to do. I wish that I could fuck you. I know that pussy good. You ain't had no dick in almost nine months, I know that pussy good and tight."

"It is...it's tight...it's real tight. Too wet. I'm too wet..."

"I want you to suck my dick so bad and ride this dick. I want to hit that pussy from the back. I want us to have some more kids."

"Me, too, baby. Me too...aww...aww...ooh...shit, I'm 'bout to cum, boy!"

"Cum for me then. Cum for me, Marnie!"

"Here it come, boy...here it come...see what you done...aww...aww...aww fuck...shit, here is comes...I'm cumming! I'm cumming!" My orgasm started in my feet and rose slowly up to my leg to my pussy. Juices poured out of me like a water faucet was on in the truck. My body shook and convulsed like I had gotten hit by a thousand volts of electricity. I came hard and long and it took a while for me to recover. I leaned back in the driver's seat with my legs wide open for the world to see. My left foot was propped up on the dashboard and my right foot was by the gear shift lever.

"Now lick your fingers clean for me." Khadafi ordered.

I put both fingers in my mouth that had just been inside me and sucked them dry. The sucking sounds I made reminiscent of me sucking Khadafi's dick. "Can I go to my doctor's appointment, now, nasty ass?"

"Yeah, go ahead. I'm about to go in the cell and beat my dick. I'ma call you back later on. And don't forget to call Pee-Wee back."

"I got you baby. Don't even trip. Talk to you later. Bye."

***

Finishing my cup of Pumpkin Spice latte from Starbucks, I sat the empty cup on the table next to the leather couch. I was tired as hell after my freak session in the truck earlier, messing with Khadafi's freaked out ass. I reclined my lazy boy chair a little and waited for Dr. Sturgil to come in. Dr. Sandra Sturgil was a beautiful woman in her early fifties that reminded me of Angela Bassett. She was a highly successful therapist and a friend of my mother's. This was my 8th visit with her and I enjoyed our talks and her simple wisdom and applications. Twenty minutes after my arrival, Dr. Sturgil walked into her office, a pangent aroma of perfume trailing behind her. Her pants suit was stylish and attractive, her heels designer, and new. Her long mane of hair was probably a weave, but she wore it well. I leaned forward to sit upright and she stopped me.

"Please, Monica, relax. I'm a little late and I apologize. I got caught up in something else and lost track of time."

Thinking about the little episode in the Escalade, I replied, "I know what you mean, believe me, I do."

"How are you this morning?"

"I'm good, Doc. You?"

"As good as can be expected. I see you gotta new hairdo, huh?"

I ran my fingers through the short, sultry do that I'd had before Khadafi went to D.C. jail in 2011. It was dyed red with black high-lights and streaks at the roots. "Yeah. I been back doing my yoga and losing the post baby weight, so I felt it was time for a change. Something short, easy to manage, and bold."

"Change is good. Red becomes you. It fits your complexion. If you look good, you feel good. How's your mother?"

"She's great. Getting on my nerves and fussing over the baby. Spoiling the heck out of him."

"So, Khamani is good, huh. Spoiled, but good. How's Khadajah?"

"Grown as hell. Three going on thirteen. She's the natural big sister to her brother and loves to touch him. They both remind me so much of their father."

"And how is he? Still incarcerated."

"Unfortunately, yes. But his lawyer says it's not as bad as it appears. Hopefully, soon he'll be here to be with his kids. The last one, he practically begged me to have."

"You sound like there may be some regrets. Are there any?"

I shifted uncomfortably in my seat, staring at my hands now setting in my laps. My marriage finger still absent of a ring." Now...no regrets. Just never expected to be a single mother with two kids...their father not present. I mean, I get support and a lot of help...but my kids need their father."

"I agree, but let me change lanes for a minute. Have you heard the voice of pain, lately?"

"Not since that day in the closet when I thought my kids father was dead."

"Good. And that's because you are not under great pressure and stress. What you see and hear is a manifestation of what you feel inside at that time. The clinical term is called 'emotional cerebrumatology. In layman's terms, when your mind reaches a point of overload, your reality becomes disrupted and you imagine that you see things that are not there."

"So, you're saying I'm crazy?"

"Absolutely not. Actually, it's a very common occurance amongst stressed out, African American women. You are..."

For the next forty minutes, I had my life dissected and psycho analyzed but Dr. Sturgil's words were comforting and therapeutic. I laughed, I cried. Lastly, me and doctor hugged and I left her office feeling reinvigorated and fresh.

***

Imperial Autos was doing good business. That was easy to see once you pulled onto its lot on New York Avenue. The selection of cars was better and more vast than the last time I'd been here. People checked out cars and talked to dudes that I figured that the car lot must have employed. I parked the Escalade on the street and walked through the chain linked fence and headed for the trailer where Khadafi's office was. His seat was now occupied by his friend Pee-Wee. I suddenly felt a little cocky and I was a lot upset that Pee Wee wasn't answering his cell phone. I walked into the trailer like I owned it. A female who sat a desk stood up and tried to stop me from going towards Khadafi's old office.

"You can't just go back there, miss. I can tell the boss that..."

I spent on that bitch in one heartbeat and spazzed out. "Boss? Where is the boss at? Back there? That ain't the boss, bitch. The is locked up at Seven Locks right now. That nigga back there is his man. So, don't you ever in your life tell me where I can't go in some shit that my man owns." I walked up the funny looking chick until I was inches away from her face. "Are we clear on that or do you need a more detailed ass whipping to make you understand me better?" The drag queen looking chick back away from me and want to her seat and sat down. "Good answer, bitch. Good answer."

I proceeded down the hall and without knocking, opened the door to Khadafi's old office. I wasn't shocked at all by what I saw. Pee-Wee creep as was legendary in our neighborhood for his predilection for young girls. Pee-Wee sat on the couch by the wall, while a young bitch that looked to be about sixteen or seventeen kneeled between his legs and sucked his dick.

When he looked up and saw me, he smiled. The girl tried to stop the sex and get up, but Pee-Wee stopped her. He grabbed her head and guided her up and down. His eyes found mine as if to say, "This could be you." Suddenly, he moved the girls head away from his lap. Then he took his time putting his dick back in his pants.

'Go wait for me in the reception area." Pee-Wee told the young girl. She scurried away like a frightened mouse. "What's up Marnie? Good to see you."

"Still up to your old tricks, huh Pee-Wee? And you still like em young."

"Well, we are who we are, you dig. Did you see something that you liked?"

I couldn't help but laugh. "Pee-Wee, you funny as shit. You ain't never had nothing that I liked. But now I see why you don't ever answer your phone for me or Khadafi."

"I be tied up in a rack of shit. Khadafi knows how that goes."

"True dat, but now that I have you in front of me, let me get that money, you got for Khadafi's lawyer."

Pee-Wee walked over to the wall safe and pulled out some money. He tossed rubber bonded stacks of money at my feet. I couldn't believe the blatant displays of disrespect that Pee-Wee was showing. "That's fifty grand right there."

With a smile on my face, but anger burning in my heart, I said. "I'ma take them two slights on the chin Pee-Wee and chalk it up to stress or something.

"What are you talking about, homegirl?" Pee-Wee asked as if he was clueless.

"When I walked in here, you made the girl continue to suck your dick, even after you saw me standing in the doorway. Then you gon take your time putting your dick up like I really wanted to see that little shit. Then to add insult to injury, you throw the money at me. You are a disrespectful muthafucka, Pee-Wee and you know that you wouldn't have tried that shit if Khadafi was home. He was loyal to you and this is how you repay him? You's awful nigga, Pee-Wee. Foul."

"Ain't nobody tell you to just bust up in here like that. You got exactly what your eyes called for. And as for all the rest of that shit you poppin' miss me with it. My gun pop just like Redd's joints do. And you and I both know that slim ain't loyal to nobody but himself. H knows that."

"I bent over at the waist and picked up the money, then dropped each roll into my purse. "Your joints bust like his. He ain't loyal to nobody but himself. I got you, brotha. I'ma make sure that he gets the message. You be easy."

"Tell slim I said I call me. I need to holla at him." Pee-Wee said to my back.

I was already walking through the trailer and headed back to the Escalade. Pulling out my cell phone, I hit the button that would call Malachi Chu. His number already programmed into my phone.

"Malachi Chu, speaking."

"Mr. Chu, this is Monica Curry, Luther Fuller's girlfriend. I have some money he told me to drop off to you. I'm on my way right now."

CHAPTER 9
DETECTIVE COREY WINSLOW

By the time I arrived at the scene of the latest homicide in the District the fact that a person was being killed at least once a day was not lost on me. But this particular man being killed at 7:30 am while getting into a car intrigued me. Usually killers didn't get out of bed this early. I ducked under yellow 'Do Not Cross' take that cordoned off a quarter mile radius now considered a crime scene. As I walked towards the victim whose body was draped with a white sheet, I was met by Detective Travis Mays.

"How's it going Winslow?" Mays asked, extending a hand.

"It's going, Mays. What's the situation here?" I replied.

"You know how life goes in the big city. The victim is forty-six year old Raymond Proctor. He had identification on him. We're all familiar with this guy. How was your basic career criminal. Drugs, assaults, guns, you name it, he did it. But old Red Ray as he was called on the streets was also a friend of the police and a government informant. Since someone went through the trouble of ambushing him at seven something in the morning, I'd wager and say that he pissed somebody off. May be his friends found out that he was a real live federali. Maybe he beat somebody out of their money. or maybe someone he ratted on got out of prison and did him in. Who knows? What we do know is that he was seen exiting that building over that at the corner of C Street and Benning Road. He walked the half a block to the BMW there which was requested to him. A witness on her way to work said that a dark colored vehicle pulls up and a lone man exits. The lone man wearing a mast, opened fire on the victim, killing him instantly. The lone man hops back into the vehicle and it pulls off. The witness…"

My cellphone vibrated. I pulled it out of my pocket and saw that it was the station calling me. "Excuse me for a minute, Mays. I gotta take this call. " I answered the phone. The caller was Captain Greg Dunlap.

"Winslow, get over to the District Attorney's office in Hyattsville…"

"I'm working a case, Cap. The Benning Road murder that happened about an hour ago."

"Not anymore, you ain't. I'm sending Dave Chave out there. He's already on the way. You get over to Hyattsville and see what's the next plan of action in regards to Luther Fuller. If they're charging him with murder, I need to know all about…"

"Murder? Luther Fuller? Who did he kill now?" I asked curiously.

"You don't know, huh?" Captain Dunlap's voice faltered and he got quiet. Then just as I thought he'd been disconnected, he spoke. "Moe Tolliver passed away last night."

"Aw, shit!" I muttered. Things were about to hit the fan literally.

***

I had only been around Moe Tolliver a few times, but his presence stuck with me. He was a legend in police circles. His homicide closure rate was unparalled in the city. His death disturbed me and upset me. It was sudden and unexpected. It was senseless. From my seat in the back of the conference room at the D.A's headquarters, I spotted two people already present in the room. The large white man, I didn't know. But the beautiful, Caucasian woman, I did know. Ann Sloan was the U.S. Attorney for the District of Columbia. She was fierce litigator and champion for all victims of crimes, no matter how big or small. Ann Sloan resembled Jenifer Aniston to me, but she was a lot prettier. Her and the other man in the room talked in hushed tones and totally ignored my presence. I wondered if anybody even knew that I was told to attend the meeting. Minutes after my arrival, the District Attorney for the state of Maryland walked into the room. Having only seen the African American woman on T.V., I realized that she looked thinner and shorter in person. Delores Monroe exuded style and grace and power.

"Please forgive my tardiness and thank you all for coming. As we all know, Maurice Tolliver passed away last night. We have already sent our condolences to his family. I did not have the luxury of knowing Maurice Tolliver personally, but I read his life and I've heard exemplary things about him. His death is a travesty. This is meeting is more of an impromptu press conference minus the press. I'm trying to decided how to proceed in this case against Luther Fuller..."

"That's simple, right?" I offered loudly.

My outburst got everybody's attention. D.A. Monroe stared me down and said "You must be the detective that I was told would be here. Detective Corey Winslow, right?"

"Yes, ma'am. I'm here..."

"You said that the decision on how to proceed is simple? How so?"

"The state of Maryland upgrades the charge against Fuller to Murder. He goes to trial and loses. Then goes off to a penitentiary in the mountains and dies tragically at the hands of a prison gang called the Aryan Brotherhood."

"That depiction of events is colorful, detective, but unfortunately, it's not that simple. Things in Maryland are done differently than the District. That's why I've asked my counterpart Ann Sloan to join me here. Hopefully, she can provide me with a little assistance and clarity with all the nuances and differences in jurisdictions. According to the Medical Examiner's office, Maurice Tolliver died of an acute hematoma miocerpathy. In translation, I'm told that means a rare viral blood infection. That may or may not been caused by the hospital and or its tools and instruments. Not the bullets that were inside his body."

"But what about the fact that Moe Tolliver wouldn't have even been in the hospital had it not been for Luther Fuller?" I blurted out. "Doesn't that make Fuller responsible indirectly?"

"Detective, you know Maurice Tolliver, correct?" the D.A. asked.

"I knew him, yes."

"So, I understand how you must feel in regards to his untimely passing. But personal feelings aside, I am an officer of the courts and I have to remain objective here. I have to go by the law and the law is that police officers cannot cross state lines and go to the rear of residences to arrest people without the proper legal documents , namely a warrant. Our investigation shows that detective Tolliver acting alone and without authority, pursued Luther Fuller to the residence on Montrose Avenue and guns were discharged causing both men to be wounded.

"In this case, Maurice Tolliver broke the law. Why he did what he did was known only to him. Since he never recovered enough to be interviewed by my office, that information died with him. In light of the findings, taking Luther Fuller to trial for murder is out. The assault with attempt to kill is even in question here.

"In trial, Fuller's attorney, a man named Malachi Chu, whom I know really well, is going to assert that Maurice Tolliver was acting as a "rogue" cop and posed a threat to Luther Fuller's safety, thereby allowing Fuller to adopt the "self-defense" statutes allowed here in the state of Maryland. I've been trying cases in this state for sixteen years and I honestly believe that if the defense strategy doesn't prevail, the liberal citizens here acting as jurors, will be hung after a trial."

"So, we charge him with nothing?" the large white man seated next to Ann Sloan asked.

The D.A. looked at me and said, "Detective Winslow, excuse my manners. This very large man at the table is Detective Jake Peters. He's the investigating officer to the shooting on Montrose." To Jake Peters, she responded, "The only criminal charges we can indict and convict Luther Fuller on is gun offenses. Possession of a firearm by a convicted felon and unlawful possession of a firearm, that sort of thing. Throw in the unregistered ammunitions and Fuller is still only facing eight years, significantly less if he pleads out. I can press for the max sentence, but if the District can't come up with something to charge Fuller with, he walks out of a Maryland prison in three years. I wish that we could do more, but legally, our hands are tied."

"Madame District Attorney," Ann Sloan said and stood up. "My office has been for the last year or so, actively investigating Luther Fuller's involvement in over thirty homicides…"

Jake Pitts whistled. DA Monroe's eyes widened.

"…We believe that Fuller and an accomplice shot up a basketball court full of people, killing nine of them. We have a witness that puts Fuller at the scene of a brazen, broad daylight kidnapping and double homicide, but the witness didn't witness the murders. And any lawyer worth his law degree could rip her apart in a witness stand. That's why we haven't indicted him on anything. Just like you are in regards to Mr. Fuller, we haven't quite gotten what we need to make sure that Luther Fuller does life in prison. But we're working on it. In closing, proceed that way you see fit and will work diligently on our end to make sure Fuller goes all the way down."

***

Outside, beside her chauffeured Lincoln Navigator SUV, Ann Sloan pulled me to the side.

"As far as you know, has anybody on the force ever tried to talk to Fuller?" Ann Sloan asked.

"You mean like get him to confess to something?"

"Yes. It's just a thought but what if someone could break Fuller and get him to tell on himself or others. What if we threaten him? Really shake him up and allege that he's facing life in Maryland and death in D.C.. do you think he'd crumble under pressure?"

"I don't know, Mrs. Sloan. I honestly don't know."

"Well, let's try it. Nothing beats a failure but a try."

"And how do you propose we do it? At Seven Locks?"

"Of course not. We get him to 555 under false pretenses, alone and then we take a crack at him. Maybe he wants to bare his soul. Who knows."

"If you put it together, I'm there. I can help convince Fuller that he's up shit creek without a paddle. I can do…why are you looking at me like that?"

"Forgive me for that, detective. While you were talking you reminded me of someone I saw on T.V., what were you saying?"

"If you set up the possible debriefing, I'm in the building."

United States Attorney Ann Sloan passed me her cell phone. "Here program your cell phone number into my phone." After I passed it back she said, "I'll be in touch." She turned and climbed into the SUV.

***

Back at the precinct, I relayed everything to my boss, Captain Dunlap.

"Moe, told me once that he tried to talk to Fuller. A few years ago while Fuller was in custody. He attempted to flip him and get him to snitch on one of his partners."

"He did? Well, what did he say happened?" I asked.

"If I remember correctly, Fuller told Moe to suck his dick."

CHAPTER 10
KHADAFI

"You gotta go to, medica, Fuller." The CO announced through my cell door. "The doctor needs to see you."

I slid out of the bunk a little lethargic from working out and beting my dick. I had to beat my dick to go to sleep. After answering the call of nature, washing my face and brushing my teeth, I was ready. I hit the intercom button in the cell. "I'm ready to go, CO."

"Okay. I'll be at your cell in two minutes."

***

"Good morning, Mr. Fuller. This morning you are scheduled for an invasive medical procedure that should aid in the healing process of that damaged value on the left side of your heart. You'll be asleep during the procedure and it shouldn't take but a couple of hours. But first I need to get you to sign and date this release form. Read it if you like but it just states that in case of a medical emergency and something happens that the medical facility here at Seven Locks is not criminally liable.

Hospitals always made muthafuckas sign shit to keep their asses outta of a sling in case shit went wrong. I'd been in enough surgeries to understand that and accept it. I signed and dated the form.

"Okay, well, I just want to tell you a little bit about the procedure...I'll make a small incision near the left nipple and insert a device called the left ventrical assist device LVAD, which is basically a small automated device that will repair whatever damage it detects to the valve. Then I'll insert a tube with a micro-camera on it to see exactly what was done. Then I suture the incision and it's over. Are you prepared for that this morning?"

"I'm as ready I'll ever be, Doc. I've been stabbed, shot and some more shit, one more surgery shouldn't kill me."

"Great. Let me ask you a few questions before we get started. Are there any other concerns...medical concerns at this time? The pelvis?"

"I'm good, doc. Some days I ache, somedays I don't."

"The shoulder is okay?"

"It's all right."

"The muscle relaxers working okay? Any ill effects from the blood thinners?"

"Everything is good. I'm straight."

"Have you been working out at all?"

"All the time." I answered, tired of the questions.

"No chest pains at all, during or after?"

"Sometimes. I just ease up when that happens."

"Well, the PA will get you prepped. I'll get prepped and we should be ready to go in like fifteen minutes."

***

Later that day, I was in the cell resting when I was called for a legal visit. I was expecting him to come one day, but I didn't know when. I put my black kufi on my head and slipped on my Prada boots. My chest was hurting a little but other than that I was good. In the small attorney visit room, my Lawyer, Malachi Chu, stood reached across the table and shook my hand.

"Luther, how are you doing?" he asked. "You look sick."

I sat in the chair across from him. "I had a minor surgery done this morning, but I'm good. What's good with you? What's new?"

Malachi Chu was a half black, half Asian criminal defense lawyer that was rumored to be the best that the state of Maryland had to offer. He came highly recommended, so I hired him. This was my third meeting with him since I'd been out of the hospital and so far, he seemed to know what he knew.

"Let me bring you up to speed on your case. There's been a development and I'm not one hundred percent sure just yet how you're going to be effected. I didn't arrange a legal call with the facility because I don't believe that their legal calls are completely unmonitored. So I will never call here and tell them to set up a call. With that said, the detective that you're charge with shooting, died at Prince George's Hospital two days ago." He paused for cause and effect, then continued, "That's the bad news. The good news is that the Medical Examiner's Office unit definitely rule that his death wasn't a result of being shot. In fact, the chief Medical Examiner, a man named Ulysses Birch concludes, that Maurice Tolliver died of a rare blood infection that can't be attributed to any bullet. So as it stands your charges will stay the same, they will stage a trial on the assault with attempt, but we will beat them in court. That I guarantee. The possession of a firearm by a convicted felon counts, we probably can't beat. Your prints were on both guns. I know the judge on this one and I think she likes me. Worst case scenario, you plead to the two counts, they drop one. You'll get three years max, but I'll argue for less. With credit for time served already, you'll be home in twenty months."

"What about the kidnapping charge in D.C.?" I asked.

"There isn't one. You said the detective told you that before y'all opened fire on each other, right? Well, he lied. He had no legal right to be in your backyard and no arrest warrant. It's been almost nine months since the shooting and no charges have been filed against you in any state. I checked this morning. The D.C. US Attorney's is notorious for holding their cards close to their chest. They may be waiting to see how your charges here pan out, then they'll charge you. Tell me about the kidnapping charge so that I won't be side swiped by anything in case they do charge you."

"Listen here, cuz. I'm not gonna sit here and pretend like I had nothing to do with it, because I was involved, but right now there's no need to talk about it. If and when D.C. decides to charge me, you and I will sit down and discuss the whole matter. But only if necessary."

"Okay, have it your way." Malachi Chu said. "In regards to that case. But in regards to your current one, tell me everything that happened from start to finish."

I did what Malachi Chu requested. It took all of ten minutes. "Your story hasn't changed once, so that make it more believable. If things with the cops death changes, you'll be the first to know. You just chill out and don't get into any trouble while you're in here. Don't give them any ammo to use against you when you go in front of the judge for a possible bond. And you know the rules, right?"

"What rules?"

"Watch what you say on the phone. Don't talk to anybody in here about your case. No jailhouse lawyers or anybody. Especially not your cellmate. Chances are he's a government plant. Jailhouse informants are credible witnesses on the stand. Whenever you need to talk to me, call my office and leave a message. I'll be to see you shortly thereafter. And I got the money that your girlfriends dropped off at my office. The fifty should cover everything. But if I have to fight a charge in D.C. with you, there will be another payment due. Other than that, anything else you wanna tell me?"

"Naw."

"Okay. I'm out of here. You take care and I'll be in touch."

***

When I back to the pod, I went directly to the phone and dialed Pee-Wee's cell phone number. After a few rings, he answered.

(To accept his call, press one now) "Hello."

"Pee Wee, what's up, cuz?"

"Ain't shit, slim. What's good with you?"

"I'm good. Tryna find out what the fuck us up with you. I got your message, cuz. That's how you really feel about me, huh?"

"Aye, slim, I was jive going through some shit that day Marnie came through here. I was outta line and I apologize. Your lawyer got that fifty stacks, right?"

I couldn't believe the level of disrespect that my homie had shown Marnie. I wanted to open his whole head up until I saw his brains ooze out of what was left of his head. After a couple .223

bullets got his mind right. Pee-Wee wasn't a killer and we both knew that. In his heart, he knew that he'd have to answer to me for the disrespect, but until that day came, I acted like all was forgiven.

"Yeah, cuz. I appreciate that. And don't even trip off that other shit, Marnie shouldn't have barged in on you like that. You throwing the money at her wasn't about nothing, you was going through some other shit. I understand."

"No bullshit slim, I owe Marnie an apology, too. As soon as I see her, I'm holla at her…"

"Not to cut you off, cuz, but shorty is tryna cap her a new whip. She got the Caddy truck and the Rover, but I don't want her to keep pushing them. You feel me?"

"I feel you, she can have anything on my lot…"

"Your lot?"

"You know what I mean. On our lot. Your lot. Whatever."

"Naw, that ain't what I had in mind. Take her to the Benz dealer out Arlington and cop her something on you. That would really make her feel better. Especially after I tell her that you didn't mean no disrespect the other day."

"Slim, how am I supposed to do that. I ain't got…"

"Not to cut you off again, cuz, but my lawyer is like that. I just went on a legal visit and it turns out that I'll be home sooner than everybody thinks. The cop I shot, wasn't supposed to be where he was, so the only thing I'm facing is gun charges. If I plead to the guns, I'll be home in twenty months, he says. Can you imagine that?"

"Yeah…I…I…can imagine that. That's what's up."

"Now what was you saying before I rudely cut you off?" I hissed through clenched teeth. "You ain't got no what?"

"I was saying that I ain't got no problem capping Marnie a new car. That's what I was saying. I'ma do that as soon as possible. Anything else."

"Naw, cuz. I'm good. You be safe out there. Oh…my bad. I almost forgot. Have you talked to Bay One?"

"Not in a minute, naw. Why?"

"Have somebody go over CTF and give her the kiss of life for me."

"You got that, slim. You got that."

"A'ight, cuz. I'm out." I hung up the phone and smiled. "Bitch ass nigga." I said to myself, then picked the phone back up to call Marnie.

CHAPTER11
BAY ONE

"Did you put the package together like I told you to?" I asked Lisa as soon as I sat down beside her in the visiting hall.

"You know I did. We only got one hour out here, so don't waste time asking me stupid shit."

Lisa Craig was my main bitch. She identified as bi-sexual, but rarely had sex with men. She was light skinned and resembled Lisa Raye in her prime. I took one look at Lisa dressed in expensive designer jeans, a bad ass blouse that showed off her cleavage and killer heels that matched her blouse and stifled my desire to smack the shit out of her because of her smart mouth. Out of all the women that I ever had, Lisa had the wettest, sweetest pussy. I tolerated all of her imperfections because of all of the above and the fact that she was always down for the struggle.

"Good. This is what I need you to do. Go in the ladies room and find the trash receptacle. Lift the plastic trash bag out of the receptacle, put the package in there and then put the bag back in. You got that?"

"I'm not retarded, Bay. I got you." Lisa said, stood up and sashayed her sexy ass across the room to the restroom. A few minutes later, she was back.

"It's done. But they need to get somebody to clean that muthafucka up because it stinks like shit in there. Smells just like funky, fish pussy in there. That's crazy!"

"You like my new hairstyle?" I asked and ran my hand over my waves.

"It makes you look mannish. Your face is pretty, so you look more like a faggie than anything."

"Sticks and stones will break my bones...you know what they say?" I joked. "Besides, getting rid of the hair is liberating."

"These muthafuckas need to liberate your ass. I miss you, Bay."

"I miss you too, baby girl, no bullshit."

"You been in this muthafucka for over two years, what the fuck they gon' do with you?"

I thought about Lisa's question and didn't have an answer for her. So I just told her what I knew. "After the cop that witnessed me kill TJ got shot, I went to court and took my cap back. Under some D.C. law that one of the girls in here found for me, I insisted that I had a right to go to trial. My shit been in limbo since then. And I just found out that the cop just died. So, the government has to find a witness willing to say that I killed TJ and I don't think they can find anybody. Wasn't nobody out there but Wayne-Wayne, Tubby, Pee-Wee, Dion, and TJ. Dion, Wayne-Wayne, and TJ are dead. Tubby and Pee-Wee are solid niggas, they can be trusted. Hopefully, I can beat the case and come home. There's nothing else to hold me on."

"I really wish you were home, Bay. Can't nobody make love to me like you do. Lick your tongue out and let me see it." Lisa said seductively.

I licked my tongue out and moved it around in the air as if I was sucking Lisa's pussy. Then I licked my lips.

"Your mouth is pretty as shit. My pussy getting wet just thinking about it."

"You put that in the package too, right?"

"The cell? Of course I did. Call me when it's activated and I'ma send you some pictures of this phat, wet pussy."

"It's a good joint with the internet and all that on it."

"Yeah. I was gonna just get a basic phone, but Pee-Wee came with that one. That and other stuff. He said that Khadafi sends his regards."

"What else did Pee-Wee say?"

"Other than the fact that he tryna fuck me? Nothing. He tried his hand, popped all this big boy shit to me about how much he can make my life better and all this and that."

"And what did you tell him?"

"I told him that I belong to you. But he knows that already."

70

"Apparently not. Disrespectful ass nigga. It's all good though. All the animals in the jungle laugh and play when the lion is away. But fuck all that, tell me some more about that phat, wet pussy."

The hour in the visiting room seemed to fly by. After hugging and kissing Lisa, I walked over to the C.O. station to get my ID card. C.O. Karen Battle gave me a look and a smirk. I gave her a wink and left the room.

***

Later that night when the unit was dark and everybody was asleep, the CO came to my door.

"You gotta a legal visit, Lake. Get dressed."

A legal visit at 11:00 o-clock at night? I wondered what the hell was going on. I got dressed and left the cell. The C.O., a lady named Tereasa Sykes, passed me a hallway pass and opened the sally port. In the sally port, there are two rooms in the hall. One functions as a breakroom for the C.O.'s and the other as a makeshift infirmary. As I walked down the sally port, the door to the CO breakroom opened and CO Karen Battle waved me into the room.

"A legal visit, huh?" was all I could say before the CO's lips locked with mine.

After a long kiss, she said, "We can talk later, I get off at midnight and I gotta be back at my post before then. Besides I had to bring your stuff to you."

I saw two condoms stuffed with drugs and the cellphone laying on the table, then I looked back at CO Battle, who was already taking her pants down. She sat up on the table and laid all the way back, pussy exposed and wet. I stomped down and put my face in the place. In seconds, she was moaning and gripping my head.

"Got damn...Lake! Don't do it...like that! I'ma cum too fast!"

I knew exactly what to do to get CO Battle off. It wasn't my first time eating her out. She had worked my unit for a whole thirty days before. She hopped on my line after observing the way I move and finding out what I was locked up for. After the thirty days of me and her sparing back and forth verbally, she came back to the unit a week later. Once everybody was locked in their cells, she let me out and told me to clean up the unit.

I went to the mop closet to get the bucket, water, and a mop. In the mop closet she cornered me and kissed me. I bent her over the deep sink, had her pants off her ankles and ate that pussy real good. That was our first sexcapade, and others followed after that. Karen Battle was a sucker for my head game and I used that to my advantage. She would do anything I asked her accept help me escape. And that was cool, because I didn't wanna escape anyway.

"A-a-r-r-g-g-h-h shit, Lake! I'm about to cum on your tongue."

I wiggled my head and stuck as much tongue as I could into CO Battle, then alternated between slobbing on and tonguing down her pussy and ass. All the while, rubbing her clit.

"Damn…here it comes, Lake. I'm cumming!"

And cum she did. All over my face, in my mouth, on my lips. I had her juices running down to my chin. I kissed her pussy one last time and stood up. "Lick the rest of your cum off my face." I commanded.

Just like I knew she would, CO Battle did exactly what I told her. Before I left the breakroom, after she'd gotten dressed, CO Battle said. "If you need anything else and I mean anything. You let me know."

"I sure will, I sure will." I told her, then bounced.

***

So, when the CO, the same one as before, CO Sykes came back to my door the next night, I thought that it was another creep session with Battle, but I was wrong.

"You got court, Lake." CO Sykes told me at the cell door.

"Go ahead with that bullshit, Sykes." I replied as I wiped sleep out of my eyes.

CO Sykes put the clipboard in her hand up to the cell door window. "I'm not bullshitting you, baby. You got court." She said and pointed at my name on the court list. "Bayona Lake. That's you right?"

"You know damn well that's me, Sykes."

"Okay, then. I'll be back in thirty minutes to get you. Be ready."

"Court? How the fuck I got court?" I asked myself repeatedly as I got up and took a bird bath in the sink. I brushed my hair and threw my kufi on, my CTF dark blue pants and shirt uniform and my butter Timberland boots. My lawyer hadn't said anything about no court date.

"You ready to go, Lake?" CO Sykes asked.

"Ready as I will ever be." I replied.

***

Downstairs in R and D, I made it to the bullpen in the first wave, so I was able to find a nice little section on the hard metal bench in the back of the pen. I laid down to prevent any other bitches from sitting next to me. Women of all races and hued, entered the bullpen in droves. I scanned faces for any that I might know but there were none. The women in the pen ran the gamut. Crackhead, dopefiends, shoplifters, homeless bitches, drug dealers, prostitutes, drunk bitches, domestic violence bitches, fighters, knifers, shooters, and killers. Some old, some young, some pretty, most of them ugly. Most of the women at CTF knew or knew of Bay One. So I had no problem reclining on a bench to myself while others were forced to stand. My thoughts were racing at a high speed and questions fueled my mind. So, I barely noticed when the US Marshal's Officer came to pick them up for court. When all the women in the bullpen names were called and they were handcuffed and shackled, I realized that I was in the pen all alone. I walked up to the bullpen bars and called out to one of the Marshalls.

"Hey Marshall?"

"Yeah."

"I'm on the court list for court, but y'all didn't call my name."

The Marshall conducted a list in his hand then counted all the women cuffed and shackled. "Forty-One. My list says forty one. I'm counting forty-one. What's your name?"

"Bayona Lake."

The Marshal doubled check the list, then shook his head. "Not on this court load. Maybe you're going to court in another jurisdiction. Don't know what to tell you, but take care."

I watched the Marshal's load the bus up with incarcerated women and then pull off. Since there were no other C.O.'s around in R and D, I took off my uniform shirt, balled it up, used it as a pillow. I laid back on the bench and went to sleep.

***

"Lake that you?" a male voice called out.

I awoke hesitantly and shot straight up. "Yeah, that's me. What's up?"

The man was black, about 6'1 and wore about 300 pounds. His hair line receded and his gut threatened to pop the buttons on his shirt.

"Come on out."

I put my uniform shirt on and exit the cage. The fat man lead me around the R and D until we reached an area where cubicles and booths were. Standing beside a finger printing machine, next to a booth, a white man that looked like Tom Cruise awaited us.

"Bayona Lake, my name is Detective Garland Smallwood and this is my partner, Chris Bellamy. We are here to escort you to your arraignment scheduled for today."

"Arraignment?" I asked, befuddled. "What arraignment?"

"The arraignment where you are about to be charged with first degree murder in the death of Mytika Lemons. So, you have the right to remain silent. Anything you say can be used against you in a court of law. You have the right to an attorney if you cannot afford one, one will be…"

******

"Bayona Lake, my name is Carlos Hamilton. I'm with the Public Defenders Service. I have been asked to represent you in this matter. Today you will be arraigned and I'm told by the Prosecutor's Office that tomorrow you will be indicted on one count of first degree murder."

"Indicted? For murder? I don't know what the hell is going on. I didn't murder anybody." I lied with conviction.

The lawyer read something from a folder then asked. "Do you know a woman by the name of Gloria Dunbar?"

My blood pressure rose immediately and my heart rate quickened. "Yeah I know Gloria."

"Were you two housed together in a unit at CTF?"

"Yeah, we was. She left and went out Maryland about two months ago. Why? Gloria didn't kill nobody either."

"Nobody's accusing Gloria of murder. According to what she's told the homicide detectives on this case, you did. She says you killed Mytika Lemons and she's willing to testify against you in court."

All I could do was take one deep breath and then exhale. My words to Lisa the other day immediately came to mind...

"...I'll beat the case and come home. There's nothing else to hold me on."

I had to laugh to keep from crying. Here I was thinking that I had met one of the realest bitches alive in Gloria Dunbar and it turns out that I had really been fraternizing with a real live rat. Wow!

Anthony Fields

CHAPTER 12
KHADAFI

Nobody told me shit. Seven Locks didn't say where I was going. Neither did the two deputies, that drove me to D.C. I was handcuffed to a bully chain and transported to a building that I didn't recognize. In an underground parking garage, I was taken out of the car and lead through a labyrinth of hallways, until we reached one that opened and became a series of offices. When I walked into one office, it was conference room style and a couple people sat around a large, wooden conference table. A feeling of dread washed over me as I was made to sit down.

"Luther Fuller?" a blonde, white woman started. "It's good to see you again."

When she said that, it hit me. How could I forget the woman who had tried to send my ass to prison for life. Ann Sloan was the prosecutor that tried my case on the double homicide almost three years ago. Her hairstyle was different, but it was her. "Ain't my lawyer supposed to be present?"

"You can call him in a few minutes, I just wanna talk to you about a few things. You don't have to sign anything, you're not charged with anything...yet and you don't have to talk to me..."

"So why did you bring me here and where the hell am I?" I asked.

"You're in a safe location. We're not going to kill you, so relax. Again, I wanted the opportunity to discuss a few things with you. All you have to do is listen. Then if you'd like to talk to me, you can. I promise you that you are not being recorded, unless you request to be recorded."

"I request that this be recorded then...because y'all muthafuckas will say that a nigga said something that he didn't say."

The prosecutor chick turned to the black dude beside her at the table and whispered in his ear. Immediately, he left the room. I wanted to bolt out of the room or force them to take me back to Seven Locks, but something inside me told me to chill out. It wouldn't hurt anything to listen to the people. A few minutes later the black dude sat a small tape recorder on the table. He pushed one of the buttons on it and said.

"This is Detective Corey Winslow, present with U.S. Attorney Ann Sloan and deputy Mike Jones from the P.G. County Sheriff's Office." He moved the recorded close to me. "State your name for the recorder."

"I ain't stating shit. Just let the recorder do what it do. Say what y'all gotta say." I barked indefinitely.

"Okay, Mr. Fuller…I know that you like to be called Khadafi, but for the benefit of those that don't know you, I'll keep it formal." Ann Sloan said, "It was my idea to bring you down here. I have been trying to get you convicted in court for years, to no avail. But this time in think I got you."

"Got me on what, cuz?"

Ann Sloan pulled a piece of paper out of a folder and read from it. "On the murder of Tashia Parker. We have a witness that'll testify that you picked her up at approximately 9:20 pm on Ely Place in Southeast, D.C. We pulled fibers of hair that your DNA matches off of her body. And her cell phone call log shows that you were the last person that she talked to alive."

"Cut the jokes." I said and laughed.

"That's funny, huh? Well how about this? I have Donna Jasper, the mother of the man you killed…Fellano Jasper, who says that you and an accomplice kidnapped her and forced her to call her son for you. She says you were wearing a disguise, but she saw enough of you to pick you out of a photo array."

"Did she see me kill somebody?"

"Unfortunately no. But the kidnapping is iron clad. The only reason you're not here in D.C. facing that charge is because it's not good enough to me. Not a severe enough charge for me. I want you on a murder. Or two. Or three. You know how you do. Let's see I have a burned out ford Crown Victoria with a body inside the trunk. The man inside the trunk was bound and gagged. The fire left the cloth that bound him intact. I have forensic evidence that links you to that murder."

Things were getting serious and my temperature was starting to rise. I felt like a turkey about to be cooked for Christmas. I smiled at the prosecutor, but kept silent.

"Still funny, huh? Okay. I have more for you. I have the triple homicide on Burns Place in Southeast. I can connect you to that house on that night. The murders on the basketball court in the Simple City area where nine people died, that was you too. And if that's not enough, one of the guns that you used to shoot Maurice Tolliver was used in a Murder in Landover Maryland and another in Northwest, on Dalefield Street. So I'm gonna pin those bad boys on you, too."

"If you're putting together all that against me, why are you wasting time by telling me about it. You threatening to pin murders on a nigga, what's wrong with you pinner? Is it broke?"

"Naw, it ain't broke, Khadafi and I'ma call you that now because you're pissing me off. I'm trying to give you a chance here. A chance to save yourself. I know that you had an accomplice in all of those murders that I mentioned. Frankly, I don't care who goes down on the murders. This is not a personal, arena styled combat situation between you and me.

"I've been trying to send you to the feds for life for years only because that's what I'm paid to do. I need to close several murder cases that I know you were involved in or knew something about. You can take the fall...and you will take the fall because it's only a matter of time before we connect the dots on all of the murders. And all I need is one to put you away for life. Detective Winslow, talk to this guy for me, will you?"

The black detective at the table leaned forward. "I just sat here and listened to USA Sloan tell you what she knows. Let me tell you what I know. I know that sixteen-year-old Kenya Dickerson was killed by a guy named Terrell 'Tyger' Holloway, because he believed that she was a witness against him in the murder of her boyfriend, Tyjuan Glover. I know that after identifying his daughter's body, Antonio Felder, went to the 4300 block of Alabama Avenue in Southeast and shot eleven people wounding four and killing seven.

"I know that at some point you and Felder hooked up. I know that in 2007 at a federal pen in Beaumont Texas, you, Felder, and a few other men were investigated for a prison murder. I know that you were at Felder's daughter's funeral. I know that Tashia Parker got involved in some kind of way and lost her life because of it. I know that you and Antonio Felder killed Linda Holloway, her son Curtis Holloway…who drove the getaway car the day Kenya Dickerson was murdered, and Holloway's girlfriend, Larcel Davis.

"I know that either you or Felder killed Frank Jasper after going to that basketball court and killing nine people. I know that you kidnapped Donna Jasper and held her hostage until she called her son, Fellano, where you lure him to First Sterling Road and killed him and Terrell Holloway. That's twenty three murders in a two week span. All committed by you and or Antonio Felder. How's that sound?"

"Like one of them urban novels I be reading. If you believe all that shit you just said you reading them joints, too. What's the name of that book you be reading?"

"Oh it's a good one. It's called ''Lock Khadafi's Stupid Ass Up Forever."

"Luther." Ann Sloan added. "give me something. Anything and I promise you that I'll drop all charges against you…"

"What charges?"

"The ones I'ma bring up on you in the future…and I'll give you complete immunity on whatever crimes you were involved in. Give me Felder. Give me some other people. I don't care who you give me. Just give me somebody and let me give some grieving families their closure. Let me give the new Mayor a high homicide closure rate so that she can look good on the news. Help me to help you.

"We can even make your Maryland charges disappear. We know you didn't mean to shoot Moe Tolliver. Your bullets didn't kill him. We know that he was obsessed with you and acted illegally

80

in trying to arrest you in Upper Marlboro. Help us and everything goes away."

I appeared to be digesting everything that the prosecutor had just said. I wanted her to think she had me. I stared down at the handcuffs in my lap. The silence in the room was thick and heavy. I looked the lady prosecutor straight in the eyes and said.

"Detective Tolliver told me to help myself a few years ago while I was in a cage being processed in a gun charge. I told him to eat my dick. I'm much smarter now, more mature. So, I'd never tell you something like that. But since, you're a woman and I believe in equal rights for everyone, I will tell you to go and fuck yourself. Now get me out of here or call my muthafuckin' lawyer. Now!"

***

On the way back to Seven Lakes, I thought about everything that I heard. The information that the cop and prosecutor had was accurate as hell. As if they'd been told the business by somebody. Knowing Ameen like I did, it was totally out of the question to think he did any talking. But if not Ameen, how? I thought about the fibers they say they got off of Tashia Parker. I thought about Donna Jasper and the fact that kidnapping carried twenty years in DC. I thought about the pizza delivery man that I killed and set the car on fire the night of the killing on Burns Place.

The prosecutor said that she could link me to that crime as well. Was she serious? What did she or could she possibly have? I thought about everything that the detective said and winced. One thing was for sure and that was that the people knew too got damn much. And that worried me. But at the end of the day, fuck it. It is what it is. Thinking about the prosecutor bitch's face turning beat red when I told her to fuck herself was the best part.

I laughed again just thinking about it. Then my thoughts shifted to something else. My going back to federal prison. I'd have to face all my men again. I thought about all the dudes in the joint that I constantly looked out for and wondered who'd do the same for me.

Who would bag up grams of dope and send them to me like I had done on numerous occasions? The answer to my question hit me in the face like a slap. No one. Those thoughts lead to ones of Mousey and from those I thought about Erykah.

I thought about all the letters and pictures I'd received of the energetic, vivacious young girl. The young girl that I was fucking like a mad man. The young girl that belonged to one of my men. For all of about two minutes I felt bad, then like always, I said fuck it. I told myself to make sure that I called Erykah. She had a way of making sounds with her pussy on the phone that I sure was sure it was talking. After the day I was having, I needed that.

CHAPTER 13
DETECTIVE COREY WINSLOW

Ann Sloan and I ended up inside her office after the meeting with Khadafi. I sat in a chair across from her desk and waited while she fielded a few phone calls and returned a few messages. I tinkered with my cell phone until she was done.

"That certainly went well, don't you think?" Ann asked.

"Depends on how you look at it. I apologize for the way he dis…"

Ann Sloan stuck her hand out, palm up as if to stop me. "Don't apologize for him. Besides, I did two years in the military before going to college and law school. I've heard way worse things before. I grew up on the south side of Chicago. I've been called every name in the book in my lifetime and I've been told to go 'fuck myself' too many times to count. And by better people. Do you think we got to him even a little bit?"

"That's hard to say. If we did, he sure didn't show it. But I believe that he's afraid. I believe the tough guy routine that culminated into the disrespect is just a façade. I think he's at Seven Locks right now thinking about everything we said. I think he knows we have him on certain things and that we're serious about everything you offered him. But there's something missing. There's no motivating factor. There's no impetus or catalyst that might push him over the edge."

"Impetus? Catalyst? Usually when you tell a man…give him a heads up at that…he's facing life in prison because of X,Y,Z that's impetus enough. I can go down the list of names of so called thorough streets dudes who turned rat to save their own hides, starting with Rayful Edmonds. For every big "Street Crew" that we prosecuted, I can give you at least three names of real gangstas who decided to play ball with the government. The impetus is the time they're facing."

"Well-spoken, counselor. And point taken. But either way you look at it, it's still early in the game. We can apply additional pressure to Khadafi and tighten the screws on the vice around his neck. Worse case, you get an indictment on the kidnapping and something else and he goes to federal prison after he does his time out Maryland. The kidnapping beef will hold him another ten to fifteen years, so that'll be at least twenty years with no Khadafi Fuller. I see a win-win for us."

"I agree." Ann Sloan retorted.

For some reason, I could feel Ann Sloan staring at me like she was looking through me. It made me a little uncomfortable. "You're staring at me again. Do I have something in my nose? Cold in my eyes?"

Ann laughed. "No, no, nothing like that. I'm sorry for staring, but you bear an uncanny resemblance to somebody I saw on T.V."

"Good thing or bad thing?" I asked.

"I'm not quite sure just yet. I'll let you know the answer to that one later."

"I have to get back to work. If anything breaks please let me know."

CHAPTER 14
AMEEN

Haynesville, Alabama...
The address on the house read *1203 CedarPine Creek Road.* I looked down in my hand and read the exact same address from the paper I'd printed out. The man driving the Uber car asked me was the address correct.

"Yeah, this is it. Gimme a minute to get myself together." I sat in the car and stared at the house. It was a red brick, two story, colonial, with black shutters attached to the windows. In the driveway, was parked a Town and Country mini-van. I looked around for any signs of anything that would tell me for sure that my family lived in the house. My heart rate increased as I got out of the car and approached the house. As I approached, I listened for sounds of familiarity, Kay Kay's cries, Shawnay's voice, Asia distinctive laughter.

I heard none. I walked up to the front door and rang the doorbell. My breath caught in my throat. Silently, I prayed that Shawnay was on the other side of the door. We had to talk, needed to talk. I missed her and my kids so much and nothing or nobody could take their place. I heard footsteps and a smile crossed my face.

It was her. It had to be her. The locks on the door clicked and the door opened. The smile on my face vanished immediately. On the other side of the door was a middle aged white woman with auburn colored hair. She stared at me through the glass of the screen door.

"May I help you?" the white lady asked.

"I'm looking for my wife. I was told she lived here." I stammered.

"Well, unless you and I was married before and nobody told me, I'd say that your information is inaccurate." The woman said with a smile. "And I've lived here for the last ten years, so I'd know if your wife lived here."

Dejected, I apologized for the intrusion and left.

"Where to now?" the Uber driver asked.

"The airport, ock. The airport."

***

My seat on the plane was a window seat. I stared out the window into the vast blue sky and wondered exactly how planes flew. Every time I rode on a plane the experience fortified my belief in the Creator. I looked into the heavens and knew that everything that beheld wasn't created by man. And the whole design of the planet spinning on its axis while evolving around the sun wasn't by accident. So nobody, could tell me that Allah didn't exist. I believed that with all my heart, but I couldn't understand his reasons for doing things.

I closed my eyes finally and thought about the three other trips I'd made to unknown cities and states all in hopes of finding Shawnay and my children. Colombia South Carolina, Smyrna Georgia, Tallahassee Florida, and now Haynesville Alabama. Four possible locations where my family resided, four wrong addresses four letdowns, four heartbreaks. I often wondered if I'd ever see them again. I wondered if Shawnay would ever forgive me and come back. I wondered if they missed me. If their lives were as miserable as mine because we weren't together.

"We're now descending to just under ten thousand feet. The weather in Washington is sunny skies, but cold. It's forty degrees on the ground. We should be landing at Reagan National Airport shortly. I hope that you have enjoyed your flight. Thank you for riding with American Airlines."

***

When I walked out of the terminal, I spotted a burgundy Audi A8 idle by the curb. The window came down and Nicole smiled at me. I walked to the Audi and tossed my overnight bag into the backseat and then I climbed into the passenger seat.

"I take it that it was another strike out, huh?" Nicole asked.

"That's the story of my life, Nic. You know that."

"I hope that you don't blame me, Antonio? I gave you the addresses that I could find and I always told you that they could be wild gooses you were chasing."

"I'm not mad at you, baby girl. Just disappointed that's all. I actually believed that that one might be it. Shawnay, has family in Alabama. It made sense for her to go there. I was all on them people's front porch cheesing and shit thinking that I'd found my family. I ring the doorbell and a white chick that looked like Rosie O' Donnell answers the door."

"I'm sorry, Antonio. But you were going to find them. I know you are." Nicole said and pulled away from the curb. "I'ma holla at my friend out Quantico again and check and see if he's got anything for me. Then I'ma..."

"Naw, I'm cool, baby girl. I kinda feel like a rabbit running on one of them circles things where they keep running but ain't going nowhere."

"Uh...I think that's a hamster, boo. Not a rabbit."

"You know what I mean." I looked over at Nicole. She was gorgeous. She had really grown into her own style of a back chick over the years. Her hair was long and straight. Hot combed to fall down her back and over her shoulders. Nicole's skin complexion was like caramel candy. Her eyes were hazle and her body was proper. I spied her shoe game and saw that her heels that she wore with her jeans were on point. Her nails were manicured and polished the same color as her car. I wondered if her feet were proper.

"Nic, take me to the 51 liquor store. I wanna get a drink and then go to my daughter's gravesite." I told her. "And if you don't mind, I'ma need you to pick me up from there in about an hour or so. Cool?"

I'ma do whatever for you, Antonio. I keep telling you that. But I gotta say that I'm not happy with the fact that you drink so much now. I know you're still hurting and you're trying to find a way to cope, but ain't no answers in the bottom of no liquor bottle."

"I hear you, baby girl. Point taken. 51 liquor store please. Thank you."

***

"Hey, baby." I said and sat down next to the gravesite tombstone that depicted my smiling daughter, Kenya. "Just got back from another wild goose chase. I went to Haynesville, Alabama. Can you believe it? Haynesville Alabama. A place down in the South that still has an old General Store, population 35,000. They probably lynched more blacks than the entire Jim Crow South. My plane ride down there and back was cool though. It's the first time I flew since being locked up in the feds.

"It was better because, you feel a little more free. When I used to fly in the feds, I was handcuffed to a belly chain and shackled at the ankles. I always felt real helpless. Like if something happened to the plane, I had no chance of survival. That was the worse." I pulled the Armadale Vodka out of the bag and unscrewed the top. After taking a generous swig and letting the liquor burn my chest, I continued talking to my daughter.

"I really hope that you can hear me, baby. 'Cause I'd hate to think that I be out here talking to myself. Hold on…let me zippen my coat all the way, it's jack frost out this piece right now, but I'm good cause the Armie is gonna warm me up." I took another swig from the bottle. "I'm good, other than the fact that everybody I love is gone. I get lonely sometimes. But mostly, I do things at the shop to keep myself busy.

"My partner Angelo Daniels, we call him Nut, he asked me to give his daughter a job. I hired her at the shop and it was a good decision. The shop needed a little estrogen in it. She's twenty-one-years old and just finished school at Morgan State. She probably won't be there long. Just until she finds something in her field that she majored in. I'm thinking about opening another store. Yeah, your pops is a success in the clothing retail business.

"I'm leaning towards calling this next store something different though." Another swig from the bottle. And another. "Live the Omerta keeps calling me and I think I'ma call it that. Put the initials LTO on everything, but let it be one of them multi-definition type things. On one shirt LTO might stand for Love Talk Only and another might say, "Limit The Opportunities. It's still a thought in progress though."

Tears formed in my eyes and fell down my face. I ignored them and threw the bottle of Vodka back again. My head was spinning and I could feel myself getting drunk. "I miss you so much, baby! I don't know what to do. I can't find a way to not miss you. If I still had your mother, sister, and brother here, it would be easier, but I don't. And you know what I'm not mad at Shawnay anymore. She did the right thing at the time. But all that's behind me, baby. Killing the green-eyed dude ended it for me.

"It's over. But your mother doesn't know that because she never gave me the chance to tell her. I came home that night and they were gone. It's been nine months and I can't believe that I haven't heard a word from them. From Asia. It's crazy baby." I cried openly for a minute or two. "Look at me, baby. I'm a broken man. Half a man. I don't pray anymore. I've lost my way. I smoke weed and I drink liquor. That's how I cope, Kenya. That's crazy, huh?

"I'm nothing, baby without you. Without your mother and my kids. That's why I can't stop looking for them. I can't give up. I won't give up trying to get my family back. Ever. One day, baby, I'ma see you again. I know I will. I love you, okay. I love you, Kenya. I love you!" I dropped the bottle of Vodka and dropped my face into my hands. My chest heaved with every violet sob that took over my body.

I leaned on my daughter's tombstone and cried like I hadn't cried in years. It was all I could do. After all of my tears had met my hands and I felt like I couldn't cry anymore. I wiped my eyes then got up off the ground and started walking towards the entrance of the cemetery. Pulling out my cellphone, I dialed Nicole. She answered on the first ring "I'm ready to go. Come and get me."

***

I climbed into the Audi and looked at Nicole behind the wheel. She was a great looking woman, I reminded myself. The music playing in the car was sexy R & B. The Canadian dude "The Weekend" sang his song with conviction. I listened to the words and leaned back in the passenger seat.

"Are you okay?" Nicole asked me.

"I'm good, Nic." I looked at Nicole again. She was sexy as hell. She had taken her heels off and was driving barefoot. I glanced over and down at her feet. Just like I figured, her feet was props. Her toenails were painted burgundy. I don't know if was the heat in the car or the music that played, but suddenly I was horny as shit.

"I never knew that your feet were that pretty."

"What?" Nicole said and then looked down at her own feet. "Don't look at my feet, Antonio. I need to get them done..."

"They proper. Just like you're proper. You look good as shit, Nic. Real sexy."

"Antonio, be quiet. You're drunk."

"I'm not drunk. I was drinking, but I'm not drunk. Believe me. I know what I am saying."

"You look good, too, Antonio. Despite the bloodshot red eyes."

"I'm hungry, Nic. I'm tryna eat."

"You're hungry? Where do you wanna eat at?" Nicole asked.

"I'm hungry, but not for food. And I'm tryna eat right here. Right now."

CHAPTER 15
NICOLE BROOKS

"You wanna eat what, Antonio? Me? In this car?"

"That's what I said. If you scared, get a dog."

"I already got a dog. His name is Gino. But I ain't never scared, baby."

"Why are we still talking, then?" Antonio asked.

"Be careful what you ask for, baby. I'ma bitch that'll make it happen."

"Make it happen, then."

I licked my lips and laughed. This nigga got me fucked up. I'ma real bitch and the realest bitches do the realest shit. I looked around for the nearest exit off of the freeway. I kept driving until I saw it. I took the exit and kept driving until we were in a residential neighborhood somewhere in Chevelly, Maryland. Since it was now dark outside and kinda late, that made finding a spot to get my freak on in the car, easy. I found it on 55th Avenue and Kenilworth. I drove the car into a parking lot and pulled behind the building there. It was dark and secluded. Killing the engine, I lifted myself up and wiggled out of my jeans. My panties came next. I handed to Antonio. "Here you keep these. Sorta like a trophy."

Antonio put the panties in his coat pocket and then unzipped it and pulled it off. He unbuttoned his shirt and pulled that off too. The sight of his chiseled chest in that tank top t-shirt got my juices flowing. I reclined my seat all the way back and moved it back closer to the backseat, to give us some room. Completely naked from the waist down, I opened my legs wide and leaned back. I looked Antonio straight in the eyes and said.

"You told me to make it happen, right? Come and get what you asked for."

With the alacrity of a cat, Antonio was out of his seat and in between my legs, head first. His tongue lapped at my soaking wet pussy like it's juices were from a fountain type soda machine and he was thirsty. I moaned and groaned and twisted myself into a frenzy. I threw my head back as far as the headrest would let me and damn near bit clean through my bottom lip. His tongue was all over my clit and inside me hitting my spot. That spot. The spot that was gonna make me wet his entire face up.

It felt so good. So damn good. I felt the sudden desire to flee. To push Antonio off me and get out the car and run. Run away from his overly aggressive tongue, his lips. Antonio's pussy eating game was mean and right then I envied his wife. She had been the recipient of his mean head game for years and I was jealous of that. I thought about all the months that had gone by without me getting any type of sexual healing and shuddered.

Then I screamed, screamed, and gripped Antonio's bald head. My screams were primal. They came from someplace deep inside me that hadn't been heard from in years. The feelings that I felt were so extreme they scared me. I became afraid. Opening my eyes I looked down at Antonio and wanted to tell him everything that I'd been hiding inside of me for months. I wanted to tell him that I'd had a crush on him since I was a young girl in the hood watching him grow into a man. I wanted to tell him how much I always wanted him for myself and how he was the epitome of the realest nigga alive to me. I'd heard all the stories about him.

How he got down in prison and on the streets. I wanted to tell him that no other nigga in the world had shit on him and that he embodied all the qualities and characteristics of a real man. Above all, I just wanted to say thank you for eating my pussy so good. But instead, I kept silent. But I moaned and periodically screamed. I gyrated my hips and then moved to get away from Antonio, but he wasn't having it.

He locked his arms around my thighs and kept me where I was. Gyrating my pussy in his face. Trapped like a wounded animal, I gave in to the reality of my situation. I submitted. Gave in.

I came all over Antonio's face, just like I knew I would. He heard me cum, felt my legs lock around his head and attempted to squeeze him to death. He heard my cries, my pleas to stop, but ignored them. He kept right on licking me, kissing me, and sucking my clit. Then it hit me.

Dawned on me like the night sky disappearing in the early morning. Antonio wanted to punish me. I was the reason that he'd taken four trips out of town and still hadn't found his family. He knew that his tongue was killing me softly and that I'd cum already. Hard. He wanted me to cum again. he wanted me ahead of the game literally because I'd been left behind for so long.

Then without warning, Antonio rose up my body and kissed me in the mouth. I opened my mouth unwittingly and gave him my tongue, tasting myself all over his lips and tongue. I was so caught up in the kiss that Antonio's dick entering me caught me off guard. But only momentarily. I wanted that dick in me. Needed it.

I opened my legs wider as Antonio grabbed my right ankle. My left foot dangled in midair as our bodies collided. The air was thick and hot. The car felt like a porn set. And I was it's star actress. But I wasn't acting. Antonio's dick was so deep inside me that it hit my deep spot and it hurt. It hurts so bad, I had to tell him. His dick felt like it was in my chest.

"Oooh…Antonio…you're hurting me! You're hurting me! Oooh…it hurts…it hurts." All I could do was grip the headrest and take the dick. In that order.

Antonio's stroke was steady and persistent. I knew that his blood was full of alcohol and that his dick would be effected by that. His liquor dick would be inside me for a while and there no getting around that. So, I relented. Accepted the painful seduction. Rotated my hips, bit my lip. I opened my eyes to see Antonio's face but my vision was blurred. I couldn't even make out the color of the polish on my toes. Good dick made my toes curl.

Great dick blurred my vision where I couldn't even see my toes. OMG. I started to feel the tension build in my core. The feeling that emanated from my mid-section and warned me that my orgasm was going to be explosive. Next came the tingles in my toes and the leg shakes. I don't think Antonio even noticed what he was doing to me.

His pursuit of an orgasm made him impervious to me. His rhythm found, held steady. His dick was like a jack hammer, driving itself in my concrete, breaking me with every stroke. I couldn't hold back any longer and told Antonio so. Then I released. A volcano inside me erupted and spew lavalike liquid out of me and all over Antonio's dick and midsection. Then as if on cue, Antonio followed. He grabbed me and held me an came deep inside of me.

***

I left my jeans, my panties, and my heels off as I drove to my apartment, Antonio asleep in the passenger seat. There was no way I was gonna let him get away from me this night. His cum seeped out of me and dried my inner thighs, but I didn't care. It made me feel extra slutty, exhilarated and free. At my apartment, we barely got through the door before round two began. Our sex started out wild and forceful with me held up in the air against the wall while Antonio fucked me deeply and animalistically for what seemed like an eternity.

Then things became calm and sensual on the living room floor as the missionary position felt like the most erotic position ever. Antonio pressed his palms into my inner thighs and pressed me to the floor and fucked me slow. That turned into a lot of kissing. I ended up on my stomach and then on my knees, carpet burns stinging like hell. At some point we stopped to shower together, but pure animal magnetism brought us back together in the bedroom.

There I faced the wall as Antonio stood behind me and blurred my vision again. I was upside down, on top of him reverse cowgirl and laid out on my side. I had both feet held by my ears. I was pretzel dipped. I was corkscrewed. In the end, my pussy was sore but satisfied. Then like a kid playing hide and seek, sleep found me and that was it.

***

I stirred a few times and then my eyes opened. The digital clock on my dresser read 8:10 am. Looking over my shoulder, I saw Antonio still knocked out sleep. His light snores music to my ears. A smile crossed my face as I remembered the night before and how it all started. Then I could hear Salt N Pepa singing in my ear... *Whatta Man, Whatta Man, Whatta Man!* When a bitch woke up thinking about rap songs from twenty years ago, she knew the dick was nuclear. Getting out of bed, I floated to the bathroom and handled all of my early morning business. All was quiet in the house and I didn't have to go to work, so I decided to fire up my laptop and check some traps. My mailbox was full, but most of it was junk mail and spam. I skimmed through all the emails deemed worthy of reading and focused mostly on just one. The one from my friend Mack at Quantico.

Nic... Hi. It's me Mack. Wonderful News. Did some extra digging and guess what? I found your girl. I'm the best, huh? Yeah, I know. Well anyway, Shawnay Felder aka Shawnay Dickerson is now going by the name Lashawn Wilson and she's living in Texas. A small town forty miles north of Houston, called Linden. She has a house there and leases a BMW under the Wilson name. She has a fourteen-year-old daughter named Asia Wilson and a four-year-old son, Khasar Wilson. She hid pretty good, but nobody can hide from Mackman. She's employed by the Presbyterian Hospital for Children. Her address is...

11012 Lonestar Lane
Linden, Texas 77762

There's a landline number listed for the residence. That number is (222)-561-0910. A cellphone under the name of Lashawn Wilson shows this number (222)-801-4632. I hope that this is all that you need because your favors have ran out. Hope to hear from you soon, though. ☺ Mack!

I reread the email over and over again. Mack had found Antonio's wife and kids. It was the information that he so desperately wanted and needed. It would reunite him with the people that he loved most in the world. It would make him the happiest man in the world. But what about me? How would him leasing a runway to Texas make me feel? What if he left and never came back? I thought about the fact that I've wanted Antonio Felder since I was twelve or thirteen and I had finally gotten him.

He wasn't mine to have completely. I wasn't naïve enough to think that, but for the moment I held a piece of him. And if that piece promised more nights like the one I'd just had, then that piece was worth holding on to. Sitting on my bed with the laptop in my lap, I glanced over my shoulders at Antonio. Then back at the email. His happiness was in that email. My happiness was lying in my bed. my decision wasn't a hard one at all. Powering down the laptop I closed it and put it under my bed.

I wanted to hold on to my piece for as long as I could. Moving the covers off of Antonio, I found his soft dick. I leaned over him and licked on his balls while gently stroking his dick. Then I started at the bottom and licked my way to the head. At the head of his dick, I swirly topped it until it grew in my hand and became hard as stone. When that happened, I put the dick in my mouth and sucked it like it was my last meal.

Antonio awoke, looked down at me and asked. "Nic, what are you doing?"

I pulled his dick out of my mouth and replied, "Eating breakfast."

CHAPTER 16
MARNIE

"Sit or lie back in a comfortable position with your eyes closed." The yoga instructor said to the class. "Place one hand on the belly and one hand over your chest, near the heart. Pay attention to the way you breathe…allow your inhalations to lengthen and your exhalations to deepen. As the breathe finds more room to expand in the body, allow it to usher in a sense of relaxation. Now the first pose that we about to go into is the SUKHASANA pose…"

I eased up off the mat and sat with my legs crossed, Indian styled. I rested my hands, palms up on my knees and closed my eyes. Then slowly I put my left hand on my right knee and twisted my body to the right.

"Inhale and lengthen the spine. Exhale and tone the belly. After five deep breaths, switch sides…now take your feet and space them three to four feet apart, bent keep them parallel. Turn the right foot out 90 degrees, and the left foot in 30 degrees. Inhale and bring the arms out to your sides, parallel to the floor…"

Going through the different yoga positions, I did it strictly on autopilot. I listened just enough to do what the instructor instructed us to do, but mind was intune with my body in today's session. Something Dr. Sturgil said to me the other day wouldn't leave my head…

"The basic aspect of life that's most important is the choices you make. Each choice you make is a choice of intention. For instance, in a particular situation, you may choose to remain silent and that action may serve the intention of penalizing, sharing compassion, extracting vengeance, showing patience, or loving. You may choose to speak forcefully and that action may serve any of the same intentions. What you choose with each action and each thought is an intention, a quality of consciousness that you bring to your action or your thought. The splintered personality that's what you have, Monica, a splintered personality…has several of many aspects. One aspect may be loving and patient, the way you were

97

when Khadafi was with Kemie and you waited your turn with love and patience.

"Another may be vindictive…remember all the days that you hated Kemie because Khadafi loved her and you prayed that she died? Another could be charitable…like when you offered to pay for Kemie's funeral and you called D.C. jail to break the news to Khadafi about her death. Each of these aspects has its own values and goals. If you aren't conscious of all the different parts of yourself, Monica, the part of you that is the strongest will win out over the other parts. It's intention will be the one you use to create its reality…"

The part of me that is the strongest is my love for Khadafi. That's my reality. The uncontrollable truth in those statements now hung around my neck like an albatross. At what point in my life had I given up so much of myself and replaced it with all things Khadafi? Did my deep seated hatred and desire to get back at Kemie make me vulnerable to a love that is absolutely no good for me? How had I allowed myself to get caught up so deeply? Here I am over five years into a destructive love and it hasn't progressed one bit. How many times had Khadafi almost been killed? How many times had he been arrested?

"Exhale and twist your upper body to your right until your hips are facing your right foot…if your hips are tight, you may need to angle the back foot in more…"

If Khadafi was sentenced to a long prison bid, can I hold him down the way he would want me too? Would it be fair to my children to have them connected to their father in prison visiting rooms? I remember in one session with the therapist, I was asked what did I forsee for my future with Khadafi. Then and now, that question remains unanswered. Why? Because I really don't know. Khadafi doesn't even know what his own future holds besides jail time. Then I thought about Khadafi's words to me about a year ago.

"Yes, I still love Kemie. I'ma always love her. Do I miss her? Yes!"

"What I wanna know is...If Kemie was alive right now, would you and I be together?"

"I...I...don't know..."

I remembered how much that conversation I had with Khadafi that morning had hurt me, ripped at my heart. But just like I always did, I forgave Khadafi and decided to overlook all of his imperfections. After all real love came with trials and tribulations, I told myself. As I stretched and went through position after yoga position, I asked myself one question. Was my dysfunctional love with Khadafi worth holding onto forever. And even as the yoga session came to a close, I still couldn't answer the questions.

***

On the way out the door of the studio, I bumped into a man and dropped my yoga mat and gym bag. We both bent down to retrieve the dropped items at the same time. The moment was awkward for me.

"I got it." I said to the man who now held my bag.

"No, I got it." he replied and smiled. "Here you go."

Standing I could see that the man was gorgeous. He was tall, at least 6'3 and thick. I could see that through the sweatshirt he wore. His eyes were grey and hypnotizing, his hair a layered Mohawk style that accented his curly hair. His almond colored complexion was unblemished.

"Thank you."

"No, thank you." Grey eyes replied and smiled at me. His teeth white and perfect.

"For what? Thank me for what?"

"Just because. You might be the prettiest woman I've seen all day. Do you come here often?"

"To this studio? Sometimes. I'ma nomad actually. I go to all different yoga studios. It just depends on where I am and how I feel that day. You?"

"Believe it or not, I'm the same as you. I've been here two times before, but I usually do the Bikhram yoga at a roof top studio on 14th Street. I work across the street at Waller and Ingram. It's an accounting firm. I'm an accountant."

"And I'm a nurse with two kids at home. It was nice meeting you." I said abruptly and walked over to my car. With the remote on the key ring, I opened the trunk to toss the gym bag inside.

"Nursing must be paying good these days." Grey eyes said as he walked over to me.

"Why do you say that?" I asked.

Grey eyes pointed to my car. "Not many nurses I know drive a new model Mercedes Benz. Paper tags too. The health care industry is a bargaining business but not many nurses can afford one of them bad baby's."

I looked at my new Mercedes S630 with the panoramic roof and thought about all of things about my life that I could never tell. Never admit to. I tossed the bag in trunk and closed it. Without another word, I walked to the driver's side door and lifted the door handle.

"Listen, I wasn't trying to be intrusive, it was just an observation about the car. Meant as a joke actually, but it didn't come across right. I don't approach a lot of women because usually I'm inundated with work. I'm single with no drama attached. And I love yoga. Every weekend, Meridian Hill Park hosts a new form of yoga in an indoors facility. It's called Acroyoga, if you're free on any weekend, I'd like you to check it out. And I'd like to be there with…well not necessarily with you like a date…I'd like to see you there. See what you think about the new Yoga craze. How about it?"

Being anywhere in half naked environment like a yoga environment around the fine ass, grey eyed man would be a hellava temptation. But one that actually made sense to me and besides, I thought to myself, what could it hurt?

"Okay brotha, you got that. Let's exchange numbers and maybe we can end up at the same yoga event. Maybe."

"Maybe is good enough for me. By the way, my name is Cree. What's yours?

"Monica, but everybody calls me Marnie. You can call me Marnie."

***

My son's tiny lips sucked at the bottle's nipple as if he hadn't eaten in days. "Ma have you been feeding my son?" I asked jokingly. "He's crushing this bottle of milk like he ain't had one in days."

"Child, that little boy is greedy as shit. Just like you was a baby." My mother called out from the kitchen.

Khamani Fuller's eyes were on mine as he greedily devoured his milk. His tiny hand tried to hold the bottle as if it was too heavy for his mother. I couldn't help but to smile as I stared down at my son, at Khadafi's son. He was perfect in every way and I loved him more than life itself.

"You talking 'bout Mani out there acting like he ain't ate in days. You should see your daughter in here punishing these chicken wings. Girlfriend got bones, fired rice, and mumbo sauce everywhere on the table and her clothes."

I picked up my son and carried him to the kitchen. Sure enough, there was my beautiful daughter, sitting in her high chair at the table, eating Chinese carryout food from a Styrofoam container. Her face had rice, sauce, and food on it along with her clothes. I laughed at the sight of her. Khadajah looked up from her meal and said.

"Chicken wings, Mommy. Chicken wings."

"I know, baby." I responded. "You like Chicken wings. You was really hungry, huh, Dada?"

My daughter nodded her head and went back to devouring her food. My mother stood at her kitchen sink washing dishes. She glanced back at me, then asked.

"What's on your mind, Marnie?"

"Why do you asked that?"

"Because I know my only child. Talk. What's on your mind?"
I pulled out a chair from under the kitchen table and sat down.
"I'm that transparent, huh? Been doing a lot of thinking, that's all."
"About what?" my mother asked, her back to me.
"My life. About my future. About me and Khadafi. About life in general."
"Does this guy that you met at the studio today figure into any of that?"
"Of course not, Ma. I been thinking a lot before today. I think it's the therapy sessions with Dr. Sturgil. A lot of what she says is thought provoking. Things might not work out for me and Khadafi."
"Marnie, did you get hands on another gun?"
"Ma! Why do you have to go there? I'm way past that stage there."
"Glad to hear that, baby. Hooking you up with Sandra was the right thing to do, but what brought these thoughts on?"
"I told you, I think it's the therapy sessions. Can you watch the kids tomorrow, while I got and see Khadafi? I have to talk to him about our future."
"You know I will. I live for my grandbabies."
"Thanks, Ma. I'ma spend the night here with you, then. Is there any more of them chicken wings that Dada is eating. She done made me hungry."

CHAPTER 17
MARNIE

"Who are you here to visit today, ma'am?" the C.O. behind the glassed asked.

"Luther Fuller." The woman about two people in front of me answered.

I had to check my ears to see if they were working properly. I couldn't have heard what I thought I just heard. The woman grabbed the visiting paperwork that she had to fill out and stepped out of the line. I stood staring at the woman, who looked a little young. Her hair was dyed purple and it matched the purple lipstick on her lips and the polish on her nails. She was pretty with dimples in her cheeks. She looked like Lauren London. My curiosity got the better of me as I stepped out of line and approached the woman as she filled out the papers.

"Uh...excuse me." I said politely to the woman. "Did I just hear you tell the guard in the booth that you're here to visit Luther Fuller?"

The young woman looked me up and down with a lot of attitude. "Yeah, that's what you heard." The woman replied aloud and went back to the papers in her hand. Under her breathe, she said. "Ear hustling ass."

Her little smart remark in conjunction with the fact that she was there to see my man made me snap. I got right up on the woman and hissed in a low voice. "Look here, you little funny looking clown ass bitch, I'm trying to be nice. But I see that you ain't accustomed to that, so I gotta be gangsta with you. I will beat your lil purple haired ass in here. Straight like that. Jump out there and say some slick shit again, if you think I'm playing. Go ahead, pop some slick shit and watch what I do." When the woman didn't respond to my challenge, I knew that I had gotten my point across. "I'ma ask you three questions and I want three answers. Simple as that. Who are you? What are you to Khadafi? And why are you here today?"

Suddenly, the sass in the woman's smart ass was back. "Who are you? What are you to Khadafi? And why are you here?"

Smack. Smack. Before I could respond my hand reacted on it's own. The woman's hand reached up to touch where I had just smacked her at. I knew that people in the lobby had heard the commotion, but I didn't care. My adrenaline was pumping and I was ready to show out. "Answer my muthafucking questions before I get locked up for crushing your stupid ass up in here."

The woman was frightened, but anger was written across her face. Tears formed in her eyes. "I'm his woman. That's who I am. You must be his baby mother. My name is Erykah and I'm here because Khadafi told me to come. The same day he asked me to play with my pussy for him over the phone..."

I had heard enough. I took both of my diamond earrings out of my ears. "Check this shit out, bitch. You go ahead and see that nigga since he told you to come. But when you finish your visit, I'ma be in the parking lot waiting for you. You got a real ass whipping coming today. I'ma see you when you get outside."

I turned on my heels and exited the Seven Locks Detention Center Lobby. There had to be steam coming out of my ears, I was so hot. My head began to ache instantly. I sat in the car and changed out of my boots into a pair of tennis shoes that I kept in the trunk for my yoga sessions.

I wasn't in the parking lot for no more than fifteen minutes before two male correctional officers walked over to my car. The short, black CO said, "Ma'am I'ma have to ask you to leave the premises. If you leave right now, we won't involve the police. The lady inside the lobby claims that you assaulted her minutes ago and that you threatened her. She's afraid of you and says she wants to leave, but she's not coming outside until you are gone. Y'all can do whatever y'all want to somewhere else, but not here. So, please get into your vehicle and leave the premises."

"Rat ass bitch." I uttered and smiled. "Okay, brotha. I'm leaving."

Getting into the Benz, I glanced over to the entrance of the jail and spotted the purple haired woman pecking out the door. We locked eyes. I mouthed the words, "You hot bitch." And pulled out of the parking lot. "This bitch think she done got away, but I gotta trick for her ass."

I turned onto the main street leaving the prison and bust a U turn. I bust another U turn and parked my car a half a block away from the turn that you had to take to get to Seven Locks. And just like I figured, about ten minutes later, a black Kia Optima got caught at the light at the intersection by the exit for the prison. The stupid bitch's purple hair stuck out like a sore thumb. It was her in the Kia. As I followed the Kia, my emotions ran the gamut. I was upset that Khadafi had the audacity to fuck around even while locked up, but relieved to know the truth ad to have a reason to bounce on his dirty dick ass.

The woman's arrogance told me that she had fucked Khadafi. And she called herself his woman. That's what fucked me up the most. Had Khadafi really told the clown bitch that she was his woman? He had to. Why would purple hair lie to me? I was sad to see that my loyalty had been taken completely for granted. The more I thought about the boldness in the broad, how messy the situation became and the fact that she called herself Khadafi's woman, enraged me more. The anger that I felt towards Khadafi was about to be taken out on Purple hair.

Tears formed in my eyes and fell down my cheeks and that made me mad. Why was I still crying over a nigga that obviously didn't give a fuck about me? The Kia entered D.C. and kept going until it reached a small street in Southwest called Galveston. I was at least four cars behind the Kia and was certain that the purple haired woman didn't know I was behind her. The majority of the drive, she had a phone to her ear. I pulled onto Galveston and stopped. I watched purple hair park her car.

I crept down the block until I saw her get out of the car. I sped up and parked. Then I shot out of the car like Alyson Felix running down a track. Purple hair stood transfixed to the sidewalk as she saw me approach her in a blur. Then I was on her ass. I looked like Mayweather on that bitch. She fell to the ground and balled up into the fetal position, hollering and screaming.

"Shut up, bitch and take this ass whipping. Where's your slick mouth at now?" I asked as I stomped a hole in her ass.

"Please stop! Please! I'm sorry!" purple hair yelled out.

I stood over her, winded. "The next time you meet a real bitch, recognize her. And stay in your place. You punk bitch." I told her then walked back to the Benz and got inside.

My forehead was sweaty and I had to wipe hair out of my eyes. I looked in the mirror and saw the mad woman that stared back at me. I was frustrated. I was hungry. And I wanted to hurt Khadafi as much as he hurt me.

***

"Hello, can I speak to Cree?"

"This is me. Hey, Monica. I was hoping that you called."

"Did I catch you at a bad time?"

"Naw. I was just catching up on some reruns of Sons of Anarchy on Netflix. Talking to you is a welcoming distraction. I was just starting to think I was a white dude in a motorcycle gang in a town called Charmin."

I laughed. "I know you told me about hooking up for yoga, but I kinda had another idea."

"Is that right? Well, do tell." Cree replied.

"There's a restaurant that I've been dying to eat at in Adams Morgan called the Spaghetti Garden. They serve pasta anyway you can imagine it, I hear. I'm hungry and thought that maybe you are too. And that we can meet there for a meal, my treat."

"Wow, a woman that pays on the first date. I would love to have a meal with you, Marnie."

"It's not a date, Cree. Just a meal. There's a difference."

"It's semantics, Marnie. You say tomato, I say tomahto. Either way, we can still slice it and put it in our salad then eat it. When would you like to treat me to a meal?"

"Right now. Tonight. Are you available?"

"And miss out on an opportunity to watch Damon Pope kill white bakers for revenge? I can meet you there in thirty minutes. How does that sound to you?"

"That sounds like exactly what I wanted to hear. See you in thirty."

***

I forked the last of the food on my plate into my mouth and chewed. "Oh my goodness…This chicken stuffed ravioli was the bombdotcom. My God!"

"My chicken and broccoli fettuccini wasn't too bad, either. You made a good choice tonight, Marnie." Cree exclaimed and wiped his mouth with a napkin.

"Did I?" I asked and sipped my glass of Malbec red wine. I almost never drunk wine with my meals, but tonight it felt right. "Are you referring to the date or the restaurant."

"Both. But I thought you were against calling this a date?"

"That's cool with me, although power dinners always end with some type of deal being closed. Do we need to make one?"

"I don't know brotha. Let me get back to you on that with you smooth ass."

"Are you going to tell me what happened to your hands?"

I glanced at my scarred knuckles and quickly pulled them out of sight and beneath the table. "Not only do I do yoga, I also do MMA." I lied. "Rhonda Rousey ain't got nothing on me. I have a heavy bag in my basement that I train on. I guess I must've worked myself to hard without the hand wraps."

Cree smiled. "Beautiful, a nice body, brains, and she's a bad ass. I like that. How long have you been into MMA and yoga?"

"Mixed Martial Arts, about a year. Yoga much longer. I haven't done anything in a while before now because I was pregnant with my son. He's almost two months old."

"Is he the only child?"

"Is this a job interview?"

"No, of course not. You already have a job. Just curious." No offense.

"None taken, just joking with you. But no, I have two children. A three-year-old and a newborn. Khadajah and Khamani."

"And their father?"

My eyes found Cree's and spoke something that words couldn't.

"I didn't mean to pry. Like I said, I'm just curious by nature. That's why I am an accountant. I love getting in people's financial affairs."

"Their father is in prison." I offered reluctantly, but glad I said it.

"I'm sorry to hear that. I hope it's nothing serious and he won't be there long."

"We'll see, but mostly likely, we'll go our separate ways, if he does come home. I'm thirty-one years old, you know and I've been knowing him since we were kids. But we've been together romantically for about five years. My life, Cree is a made for T.V. movie.

"Which channel would it come on? E channel or Oprah's Own Network." Cree asked and smiled.

His smile was beautiful and it made my heart flutter. The more wine I sipped, the more irresistible he became. "Probably, the Lifetime channel. With one of them 'Mama I'm in love with a Gangsta' type titles. But that's enough about that, Christmas is in ten days, what do you have planned?"

"Spending time with the family in Arlington, exchanging gifts. You know, that whole scene that makes me feel like I'm eleven years old again."

We both laughed. "I know what you mean. Well Mr. Cree, you have a beautiful name, tell me how you got it and whatever else you want to share about you."

And for the next thirty minutes, that's exactly what he did.

***

It was a little after one in the morning, by the time I pulled into the carport adjacent to my house. The Escalade was parked in front of the house on the street, so I had to squeeze in next to the Range Rover. My date with Cree went great and I was still smiling as I stepped out of the car. I glanced at my cell phone that was in my hand before fishing inside my purse for my door keys. From my peripheral vision I saw something move beside me and then a hand covered my mouth.

It's grip was vicelike. Fear gripped me and all I could think was that I was about to be raped and killed. The body of a man pressed up against my backside. The strength in the arm that held me was undeniable. I thought about the lie I'd told Cree about me being a MMA fighter and wished that it had been true. I struggled against my attacker, deciding that I couldn't just stand there and be killed. I had to do something.

"If you continue to fight me, I'ma kill you." A voice whispered in my ear. "I'm not going to hurt you unless you make me. Be still now and or die."

Something in the way the man spoke made me believe what he was saying. I stopped moving.

"And don't worry, it's not your body that I'm after. I'm not that dude. I'm a taker, I take, but not pussy. I take money and lives. I can take one or the other or both it makes no difference to me. Now, we can do this two ways. We do it the easy way and you'll live through it. If we have to do it the hard way, you die. It's just that simple. I'm here for the money that Khadafi has in the house. And the drugs. Don't bullshit me and tell me that they are not in there because I know they are. We can go inside and get what I want or I can kill you right here and then still go inside and get what I want. It'll just take me longer. Either way, I get what I came here to get. Make a decision right now. Easy way or the hard way."

The man lifted his hand from my mouth. I was terrified, but I still managed to say, "The easy way."

"Good decision. You're smart. I like that." To the man that appeared out of nowhere my attacker said, "Search the trucks, and the Benz. Look for a stash spot." In my ear, he whispered. "Is there a stash spot in any of the vehicles?"

"No." I said voice quivering.

"Put the key in the door and let's go in the house. You scream or try anything you die."

Once we were inside the house, the man shut the door, but left it unlocked. "Where is the weed at? And the money?"

"The drugs are in boxes downstairs in the basement. The only money that he has here is upstairs in the bedroom. In a duffle bag under the bed."

"Is that all the money in the house? Don't lie."

"Yes."

"I think you're lying." The man said.

"I'm not lying." I pleaded. "Please believe me."

"Okay. I believe you. Let's go get the money."

I lead the man upstairs to my bedroom. "It's under the bed."

It was then that I saw the gun. It was chrome and black. And big as hell. "You get it. And I'm telling you, if you pull anything besides a bag of money from under that bed, I'ma split your shit open. Closed casket shit."

"I wouldn't risk my life for no amount of money." I went under the bed and grabbed the bag. I handed it to the masked gunman. A few minutes later, we were back in the living room. His partner was there now. Sitting on one of my couches.

"The weed and shit is in some boxes down in the basement. Go get it." the man with me said to the other masked man. "How many boxes is there?" he asked me.

"Three. Over by the washing machine in the corner."

110

"Three boxes. Over by the washing machine in the corner." He called out.

I was held at gunpoint until all three boxes had beed carried outside.

"You did good, boo. I'm glad that I didn't have to kill you. And I'm glad that you didn't have your children with you. But if I find out later that you withheld anything from me, I'ma come back and I'ma be pissed. Go down into the basement and stay there. Count to one thousand and then come out, but not a minute sooner. You try to involve the police, I'll be back. Don't make me come back. Now go. Get in the basement."

I ran down the basement stairs and stood stick still in the dark. I did as I was told and started counting. I was afraid, almost traumatized, hurt, and upset. There was no way that I'd staying in this house tonight, if ever again. When my count reached a thousand, I walked back upstairs. The door was closed but unlocked. I peered out the window to see if anybody was there. They wasn't. my purse was still where I'd left it. On the table by the stairs. Grabbing it, I fished my cell phone. Only then did I realize that my hands were shaking. I knew that I had to get out of the house, but I didn't want to go to my mother's. I didn't want her to see me like I was and I didn't want to wake the kids. So, I dialed a different number.

"Hello, Cree? Are you alone?"

"I was just on my way to bed and yes I'm alone. Why, what's up?"

"Can I come over? I'm not tryna be alone right now."

"Sure, you can. The address is…"

***

When I walked into Cree's apartment, he started with the questions. Questions that I wasn't willing to answer just yet. So, I did the next best thing I could think of to quiet him. I grabbed him, stood on my tip toes and pulled him into a kiss. And from there one thing lead to another…

Anthony Fields

CHAPTER 18
KHADAFI

"Where the fuck you been at cuz? Why haven't you been answering the house phone or your cell phone? It's been like five days since I talked to you. What the fuck is up with you?" I exploded into the phone as soon as I heard Marnie's voice.

"I haven't answered the phone at home because I haven't been at home. My cell phone been on the charger. I left it there because I didn't feel like being bothered with nobody. I been here over my mother's house with the kids."

"Why haven't you been home, cuz?"

"Because I'm never going back there. Not even to get my shit. Or the kids shit."

"Marnie, what the fuck are you talkin' bout? You ain't never going back home and all that. What happened at the house to make you not wanna go back there?"

"I got robbed in there, that's what. We got robbed. Me, you, the house."

"What?" I asked. I couldn't believe what Marnie had just said. "You got robbed? The house got robbed? What the fuck are you saying, cuz? Spit that shit out."

"You heard me right. Every fuckin' word I just said. The house got robbed. I was coming in the door and got ambushed by two niggas. They took me in the house asking about money and drugs. He… the dude holding me…threatened to kill me if he didn't get what he'd come for. I told them where the stuff was. The money and the boxes in the basement. They took it and left."

I was beyond livid. All I could do to contain my anger was breathe. Inhale. Exhale.

"Hold on, cuz…let me make sure I heard you correctly. Two niggas caught you going in the house… my house… and robbed you? Took my shit out of the house on some home invasion type shit? Is that what you're telling me?"

It happened like I just said and I haven't been back there since.

"Man, them niggas got me fucked up out there. I'ma kill…"

"You can't kill nobody from in there, so just calm down. But I gotta tell you this, whoever it was knew you and they knew me."

"Why would you say that? It had to be random. You pushing that brand new Benz…"

"Fuck that Benz. I never asked for that shit. It was somebody that know both of us. How do I know? Because the dude that grabbed me by the neck mentioned you by name. He said, I'm here for the money Khadafi has in the house… Those were his exact words. Then once we got in the house, he asked me specially where the weed at? How the fuck would an anonymous robber know there was weed in the house? Then before he left he said, "I'm glad that you didn't have your children with you. Whoever it was knew that I had more than one child. I'm telling you, they know us."

Marnie's words crashed down on me like a ton of bricks. She was right. Whoever had invaded my house had to have been close to me. "Did you talk to the neighbors? They didn't see nobody hanging around the house?"

"It was late when I got in." Marnie said without realizing what she said. "It was after midnight the neighbors were probably asleep."

"What the fuck was you doing outside after midnight? And where was my kids?"

"The kids were with my mother. Where else would they be?" Marnie replied sassily. "I was out. I lost track of time."

Suspicion crept into my entire being and made me wanna kill somebody. "You was out where at midnight?"

"Khadafi, please leave it alone."

"Leave it alone. Bitch if you don't answer my muthafuckin' question…"

"You gon do what? Huh? Kill me, too? I ain't tryna hear that shit. I'm not scared of you. I told your ass that before."

"Where were you at, Marnie? You say you was out. Out where?"

"I just told you that a muthafucka had a gun in my face and all you keep hollering about is where was I at. Don't worry about where I was at. Do you ask Erykah where she be at?"

I almost dropped the phone in my hand. How the fuck did Marnie know about Erykah? Had I mistakenly written Erykah and sent it to Marnie? Had the people at the jail intentionally switched my mail? "Erykah? Who the fuck is Erykah?"

Marnie laughed in my ear. "Nigga, you know who the fuck Erykah is. You gon' sit on this phone and lie. Sucka ass nigga. Well if you can fuck bitches on the side, brotha. I can do the same thing."

"Marnie, stop playing with me, cuz." I said trying to calm down.

"Think what you wanna think, but two can definitely play that game."

"What?" I exploded, but then told myself to ease up. "Stop playing with me, cuz. No bullshit. Where you was at?"

"Nigga, I just told you where the fuck I was at. Out doing me. If you can fuck bitches while we together, then I can fuck niggas, too. And that's where I was. Out getting fucked."

"Oh, yeah? You was getting fucked, huh? Because of Erykah?"

"So you know her now, huh? A few minutes ago, you didn't know no Erykah."

"That's my man Mousey's woman. That's how I know her. She be relaying messages to me from Mousey. I was giving her shit to take Mousey. That's it."

"Nigga, you lying and the truth ain't in you. I ran into the bitch in the lobby of the prison. She was on her way into visit you."

"So? Mousey must've sent her up here to...(beep). "This phone is about to hang up, I'ma call you right back. As I hung up the phone and attempted to dial Marnie back again, I heard...

"Aye moe, I'm next on the phone."

I ignored whoever it was talking and kept dialing. The next thing I know, the lever that hangs up the phone depressed. I looked up and saw a hand attached to the fingers that depressed it. I shook my head and laughed. I couldn't believe the way my life was going. First my house gets robbed by some niggas, then my bitch tells me she fucking another nigga, and when things couldn't possibly get any worse, somebody had the balls to hang up the phone on me. A cold blooded killer. I reigned in my temper as I turned to look at the face that was attached to the hand and fingers. A fire kindled in my eyes that didn't match my smile. "Cuz, this ain't what you want."

"Nigga, fuck all that. You gotta respect the phone line like everybody else. We tryna get on that joint, too, kill." The dude with the long dreads said.

From the way the dude said kill at the end of his sentence told me that he was from D.C., too. He was about an inch taller than me and a few pounds heavier. His long dreads were dyed light brown at the tips. He had no idea who he was fucking with.

"Aye, cuz, check this out, I'm going through an emergency and I need to use the phone again. Let me make it and I promise you that I got something you gon' like when I get off."

The dude removed his fingers from the phone lever and I dialed Marnie back.

"Hello?"

"Now, what was you saying, cuz?"

"I wasn't talking, you was. Lying about that bitch Erykah. You forgot that fast?"

"I'm not lying. Mousey must've sent her up here to tell me..."

"Stupid ass nigga, I talked to the bitch. The lil purple haired bitch told me that she was your woman. Said you told her to come down there after she played with her pussy over the phone for you."

"She's lying if she said that. I swear..."

"Nigga, you busted. Simple as that. And speaking of busted, that's what she is too. I followed her ass to Galveston Street, jumped out of the car and whipped her ass. Lil punk bitch talked that slick shit at the jail and then balled up on the ground and hollered like a bitch when I got on that ass. And you're foul for fucking your man Mousey's woman.

"What the fuck is it with you and your fetish for fucking your friends women? Huh? Ain't that what almost got your ass killed twice by Ameen? You fucked his woman after he took a body for

116

you, made the ultimate sacrifice for you. Your stupid ass should've learned from that situation, because the nigga could've killed your stupid ass that night outside the jail, but naw, not you. Not super bad ass Khadafi. You turn right around and start fucking Mousey's woman, too. Now you about to go back to prison and he might kill your dumb ass. Disloyal, disrespectful, dirty dick ass nigga. I hate your ass. That's why I went and got some new dick.

"Aye, cuz." I hissed through clenched teeth. "Listen to me, carefully and believe me when I tell you that the screws on my cage are gonna come loose one day and when they do, I'ma remember every word you just said to me on this phone. You gon' answer for the disrespect..."

"Answer to you!" Marnie exploded. "Nigga, fuck you! I—AM—NOT—SCARED—OF—YOU! I keep telling you that shit. I don't have to answer to nobody but God! And you ain't him! Stupid as Me, I been by your side, holding you down through all the bullshit for years and you have the balls to sit here and threaten me. The mother of your muthafuckin' children, nigga. I got muthafuckas out here putting pistols and shit in my face and threatening to kill me because of you. Your stupid ass gets busted because you can't control your bitches and you mad at me?

"You mad because I beat that bitch's ass? Is that it? Talking about a bitch gon answer to you. Nigga, fuck you! Real talk! I'm sick of your shit. You treat me like shit and think I'm supposed to just stay around and accept that shit. Well, I'm through doing that. Call my mother's number when you wanna talk to your kids for now on. Don't call me no muthafuckin' more because I don't have shit to say to your ass. I mean that. And I guess, I'll see you when the screws on your cage come loose."

"Aye, Marnie...(click). Marnie? Marnie?" The line went dead. I sat there holding the phone for a minute as Marnie's words apped through me worse than any knife or bullet could. Finally, I put the phone receiver onto the grey, metal tongs that held the receiver. The dude with the dreads approached and reached for the phone.

"Oh my bad, cuz." I told the dude feigning politeness. "I got something for you for being so patient with me." The dude went for my ruse.

I acted like I was about to walk off, but span quickly and hit the dude with a lightning fast two piece combination that made his head bounce off the wall. Reaching out while he was still dazed, I grabbed his dreads and smashed his face into the phone.

"You want the phone?" I asked as I removed the receiver and let it fall.

I smashed his face into the metal tongs that held the phone. Blood sprayed from the gaping wounds that the metal tongs put there. When his body became too heavy, I let it drop. The man was unconscious, but that didn't stop me from pummeling his face further. Blood was pooling beneath him and blood was all over my hands, my clothes. I was in a zone. All I saw was red. When I tired of beating the dude's ass, I stood there resembling a blood thirsty monster from a movie. I turned and faced the crowd of inmates who waited for the phone.

"Who else is trying to use this phone?" Nobody said a word. "That's what I thought."

The slider door to the unit opened suddenly and forty correctional officers stormed the unit. "Everybody on the ground, Now!"

I lay on the ground and put my hands behind me to be cuffed. I looked at the dude that had hung the phone up on me. He was barely breathing.

"Get the stretcher in here, Now! Emergency code! Emergency code! Code blue! Code blue! Tell medical to get an ambulance! Emergency code! Emergency code!"

***

"You are a savage Fuller. A real sociopath." The white CO whose name tag read P. Quebecky, said. "You did that guy like that because he wanted to use the phone. That's a crying shame."

I paid the redneck CO no attention as the African P.A. silently cleansed my hands and put band aids on the open cuts. I was handcuffed to a long metal bench in the infirmary's isolation bullpen. Six correctional officers were in the tight space watching my every move.

"And if that poor guy dies." Quebecky continued, "I hope that they give your ass the needle. And what's crazy is that...heck, I don't even know you and I hate you. You shot that fuckin' cop and it looks like you're gonna get off on that, God bless that poor guy's family. The big guy upstairs doesn't like ugly, though and everything about you is ugly, Fuller. Ugly and rotten to the core. Cumberland and them Baltimore boys don't like you D.C. boys. So when you get to the Ultra Max or WCI, they're probably gonna kill you anyway. At least..."

What Marnie had said to me on the phone was now ingrained in my whole existence. Especially the home invasion, part.

"...I'm here for the money that Khadafi has in the house...where is the weed at?"

There was only one person alive that knew about me, TJ, and LaLa hitting Black Woozie's house on Canal Street and getting away with guns and drugs, mostly pounds of weed. That same person was the only one who knew where I lived, that I kept money in the house, and that Marnie had had another baby. He was the Godfather to my son. One man. My man, Pee-Wee. I never thought that Pee Wee would cross me like that. I knew that I'd went a little hard on him after I found out how he carried Marnie, but I never thought he'd develop balls of steel. Pee Wee had to know that I would figure out that he was behind the move. He was a smart street nigga. He knew that all fingers would point directly at him. So, why would he do that? Why risk his life like that when he knows that I will take it in a heartbeat and not lose a wink of sleep? The answer descended down upon me like a divine spirit. He did it because he thought I was finished. Pee Wee believed in his heart that I would never see the streets again. My heart was broken. I'd left the man financially over the top with my car dealership, the safe was full of money and

119

all I asked was for him to take care of my lawyers. Then one misstep on my part caused the man to invaded my home. The pain of Pee Wee's betrayal hurt more than all the others. More that TJ's, more than Bean's, more than Theodore's. The damage ventricle on my heart had to have been bleeding, because I felt like the band aids on my hands were needed there.

"Come on, Fuller." Quebecky said as he unlocked the chain that held me to the bench. "To the hole you go, and please, please make my day by giving me a reason to slum your ass to the ground and stomp it. Please make my day."

"Fuck you, cracka." I told the CO. "You can suck my dick."

The next thing I knew, I was on the ground face down with hands and feet colliding against me.

"Stop resisting Fuller." Quebecky shouted as they fucked me up. "Stop resisting!"

CHAPTER 19
KHADAFI

Them goon squad CO's fucked me up in the infirmary, but it's cool. Goes with the territory. The one named Quebecky was the most aggressive, the most unrelenting. I filed his name and face in my memory bank with Pee-Wee's and the other people I plan to kill when I get to the streets again. If I ever do. It took me about three days to fully heal. I did a lot of sleeping due to the pills that medical gave me. My shoulder was fucked up and my eye had a blood clot in it, but other than that the three days of bed rest did my body good.

A few minutes later, the CO slid two pieces of mail under my door. I got off my bunk and picked it up. I thought that it would be something from Marnie, telling me that she was sorry and that my kids were okay, but it wasn't. Both pieces of mail were cards from my aunt Mary. I opened them to discover that they were Christmas cards.

Days went by so fast in jail that I never even realized that the fake ass holiday season was upon us. I tore up both cards and flushed them down the toilet. Aunt Mary knew that I was Muslim and didn't want to accept it. I loved her with all my heart, but her 'come home to Jesus' antics were getting old. I laid back on the bunk, thoughts filled with my situation, my baby mother, my partner Pee-Wee, and my children.

***

Fifty...forty nine...forty eight...forty seven...forty six...the push-ups hurt my shoulder, but pain is what I needed, what fueled me to continue. I put my feet up on the desk in my cell and placed my palms flat on the floor. The fifty countdown was the third part of a vigorous workout regimen that I had been doing for the last two days. The kickouts, burpies, and bridges were behind me. No matter how many times I cleaned the tiny solitary confinement cell, it still wreaked of urine, sweat, and feces. The small window in the cell let me know that darkness has descended upon the outside.

Having been up all day pacing the floor and then working out, had my boy wearing, but fatigue was not a friend of mine today. I could not rest. I would not rest. My mind rejected my body's request for warmth and sleep's embrace...forty five... forty four...forty three...forty two...in between sets of push-ups, I'd stand up and do fifty jumping jacks and fifty squats and then the next set of push-ups.

The concrete floor on the cell was cold, but the cotton socks that I had on made it bearable. Sweat formed on my forehead and ran down my face despite the frigid temperature outside that seeped into the cell and made it cold. My muscles strained against the small t-shirt I was issued upon my arrival to the hole. My arms, chest, shoulders, and wrists screamed out in pain and reminded me that I hadn't done the fifty countdown in years, but I pushed on...forty one...thirty nine...

Pictures of my children took over my mind. Visions of another man raising my kids paralyzed me with emotion. It was bad enough that my oldest son Kashon was with his mother and Ameen. The thought of Khadajah and Khamani being raised by another dude was too much to bear...thirty eight...thirty seven... I need my children and they need me. Why hadn't I thought about that then, though? Back when Ameen first came to me for help? Why didn't I just say No? Why did I let him and his desperado desire for vengeance for what happened to his daughter, jeopardize my position with being with mine?

"Because that's the way you are?" an inner voice called out to me. "You live for killing. For shedding blood. It's who you are."

Thirty six...thirty five...thirty four...and where was Ameen now? In the streets living his life. Probably back with Shawnay. Or probably fucking Marnie as get back. I shook my head to clear it of those thoughts, but they wouldn't leave. Images of Ameen behind Marnie fucking her from the back played on my minds big screen in HD. No matter what I did, the images wouldn't leave.

Ameen was on top of Marnie. Her legs opened wide as he cuffed one leg in the crook of his arm and pushed it down. I could see her pretty feet as the toes curled with every thrust into her wetness. As images of Marnie on her knees with Ameen's dick in her mouth played out the longest...thirty four...thirty three... Could Ameen be the one that Marnie was fucking? Was it possible? My mind said no, but my heart said, 'yes'. I'd been in the hospital for four months and never heard a word from Ameen. I'd been at Seven Locks for almost five months and yet no word, no visit, no money, no nothing.

Thirty two...thirty one...I had to fight back tears. I was tired of crying. I was tired of feeling weak and I was tired of feeling hopeless. So, I wiped away the tears and kept doing push-ups. I thought about what the prosecutor had said the other day. About the kidnapping charge... *"the kidnapping is iron clad. The only reason you're not here in D.C. facing that charge is because it's not good enough to me. Not a severe enough charge for me."*

Kidnapping carried twenty years in D.C. and according to her, her case was iron clad. I thought about Donna Jasper and cussed myself for not killing her sooner. How had I let her get out of the can and get away that night? That situation befuddled me to this day...

"...I'm trying to give you a chance here. A chance to save yourself. I know that you had an accomplice in all the murders that I mentioned. Frankly, I don't care who goes down on the murders. This is not a personal, arena styled combat situation between you and me. I've been trying to send you to the feds for life, because that's because that's what I'm paid to do. But I don't give a damn if you or the other guy takes the fall for the murders. If you don't want to take the fall, give me the other guy."

Twenty nine...twenty eight...twenty seven...I thought about everything the black detective dude said... *"I know that you kidnapped Donna Jasper and held her hostage until she called her son, Fellano, who you lured to Firth Sterling and killed. Him and Terrell*

Holloway. That's twenty murders in a two week span. All committed by you and Antonio Felder..."

Twenty six push-ups...twenty five...twenty four...twenty three...

"Luther," Ann Sloan has said, *"give me something. Anything and I promise I will drop the charges against you..."*

"What charges."

"The ones that I'ma bring up on you in the near future and I'll give you complete immunity in all the crimes you were involved in. give me Antonio Felder. Give me some other people...help me to help you. We can even make your Maryland charges disappear..."

Twenty two...twenty one...twenty...nineteen...eighteen...seventeen...

I need to get home to kill people, to avenge all the wrongs committed against me. I needed to be with my children. I needed to fuck Marnie up...all of that weighed heavy on my mind as things that I'd heard from Marnie and the prosecutor kept playing in my mind. All audio, no video. The only video in my head was of Ameen and Marnie. Ameen didn't care anything about me. And he was probably fucking my bitch.

I paced the floor in between sets and got more upset by the minute. I was starting to listen to the beast inside me that told me as always, I was on my own. I had to make a decision that would change my life forever. Sixteen...fifteen...fourteen...thirteen...twelve...eleven...ten...nine... I combined the last eight sets and did thirty six push-ups. 1280 push-ups. Pulling off my clothes, I stood naked in front of the sink in the cell, my wounds, my tattoos, my emotions visible for whoever to see if they looked in the cell. I scooped up a rag and washed my body, slowly, methodically. All the while listening to the two conflicting voices in my head...

"There's only one way to get back at everybody who's crossed you. One way to extract the revenge that you seek." Yeah, that's true, but you can't dishonor yourself to get revenge.

"The prosecutor said that if you give up Ameen, she'd give you complete immunity for any other crimes you committed. And she can make the Maryland gun charges disappear. How sweet is that?" the prosecutor bitch is trying to trick you. You know how they do niggas. Claw 'em up and spit em out. You can't tell on Ameen, that ain't how you're built. Remember the death before dishonor.

"The death before dishonor is a relic, a passed time. Something that the mob made popular. It's over now. Nobody follows that shit anymore. It's 2013, there are more rats around then good men. And they're eating good, still in the hood and all that shit. Ratting is chic now, it's the new thing to do." The death before dishonor is alive and well. A rat dies a thousand deaths, a good man only once. Live the Omerta.

"Fuck the Omerta and the death before dishonor. Ain't Rayful in the streets? Ain't Alpo in the streets? Wasn't Sonny the Bull in the streets eating good until the Ecstasy pill shit got him caught up? Don't make me go down the list of rats that are in the streets living good."

That's true, but you come from a different fiber of niggas. You killed Keith Barnes for being a rat. You killed Eric Frazier and Mark Johnson because they were rats. Didn't you kill potential witnesses to keep them from telling? Didn't you kill Lil Cee's mother and baby sister because believe he ratted?

"Fuck all that, cuz. What's more important to you? Being known as a rat, but living in the streets with your kids or being a good man, upholding the death before dishonor while doing a million years in prison?" The million years is better if you live each day knowing that you never folded. You can hold your head high and respect the fact that you are a man of morals and principles. A man worthy of respect.

"And none of that morals, principles, or respect shit will get you a case of Roman noodles when you're hungry in prison. You need to get home to your kids. The rest will take care of itself." Don't let your kids grow up knowing that their father was a rat. Think about your son. Your legacy will affect him.

"Not if you move him out of D.C. it won't. He never has to know." Everybody will know.

Anthony Fields

"Fuck everybody else. Save yourself. It's the first law of nature." Don't become no rat.

"Give me Antonio Felder...give me some other people...we can even make you Maryland charges disappear..."

After washing my entire body, I dressed in fresh clothes. I wrapped myself in the thick wool blanket that I slept under. I leaned on the wall and cried. I cried because of all the pain and hurt I'd felt in my life. I cried for all the friends I'd killed. I cried for my mother and uncle. I cried for Kemie. I cried for Marnie and all that I put her through. I cried for my children and their future in an unjust world. I cried for Ameen. I cried about the decision I'd made. What I had to do. I cried for all the people that had been told on. I cried for what I was about to become.

***

Christmas came and went in Seven Locks with no jingle bells, no lights, no gifts, no songs, no carols, no holiday cheer. On the 26th, I requested the phone. The CO brought the phone to my cell and popped my food slot. It took me a few minutes to get a number for the U.S. Attorney's office, but I finally got it.

"Hello? I'm trying to reach US Attorney Ann Sloan." I told the switchboard operator.

"The US Attorney may be busy, who may I ask is calling?" the operator replied.

"Luther Fuller. Get her to the phone. She would love to speak to me."

The line went blank for a few minutes and then a female voice said. "Luther Fuller, what can I do for you?" It was Ann Sloan.

"You win. I wanna come in and talk. Make it happen before I change my mind."

***

The next day, I was seated in the same room as before, in the same chair. But this time the US Attorney and I were in the room. Ann Sloan placed a small recorder on the table and said, "What do you want to talk about today, Mr. Fuller?"

There was no turning back now. I had people to get home and kill. "Today, I wanna tell you who killed that police officer Emily Perez and the witness against me, Latasha Allison last year..."

"OH...MY...GOD!" Ann Sloan proclaimed, grabbed her cell phone and dialed a number. "Maggie, get Howard Easley in here right now and call Delores Monroe, the District Attorney for Southern District of Maryland and tell her we need to meet as soon as possible. Do it now! Bye. Tell me everything Khadafi you're doing the right thing..."

Anthony Fields

CHAPTER 20
DETECTIVE COREY WINSLOW

"Detective Winslow, Ann Sloan, are you in the area?"

"When you say, in the area, what area are you referring to?"

"The area near my office on 4th Street."

"I'm not, but I can be. Do you need me to come and see you?"

"You told me to let you know when something in the Luther Fuller case broke, well I'm doing that now. When you get downstairs tell Henry the head security guy at the desk, that you're here to see and he'll let you right up."

"Okay. I'm on my way."

I disconnected the call and glanced at my watch. It was 7:20 pm and the sun had already set making the sky turn a pretty dark purple color. I drove through Congress Park and wondered what part of Alabama Avenue were they beefing with. In the last 72 hours, the war between the two neighborhoods had left five people dead, including an eight year old and a thirty-one year old mother of two. According to the unofficial talley, it was Alabama Avenue three, and Congress Park two.

I knew that sometimes soon we'd be called to Congress Heights to scrape another young black kid off the pavement and the suspects would be from Congress Park evening the score. Twenty minutes later, I pulled into a parking space near 555 4th Street. Doing exactly as I was told, I found myself knocking on United States Attorney Ann Sloan's door to her office. Ann Sloan opened the door and stepped aside to let me pass.

"Have a seat." She said and walked past me to her desk. She held a phone to her ear. "I'll only be a minute or two."

I sat in a chair facing her desk and noticed that a pair of black designer heels sat beside the desk, one heel on its side. It was trying not to eavesdrop on her conversation but I couldn't help it once I heard the names Luther Fuller and Antonio Felder thrown around. The grin that crossed Ann Sloan's face reminded me of Sylvester the cat grin after he'd popped Tweety bird the canary into his mouth.

Ending the call Ann Sloan sat the phone down and pulled it aside on top of her desk. She looked at me and smiled. Then she said, "I have good news that I want you to hear before I announce it to the power meeting tomorrow. But before I tell you my good news, I need to tell you something else."

As I watched from my seat, Ann Sloan stood up, lifted her skirt and pulled down her panty hose and took them off. She walked around the desk and stood about three feet in front of me. My eyes dropped to her tiny, pretty feet, and noticed that they were painted a bright shade of red, the same color polish that adorned her fingernails.

"There's this show on the Starz channel that I am absolutely obsessed with called Power. The main character Omari Hardwick is one of the most handsomest, sexiest men that I have ever seen in my life. And you, detective happen to look just like him. That's why I stare at you so often. I couldn't believe your uncanny resemblance to Omari Hardwick. Am I making you uncomfortable, detective?"

After I picked my jaw up off the floor, I replied, "Uh, not at all. Power huh? I've been told that I resemble Ghost before." I won't lie and say that I wasn't a little afraid. The woman standing in front of me in a seductive manner was one of the most powerful women in the city. My eyes followed her to the office door as she turned the bolt lock, locking the door. She turned and leaned on the door. "You must think I'm crazy, right?"

"Crazy? No. Spontaneous, bold and incredibly sexy? Yes! But not crazy."

"Good." Ann Sloan said and reached behind her to unzip her skirt. It fell down her body and lay in a heap at her feet. She stepped out of it and walked towards me. Her panties were black lace and hugged her petite frame. They gripped her like a small hand. Standing in front of me, her shirt was removed next. I couldn't believe my good fortune. The United States Attorney for the District of Columbia was inside her office stripping out of her clothes in front of me. Her strip tease was slow and deliberate. My dick rose in my pants. Ann Sloan unclasped her bra in front and pulled her arms through it until it lay at her feet. Our eyes locked as she covered the space between us and dropped to her knees in front of me. Her eyes on mine, she unzipped my pants and pulled my hard dick out. She looked at it and said, "Beautiful."

I exhaled in anticipation of what came next. With her eyes back on mine, Ann Sloan put me into her mouth and sucked me deep. Sloppily, Noisily, Greedily. My back arched in my chair and my toes curled in my Louis Vuitton Loafers. Her eyes never left mines as she sucked me, stroked me, twisted her fist around me. I saw the excess saliva build at the area about her fist as she grip me with a firm grasp. My dick disappeared deeper and deeper into her hungry mouth.

Ann Sloan would alternate between trying to swallow all of me to rising up and twirling her tongue around the head. She would let me slip from her mouth as she licked my entire length from base to head. Then she'd suck me at the base as if trying to put a passion mark on me there. That lead to her holding me gently in her hand and her tonguing every inch of my dick. It took everything inside me to resist the urge to cum. I didn't want to ruin the moment by coming too fast.

I wanted the oral gymnastics to continue for as long as possible. But Anne Sloan had other plans. She looked up into my eyes and held my gaze as she slowly, passionately sucked me deeply with no hands. I could feel my dick trapped in her throat. The muscles massaging the head of my dick like a pussy. That's when I lost my composure battle as I felt the familiar stirring in my loins. As the cum rose from its depths, my hips rose.

I gripped Ann Sloan's head and pulled her down feeling every fiber of tightness in her throat gripping me. A guttural moan escaped my mouth as I erupted in the US Attorney's mouth and throat. Ann Sloan continued to suckle me like a newborn baby on a nipple, swallowing my cum as if she needed it to sustain her life. Finally, she released my flaccid member from her mouth.

I stood up and removed my pants entirely. Without saying a word, I lifted Ann Sloan from her knees until she stood on two feet.

Weighing no more than a hundred and twenty pounds, the US Attorney was light in my arms as lifted her and carried her to her desk. I sat Ann Sloan down on the desk. I removed her panties an forced her body back on the desk in a supine position.

I sat down in the seat that she had just occupied as she talked on the phone moments earlier. The wheels on the comfortable chair rolled with me as I moved up until I was within inches of a shaved pussy that had to be one of the prettiest that I'd ever seen. I gripped Ann's hips and pulled her body further to the edge of the desk. Her legs opened wider, her feet suspended in air. My tongue found her pussy and savored the taste of it.

"Don't lick me like that, detective!" Ann pleaded. "Please! Don't!"

Her please went unheard as I spat excess spit all over her pussy and then licked and slurped it back into my mouth. My tongue dancing around her clit expertly.

"Oh shit! Oh shit! I wanna feel your dick inside me! Detective, please put your dick in me! I need to feel that big, black dick in me! Oh shit...you're going to make me cum so hard, detective! I'm gonna cum if you don't..."

Ann Sloan's body rocked, shook, and convulsed like she was being electrocuted. Her words were no longer coherent and understandable.

"Oh my muthafuckin'...Oh...shit...shit...a-r-r-g-g-h!"

My dick got hard as I listed to Ann Sloan's cries of passion. I was ready to fuck her. Raising up out of the chair, I positioned my dick at her pussy as I stood between her legs. I slid my dick slowly into her while grabbing both of her small feet, holding them up as I pounded myself into her. I couldn't believe where I was and what I was doing.

Nobody in the force would believe me if I told them where I was and what I was doing. But it really didn't matter because I'd never tell a soul about my night at 555. I brought one of Ann Sloan's feet up to my mouth. I licked each toe before sucking on the big toe while still pounding her pussy.

"Fuck me, detective! Fuck me! Your dick is so deep inside me!"
I switched feet as my tongue bathed her other foot and toes.
Looking down into Ann's face, the way her forehead creased, the
expression on her face almost made me cum again. I had to stop for
a minute and pull out to keep from coming. It was time to change
positions. Grabbing her hand, I pulled Ann until she sat up on the
desk. I attacked her breast then. One by one, I kissed, licked, and
sucked all over each of them. All the while, simultaneously rubbing
Ann's clit with my free hand.

"I'm about to cum again...dammit! I'm cumming again!" Ann
announced.

The convulsions started again, then quickly subsided. I pulled
Ann until she was off the desk and standing.

"Turn around and bend over the desk." I commanded.

Ann Sloan complied like an obedient pupil. I rubbed the head
of my dick between the crack of her ass a few times, tempted to try
and fuck Ann Sloan's ass. But instead I slid my dick into her wetness and pushed until I was deep inside her. I gripped her waist as I
moved in and out until I built a rhythm. Ann Sloan tried to do everything she could not to scream from the painful pleasure she felt.
She made a fist and bit down on it as her body rocked with each
convulsion of our flesh. Ann turned around and watched as I jerked
my dick until thick cum shot all over her office carpet.

"I'm sorry I did that on your carper." I stated. "I can get it up."

"Leave it." Ann replied. "It's a reminded of what just happened."

I smiled. "What the hell just happened?"

Ann Sloan didn't respond. Instead she walked around the desk
to her clothes. Silently, she dressed herself. After finding her panty
hose and putting them on, she spoke. "What just happened was me
fulfilling a fantasy. You must think I do this all the time, huh? Well,
I don't. Actually, I have never done anything as spontaneous in my
life. Until tonight I had never slept with a black man before. Ever.
And I've never cheated on my husband. Ever. Speaking of my husband he's working late at GW tonight and he thinks I'm working

late too. What we just did was awesome. It was liberating. I have never cum three times in one sexcapade like that. It was amazing. But it can never happen again. You do understand that, right detective Winslow?"

"I'm cool with that. I'm not a stalker. Don't worry."

Ann Sloan laughed at that. "Two great things happened for me today, detective. One obviously being the mind blowing sex I just had and the other is what I wanted you to hear before everybody else. Today, we broke a real serial killer. Luther Fuller is on our side. Today, he agreed to give us Antonio Felder and help us solve over forty murders. How's that for good news."

***

The evening that I'd spent with Ann Sloan was still on my mind the next morning as I showered, dressed, and headed to the meeting at Triple Nickel. I stopped at Dunkin Donuts for a breakfast sandwich and coffee then proceeded to 555 4th Street. When I walked into the room, I recognized that this meeting, unlike the last one, contained all of the big wigs in the DC government infrastructure. Sitting around the conference table was the Mayor-elect Mary Bowser, the chief of Police Katherine Laney, a City Councilman Chris Berry, Captain Greg Dunlap, Rio Jefferson, US Attorney Ann Sloan, and another man that I didn't recognize.

I moved to the back of the room as not to be recognized. No one paid me any mind as I walked by. But as I grabbed the chair on the back and placed it against the wall, US Attorney Ann Sloan glanced back at me and held my gaze for a moment, smiled, and then turned away. Seated next to her was the Mayor—Elect and they engaged each other in conversation.

After a few minutes went by, Ann Sloan rose and got everyone's attention. "The recent uptick in violence in the city has perplexed every one of us in this room. Collectively and individually, we've all discussed in one or another what the problem could be. The Mayor has enacted a law that enables law enforcement to actively pursue and detain drug dealers and gang members at the D.C. jail for up to sixty days without any charges being filed. The initiative that we have implemented to fight crime is aggressive and needed.

"Councilman Barry, I wanted you here because your ward has been most effected by the onslaught of murders over the last year or so. And I want you to know that arrests are about to be made, homicide cases will be closed and you can give the myriad families in your ward closure they need by knowing that their loved ones did not die without justice being served. Chief Laney has worked tirelessly to put officers in the appropriate hot spots in the city where crime is prevalent. Her efforts will get a jolt today because of one man. To my left, here is Attorney Malachi Chu.

"He's a defense attorney and he represents the man that I'm referencing. Mr. Chu and I have spoken at length and just to give you all a tidbit of the information that we now have…we know who ambushed and killed Officer Emily Perez and the witness that she was protecting, Latasha Allison. We know who killed nine people on a basketball court last year. We know who killed seven people on Alabama Avenue last year, we know who killed three people in a house on Burns Place a little more than a year ago. With the help of this one man we are about to solve close to seventy murders that happened over the last five years.

"Thanks to the relentless pursuit of justice by Detectives Rio Jefferson, Corey Winslow, and the later Maurice Tolliver. This one man, Luther Fuller, will help us connect the dots that solve puzzles that have bewildered us all for years. I've made a deal with Luther Fuller, through his attorney, Malachi Chu…"

"Wait, wait." Rio Jefferson interjected. "Did I just hear you say that you made a deal with Luther Fuller?" All eyes fell onto Rio.

"Yes, detective. That's what I said." Ann Sloan replied.

"And does this deal…for all this information…come with an agreement that for it, Luther Fuller gets full immunity from his crimes?"

"It does. But I fail to see where your question is headed."

"Where it's headed? How could you do this to Moe Tolliver? Luther Fuller killed him..."

"The medical examiner's office for the state of Maryland says otherwise."

"I don't care what the state of Maryland says, everybody here who knew Moe..."

"Detective." Greg Dunlap said. "You are out of line and treading down on a slippery slope."

"Captain, you know what I'm saying is true. How do we give a get out of jail free card to the most notorious killer D.C. has ever seen?"

"Detective Jefferson, we all share in your grief for our Colleague Maurice Tolliver, but in the interest of Justice..."

"In the interest of Justice? What about Justice for Moe?"

Chief Kathy Laney rose from her seat and exploded. "I will not sit here and tolerate this level of disrespect from one of my officers. We are fighting a war out there in them streets and sometimes we have to make critical game time decisions. Luther Fuller is one man. If we can use him to lock up others, well, we're all for giving him a slap on the wrist."

"Even at the risk of him killing more people?"

Before the Chief of Police could say another word, Rio Jefferson stood up and left the conference room. I understood exactly what Rio was saying and I agreed with him wholeheartedly, but to voice that position in front of such a hostile crowd was akin to suicide. So instead I just kept quiet and took notes.

"Detective Winslow, would you please go and find Antonio Felder, so that we can lock his ass up." Ann Sloan told me.

I rose and left the room.

CHAPTER 20
AMEEN

"Wu where are my coats? My jackets, hats, and sweaters?"

"Antonio, my man, they're coming." My Chinese manufacturer said.

"You told me that last week, Wu. I believed you. Stop fucking with me, Wu and get my shit. Your company is based in Stafford, Virginia, Wu. Not overseas. Where is my shit coming from? China by boat?"

"Antonio, my man, please calm down. Have I ever done bad business with you? No, right? I just got a little back up on some orders. Today is Tuesday, your order will be there by Thursday. You have my word on that."

"I don't want your word, Wu. I want my shit I paid for."

"Thursday, my man and no later. Your next order gets a discount."

"Now, you're speaking my language. Take care, Wu." I ended the call.

"The Redskins are sorry as shit and that's all there is to it." Angenic was saying.

"Hey, hey." I called out to her. "Watch your mouth in here."

Angenic moved from behind the cash register and said, "I'm sorry, Ameen. Didn't mean to curse like that."

"Babygirl, I don't give a damn about you cursing, just watch what you say about skins." I told her, smiling. "I don't play about them Skins."

"She's right, though, ock. You know the Deadskins ain't hitting on nothing." Furquan added.

"Yeah, says the Dallas Cowgirl fan. Y'all ain't on nothing either. Tony Homo is a fag. Him and Dez Bryant mess with each other." We all laughed at that.

"Spoken like a true Deadskin fan. We like that and you know it. Don't pound and stick with a losing Mob. We got room for you on the bandwagon. Get on it."

"I might not never."

"Look, last year for his rookie season, RG III was the man until he got hurt. This year, he's back from injury and supposed to be healthy and he's playing like a bum. That's why they put the white boy in there. But he ain't no better..."

"Kirk Cousins. The white boy's name Kirk Cousins." I said.

"Yeah, whatever. He's a bum too. We just lost to Tampa Bay last night. On Monday night football. The biggest state and we lose to the worst team in the league at home. A Canadian Football team can beat the Buccaneers. How do we lose to them at him by seventeen?"

"My man RGIII is..." the door chimes, chimed catching my attention. A battalion of cops, uniformed and plain clothed walked into the store. I quickly noticed that the uniforms the cops wore were metropolitan. They were D.C.. cops. A light browned skinned dude with a detective badge hanging around his neck walked straight over to me. They were there for me. I knew it. I felt it.

"Antonio Felder?" the black detective asked.

I nodded. "Yeah, that's me. What's up?"

"Antonio Felder, you are under arrest for multiple counts of first degree murder. You have the right to remain silent..."

Uniformed officers closed in on me from all sides. "Furquan, get my phone and call Nicole. Tell her to call Rudy Subino and tell him I'm being arrested." I was grabbed roughly and my hands were put behind my back and cuffed. "Keep running the store, both of you. I trust y'all. Get the phone. Call Nicole. Tell her to call my lawyer."

"I got you, ock. I'm on it right now." Furquan said and disappeared.

Then I was led out of the store and put into the back of a Ford Crown Victoria.

***

138

I was taken to the Homicide Building at Penn Branch first. There I was fingerprinted and mugshotted. Whenever I asked who I was supposed to have killed, nobody seemed to know anything. When I saw the black detective that arrested me, I asked to speak to him. He came into the room they had me in.

"Antonio Felder. Good to see you again." the detective said.

"Who did I kill, slim? I'm locked for murder, you said, right? So who am I supposed to have killed?"

"You don't remember me, huh?"

The detective looked familiar, but I couldn't place him. Where did I know him from? I searched his face for some kind of recognition switch to go off in my head, but I drew a blank.

"Under the circumstances that we met under, I can understand why you can't recall my face. I was the detective at the morgue when you identified your daughter, Kenya. I tried to talk to her to find out who killed her boyfriend, Tyjuan, but you blocked all communications with her. Maybe if you had…well that's neither here nor there. My name is Corey Winslow."

"I remember you, now." I told him.

"Good, because you're going to be seeing a lot of me. You've been read your Miranda rights. Do you want to talk to me?"

"I just wanna know who I'm accused of killing, that's all."

"So, you don't want to talk, but you want answers? It don't work like that, dawg."

"I get a phone call, right? A chance to call my lawyer?"

"Here, you won't. Once you get to D.C. Jail, you will. Sure you don't wanna talk?"

"Positive."

"Okay. Have it your way. And for what it's worth, I'm still sorry about your daughter."

***

From Homicide, I was taken to the Superior Court building and arraigned. On sixteen counts of murder. I smiled the entire time. I arrived at the D.C. Jail on the last court load of the day. Things moved at a whirlwind pace for me as I went through intake screening at the jail. I couldn't believe that I was back inside in the infirmary, I laid on my bedroll and tried to make sense out of all that had happened. Somehow, someway, the cops had pieced together the string of murders I had committed. Sixteen murders.

I mentally tallied up the bodies I caught and the math didn't come out right. I had to be charged with the seven murders on Alabama Avenue, the three on Burns Place, a couple on the basketball court, maybe and Tyger. That wasn't sixteen. Unless I was charged with five of the basketball court murders. But how could they possibly know how many I'd killed and how many Khadafi bodied? And where was he anyway? Still out Maryland, I figured. I wondered when I'd see him, since we were definitely going to be codefendants.

I wondered what evidence the government had against me. The guns from the Alabama Avenue murders were gone. What could they have besides a muthafucka saying they saw me that night? That wasn't enough to convict me of seven counts of murder. I thought back to the Tashia Parker Murder. I hadn't touched her or anything in that hotel room and I didn't kill her. She couldn't be on my body count.

I relived the scene on Burns Place in my head. I had on gloves that night. I'm absolutely sure of that. Could it be a partial print off of a shell casing? Did I leave something behind? I didn't think I did. There was positively no connection of me and them basketball court murders. I'd gotten rid of the burgas and nigabs myself. And the guns were in the Potomac. Even the gun that I killed Tyger with was gone.

Then I remembered the van. The van that we kidnapped Fella's mother in. Could something in the van have linked me to the murders on Firth Sterling? Did Donna Jasper I.D. me to the cops? There was no way that she could have. I was in disguise the entire time we had her. Once I eliminated all those questions from my mind, an eery feeling washed over me. The unthinkable crept into my head and made me unsettled.

"Hell, naw. Ain't no way in the world." I said aloud to myself an shook my crazy thoughts from my head. The next thing I know I fell asleep.

***

"Ameen! Ameen, wake up, Moe. Ameen!"

I opened my eyes and tried to focus in the darkness of the cell. Somebody was at the cell door calling my name. "What's up?"

"Kill, I knew that was you when you came in the block. What the fuck, Moe. What you back in here for?"

Sitting up in the bunk, I tried to see who was at the door, but the lights were out in the block, obscuring the face. "Who is that?"

"This is Big Syke, Moe. The big youngin' from Hanover Street. That was down South One with you when you was on the writ. Before you beat the case and went home. Big Syke man."

"Oh...yeah...yeah. I'm hip to you, big boy." I said remembering. "What's up with you?"

"Still fighting this case. I went out the feds to Victorville pen, but they brought me right back here. I got some affidavits and shit, so I might be good in my actual innocence claim. But fuck all that, what are you back in for?"

"A couple bodies. But I ain't kilt nobody. They know that. Them people just mad cause I got back on the last joint. They tryna pin anything on me now. You on detail?"

"Naw, but Sarge fuck with me. So he let me out my cell every night to stretch my legs. I know you ain't got shit in that cell, so I'ma go and get you a care package."

"That's a bet, slim. I 'preciate it." I said and laid back down.

But before I could go back to sleep, Big Syke was back at the cell door.

"Here you go, Moe." He said and passed a rack of cosmetics and food through the cell window." I'm a young nigga, but I know

141

how to do my part. Especially for a good man like you. I got an extra bone crusher, too. You want that?"

"Most definitely, but hold it down for me. Let me holla at my lawyer tomorrow see what my story gon be like, then I'ma come and get that."

"I feel that, big homie. Go head and get you some rest. I'ma holla back in the AM."

"Respect, big boy. Respect. What cell are you in?"

"I'm in 72 cell. I'm out. Love and loyalty."

***

"Felder! Antonio Felder! You got a legal visit. Stick your arm out when you're ready."

I got up and stretched. Took care of my personals and stepped into my bright orange D.C. Jail jumpsuit. My breakfast tray sat on the floor by the door untouched. It would be a minute before I could stomach jail food again. I walked to the door and stuck my arm out and waved it. Seconds, later my door opened. At the bubble, I got my legal visit pass and left the block.

***

"Hey big guy." Rudy Sabino said as soon as I walked in the legal room.

"What's up Rudy?" I responded, walked over and embraced my lawyer.

He had an open file sitting in front of him and a grim look on his face. That was not a good sign. I sat down in the chair across the table, eyes on Rudy.

"Give it to me straight, Rudy. No chaser. What do they have me on?"

"They have a witness that can connect you to some murders. Multiple murders." Rudy's pen went down the list. "Demarcus Stevenson, Carlos Taylor, Leontaye Wilder, Smith Jones. Jonathan

Plumber, Anthony Simmons, James Burke, Curtis Holloway, Linda Holloway, Larcel Davis, Terrell Holloway, William Morris, Xavier Unger, Michael Long, Octavious Bellinger, Charles Gooding..."

"Wait." I said. "What was that last name?"

"Charles Gooding. Says here he was killed February 17th, 2012, right outside the D.C. Jail.

That when I knew. The creepy eerie feeling that I had last night was on point. There was only one person alive that could connect me to the murders of all the people on that list that Rudy read to me. The only man that witnessed me kill Charles 'Lil Cee' Gooding. No one else was there but me and him. Nobody was in that house on Burns Place but me and him.

Nobody was on Firth Sterling that night I killed Tyger, but me and him. Nobody fired a shot on that basketball court but me and him. And nobody knew that I killed seven people on Alabama Avenue the day my daughter was killed, but me and him. The unthinkable had happened. In my wildest dreams, I never could imagine it. I thought back to what I'd said, the day I went to the car lot to enlist his help...

"I'ma go back through there every day until I get him. That's why I'm here. I need you, ock. I can't trust nobody in the world on something like this but you. I know you and I know what you're made of. I know if you get caught, or we get caught, that you ain't gon' snitch..."

The stark realization of what was at hand, was a blow from an invisible fist that knocked all the wind out of me. All I could so was drop my head and shake it from side to side.

"From the look on your face, I take it that you know exactly who the witness is that connects you to all these murders?" Rudy asked.

"Yeah." I replied still shaking my head. "I know exactly who it is."

"Well, all I have here is the charging documents and some stuff from your arraignment. Do you wanna give me a heads ups on who that witness is?"

143

"Luther Fuller. The witness against me is Luther Fuller."

"Why does that name ring a bell to me? Wait...no. Khadafi?"

I nodded my head. The bond that I had with Khadafi started with a prison murder. In a shower room in a unit in Beaumont Penitentiary. The murder of a rat who had told on Khadafi's man. After that came the sacrifice. Six years. Blood, Sweat, Sacrifice. One murder. Five men. Umar, Boo, Lil Cee, Khadafi and Me. Only two of us left. Me and Khadafi. And Khadafi had just become Keith Barnett.

CHAPTER 22
NICOLE

"I'm an investigator for the Public Defender's Service." I told the CO at Visitor Control, in the lobby of the DC jail. "'Here to see Antonio Felder."

The CO consulted a computer. "He had one legal visit earlier and his lawyer's listed as Rudolph Sabino, Esquire with an address for Georgetown. He's not listed as a PDS attorney. His..."

I slid my official PDS identification and credentials through the opening in the glass of the booth. "I don't care what his lawyer is listed as, I work for the city and freelance for Mr. Sabino. He asked me to come and take an official statement from Mr. Felder. Do I need to call him?"

The female CO, a fat chick that looked like Precious, passed the credentials and I.D. back and said, "That won't be necessary. You're official. Antonio Felder is on the 3rd floor. Have you been to the jail to visit an inmate before?"

"Numerous, occasions. Too many actually." I replied and smiled.

The CO smiled back. "So you know the way up. Sorry for the delay. Have a nice day."

Everything that I told the CO was true. I'd been to the DC Jail on too many occasions, but never with the intentions that I had to-day. Getting there early, I knew that I'd be able to pick which small lawyer visit room I wanted. I knew that since the four o-clock count was imminent, that all other attorneys would be leaving and I'd be alone. Getting off the elevator, I approached the CO behind the glass on the 3rd floor's visiting area.

After a brief conversation, I was told to select anyone of the empty rooms. I selected one around the corner from the CO's booth and out of sight of every other room, and prying eye. Once inside the room, I lifted my skirt and moved my panties to the side. Then I pushed the cellphone insulated by two condoms out of my pussy. Quickly, I pulled the condom off he small flip phone and put them into my jacket pocket. The cell phone I put into my leather bag. Taking my jacket off I hung it over the back of the chair and then went back to the CO's booth.

"Does he have to wait until the count clears to come down here or can he come here and be counted down here." I asked the male CO. "We have a lot to do and very little time to get it done. Since it's only 3:45pm, the count hasn't even begun right?"

"I just called Northwest 3 and told the officer in the block to send him down. He should be here any minute now." The CO replied.

Smiling, I thanked the CO and walked back to my room. Butterflies invaded my middle. What I was about to do was bold, spontaneous, and slutty. I love slutty. I sat down in my chair and removed my panties. My pussy was soaking wet just thinking about Antonio's dick. A few minutes later, he walked in. Even in an orange jumpsuit, that man was all of it. After one day in custody, he still looked the same physically. I rushed into his arms and held him and kissed.

I didn't want the kiss to end, but I broke it. "Whew! Listen, they are about to count you in here, so sit down and act normal. But as soon as they leave, I'm giving you this pussy. And I get something else for you."

***

When I looked down, all I could see was my right barefoot and Antonio's right thigh and my left one on his left thigh. My skirt was at my waist and my legs were wide open, shaved pussy on display taking that dick. Antonio held me by my middle as I leaned my head back onto his shoulder. He bounced me up and down on that dick at a fast pace that drove me crazy. I couldn't make noise, so I put a finger in my mouth to bite down on. It didn't take long for me to cum all over Antonio's dick. Or for him to follow suit.

"Damn, that shit was the bomb diggity." I eclaimed as I fixed my clothes and put my panties back on.

146

"Say what you gon say, baby girl, but leave them heels off so I can see them pretty toes."

"Your wish is my command." I replied and positioned myself so that my feet stuck out from under the table. "Seriously, though, what did Rudy say? What the fuck is the government tryna pull?"

"There's a lot of stuff that me and you ain't never talked about Nic. I wanted it that way to protect you. But the long and the short of it is that after Kenya got killed, I went on a nut. I zoned out. You know how I get down..."

"I definitely know that." I agreed.

"Well, I did some things on the streets when I was in that zone. Things I don't apologize for or regret. My biggest regret now is the dude I took with me on my mission. The dude is working with the people and I'm the fatted cow that they want to slaughter. They want somebody's head for all them murders earlier this year. And my partner is going to give them Me."

"Not the dude with the car lot on New York Avenue that you said was your man? The dude you spoke so highly of all the time?"

"Yep. That's him. He's the one that got into that gunfight with the D.C. detective in March, out Upper Marlboro. Remember that?"

I nodded my head. "It was all over the news. That's a shame. So now he's tryna save his own ass because that detective died and give you up. That's fucked up. Bitch made nigga. So, what's the plan?"

"I'm stuck as far as I know, at least until trial. But I want you to do me a favor."

"Anything. Just ask."

"Since you ain't connected to me officially and you are a real investigatory. You can go and visit Khadafi. It would be a conflict of interest if you worked for Rudy but you don't. Feel me? I need you to go and breathe on slim. Try to talk him outta what they're making him do."

"And give him what alternative? We can't offer him a thing. Besides what? Some money? I'm not going to go and threaten him and risk going to jail for some bullshit destruction charge. What do you want me to tell him?"

Antonio paused before speaking again. "I feel what you say and you're right, but I just wanna know why he's doing it? Why he's going on me? What did I do to him?"

"Cool. Fuck it. I'll do it. Where is he? CTF? Still out Maryland?"

"I have no clue. Let me know when you find out. Have you talked to Furquan at my store?"

"Yeah, I did. He called me earlier and asked what's up with you. And he told me that the cops descended upon your shop and searched it. He said they didn't take anything."

"Wasn't shit in there. I'm smarter than that."

"That's good. Do you want me to tell him something? Better yet." I said remembering what was in my bag. I reached in the bag and pulled out the small Tracfone. "Here, put this somewhere. You can call him yourself and talk to him. And me. I want you to call me every day. If they shake down or something, get rid of it, I can bring you one of them when you need it. Is there anything else you need or want me to bring? Drugs? A fold out street knife, to keep you safe in here? What?"

"Damn, bro, you cold blooded trained to go and know exactly what to do, huh? That's what's up. But I thought you said you don't do jails?"

"I know what I said, Antonio. But that was before you put that tongue on me and dicknotized me. As a matter of fact..." I stripped mid-sentence and opened the doors of the small room. I went and looked to see where the CO was, and what he was doing. I saw that he was in the booth sleeping. "Perfect." I said to myself and went back to the legal room. I lifted my skirt and pulled my panties to the side. "I need some more of that dick before I go."

"Nic, you freaky as shit." Antonio said as he slid in behind me.

I bent over and grabbed the chair. I lifted up onto my tip toes as Antonio slid deep inside my walls. "Damn, a bitch can get use to this. Fuck this pussy, baby!"

***

I was at the Wendy's on New York Avenue ordering rood when Antonio's call came through to my phone. "Hey baby, what's up?"

"You. Did you find out where Khadafi is?"

"I did. He's still at the Seven Locks Detention Center in Clarksburg."

"When are you going to check him out?"

"Tomorrow. After I get off work. Then I'm coming back to see you. I think I'm ahdickted to you, boyfriend. Fucking with you, I'ma get my ass fired and my credentials taken away. But you know what? Fuck it. You only live once."

"YOLO."

"You gotta celly in there with you?" I asked Antonio, slutty thoughts on my mind.

"Naw. I'm in here by myself. Why?"

"I want you to pull that dick out and stroke it for me."

"It's already out. It's been out since you answered the call. I can't stop thinking about what you did to me in that room. You go hard as shit and your pussy is a torch."

"Imagine my lips on your dick, right now. You remember the last time I sucked that dick?"

"How could I not? It was only two days ago. You ate breakfast in bed."

"Well, that's what I'ma do for you tomorrow. Stroke that dick for me."

Anthony Fields

CHAPTER 23
KHADAFI

"Luther Fuller, how are you today?" Ann Sloan asked as she sat down.

"I'm good." I replied.

"I wanted to talk to you again before the New Year because I'm going out of town, but I'll be back on the 4th. We arrested Antonio Felder two days ago. Did you know that?"

"I heard about it. So, I guess there's no turning back, huh?"

"Not hardly. Hey…are you comfortable? We're gonna be in here a while would you like a more comfortable chair? Something to drink? Eat?"

"Since you asked, yeah, I'd like something to eat and drink."

"What would you like?"

"Some Kentucky Fried Chicken. A five piece with biscuits. And some fried shrimps from the carryout, with mumbo sauce on the side. A strawberry kiwi Nantucket to drink, too."

Ann Sloan wrote down what I said and passed the paper to her assistant, a man named Howard Easley. "Send somebody to get that. Have it here in the next thirty minutes. Go." She flipped through some papers in front of her and said. "Hungry today, huh?"

"Yeah, cuz, prison food is garbage."

"Okay, listen, take me back to the shooting of Emily Perez and go from there."

"After Keith Barnett was killed in Beaumont, the prison snatched us off the compound. Me, Ameen… Antonio Felder, Boo and Umar. There was one more person with us for the murder, but for some reason the prison separated him from us. Leading us to believe that he had snitched on us. Antonio Felder told the people that he committed the murder to free us…"

"And did he commit the murder?"

"Hold on…let me make sure that you and me are on the same page. Since I agreed to cooperate with you and tell you everything

151

I know. I have full and total immunity from prosecution right? No matter what is was? Or how long ago the crime was, right?"

"That's correct. It's a part of the deal you signed."

"Okay. I killed Keith Barnett in the shower room, not Ameen. He just took the beef to let me and my men go home. He had the most time out of all of us and it made sense back then. Well, to make a long story short, when I came home in 2000, I killed Lil Cee's…"

"And Lil Cee is Charles Gooding, right?"

"Right. I killed his mother and sister."

"Charlene Gooding and Charity Gooding, killed in their home on S Street in Southeast?"

"Yeah. I killed them because I thought Lil Cee told on us. Years later Lil Cee came home. He knew it was me that killed his peoples and he wanted revenge. He tried to ambush me on 7th Street in my hood and failed. Then he tried again at a hotel called the Omni Shoreham. A lot of people died in the parking lot that night, but not me."

"I remember the incident. Charles Gooding was trying to kill you that night?"

"Yeah. He disappeared for a while, but resurfaced when I got locked up for the double homicide you prosecuted me on. I was over the jail and had no clue about who killed Emily Perez and Latasha Allison, Strong's girlfriend. Although, it benefited me, I never knew who did it. The night I was leaving the DC jail, Lil Cee…Charles Gooding was waiting for me. He would have killed me had it not been for Ameen. Ameen came out of nowhere and killed Lil Cee. Then…"

"So, you witnessed Antonio Felder killed Charles Gooding?"

"Yeah, I was right there. After he did it, he told me that Lil Cee had killed the lady cop and the witness against me."

"Why did he say that Lil Cee killed Emily and Latasha?"

"He didn't know for sure, but Ameen said it was to keep me from being convicted on that double. Lil Cee needed me to beat the case so that he could kill me for killing his mother and sister."

"That makes sense. Who else did you say Lil Cee killed?"

"He killed both of Ameen's brothers. Thomas and Daniel Felder. On the same day. He did it to get back at Ameen because he thought Ameen told me to kill his family."

"And that happened in 2010, right?"

"Yeah, 2010."

Ann Sloan looked up from her notes she took. "The murders on Alabama Avenue, were you there for them?"

"Naw. When Ameen came to my lot days later, he told me that he killed them dudes out there because the green eyed dude that killed his daughter hung out right there."

"Your word against his. It's gonna be tough to prove that he did it. Do you know what he did with the guns he used that night?"

"Naw."

"Okay. Now, you were present for the Burns Place murders, right?"

"Yeah. I was right there when he killed all three of them people. He cut the dude's finger off and wrote a message on the wall in blood."

"Now, I'm hunting Tygers is what he wrote, correct?"

"Yeah."

"Alrighty...Let me go and check on that food for you, okay? Well, let me tell you this so you'll know. I talked to Delores Monroe, the District Attorney for Upper Marlboro and she's agreed to drop your charges to a misdemeanor. So you'll go to court there and be sentenced to time served, at some point. In a few days, you'll be moved from Seven Locks to the Central Treatment Facility..."

"Cuz, I ain't tryna go over there! I can't go on no fourth floor..."

Ann Sloan shot up outta her seat. "You can go there and you will. You don't have a say so in the matter. Let's get one thing clear between us, Luther. I offered you this deal to close some cases. While I appreciate you taking it, I can resend it at any time and prosecute your ass to the fullest extent of the law. I'm going to do everything I can to accommodate you however I can, but make no mistaking this, I run this shit. I'm the HBIC...the head bitch in charge and whatever I say goes. When I say move, you move. When I say talk, you talk. This is the Ann Sloan show, not the Luther Fuller show. Do you understand me? Are we clear on that?" When I didn't respond, Ann Sloan bellowed. "Are we clear?"

"Yeah, cuz. We're clear. I got you." I responded with humility but deep inside I was seething. Right then I became more mad at myself than I had ever been. I had sold my soul for a jelly roll and now this cracker bitch was talking to me like I was shit beneath her expensive shoes. But as mad as I was, I knew that I had come too far to turn back now.

"Glad to hear it. Now let me go and check on your chicken."

***

As soon as I got back to the hole at Seven Locks, one of the CO's said, "Fuller ain't no sense in you taking them cuffs off. You got a legal visit and apparently she's been here for about two hours waiting for you to get back from court."

A legal visit? What was Malachi Chu doing here? Wait, didn't the cop say she's been waiting for two hours? She? Who could the she be? "I'm ready go to, then."

The woman waiting inside the room reserved for lawyer visits was a bad muthafucka. She was pretty as hell and reminded me of a broad I'd seen on The Bad Girls Club show from the Oxygen channel. She appeared to be about my age or younger. Her hair was long and straight and from what I could see of her body, it looked like she was curvaceous. The CO opened the door and I walked into the room with my wrists cuffed behind my back. I sat in one of the chairs at the table across from her and waited for her to say something.

"Luther Khadafi Fuller, right?" the woman asked.

"That's me. Who you is?" I asked.

"My name is Nicole Brooks and I'm an investigator for the Public Defender's Service in D.C..."

"Who do you work for? Whose your client with PDS?"

"I have several clients with PDS, but mostly I'm an independent investigator. One of your friends sent me here to see you and ask you a few questions."

"Who sent you, cuz?"

"Cuz?"

"I call everybody cuz, don't pay that any mind. Who sent you, though?"

"Ameen sent me."

I had to be impressed by my old friend Ameen and his ability to reach out to me. He couldn't get to me so he sent an investigator. A pretty one at that. To disarm me. A smile crossed my face. "Is that right? How is my man doing?"

"Under the circumstances, he's not so good. He's hurting. Feels betrayed and wants to know why you're doing this."

"Tell him to join the club on the hurt and betrayed part. As for why I'm doing this, I have my reasons. Just let him know that this ain't personal. This shit is way bigger than him."

"Okay, Nino Brown...my bad. I mean Khadafi. Are you really gonna take the stand against him after all he's done for you? And that's me asking that, not him?"

"I'ma do whatever I gotta do to get out of jail. If that means rocking the woo to scorch an old friend, then it is what it is. And as for your comment about all he's done for me, I've done equal for him. I don't owe him shit. If anything he owes me, cuz. Look, I've had a long day today and I'm tired. Are you done. Because I am."

"Yeah, I'm done. Your answer to his question is that you ratting on him is not personal and that you're gonna d whatever to get out of jail." The woman said.

Again I smiled, but was sick on the inside. "Call me whatever you want to, bitch. In a few months hopefully you'll get the chance to call me a rat to my face while I'm not in hand cuffs. Then I'ma blow your muthafucka head off. You and everybody that you love. You better ask Ameen about me. Talkin' that shit."

"Yeah, whatever. I'm scared." The woman said as she gathered her things and stood up to leave. "Tough talk from a weak nigga.

Can't hold your own, so you roll over on a good dude. Then you wanna still talk gangsta. Still be gangsta. But guess what? You can't have it both ways. Either you're a rat or a gangsta. And you, you're a rat. Cheese eating ass nigga. Fuck you."

The female investigator turned her back to me and disappeared out of the room. I laid in the bed and tried not to think of what the investigator bitch had said to me, but I couldn't help but hear her words. My ego was bruised and my pride was wounded. But I couldn't undo what I'd already done. Plenty of mornings I awoke and wanted to do just that, but realistically, I knew that there was no way to recover from what I'd already done, what I'd already said to the prosecutor. I was now officially a rat and that distinction, I had to accept and wear like a scarlet letter pinned to my chest for all to see. Suddenly banging and kicking on all the doors on the tier got my attention.

"Happy New Year!" inmates called out on the tier.

"Fuck the New Year." I mumbled to myself. I thought about my kids and how long it would be before I could hold them again. Then my mind drifted to their mother. I had heard absolutely nothing from Marnie. She had moved on with her life. But it was all good because she had no clue that she'd be seeing me sooner than she thinks. I pictured Marnie with some nigga at a hotel getting fucked real good and bringing the New Year in with a dick in her mouth.

"I'ma kill that bitch." I said aloud and grabbed the book off the floor. I had the book opened to the page that I had left off on. I read one paragraph and got frustrated. Tossing the book aside, I got up and went to the wall. I banged on the wall until my neighbor, Marquis "Kilo" Venable answered.

"Yeah, what's up, Moe?" he shouted through the wall.

I picked up both books. "And they Call me God and Goon."

Kilo busted out laughing. "Hey Moe…kill my mother, them joints some cold blooded boo boo. That bitch need to stop that shit, huh? That 'Goon' joint cover is wet as shit. Got a nigga thinking that that joint gonna be a mean demo. And you get reading that shit and find out it's some shit. What part did you stop at?"

"The joint had me fucked up at the part where the little girl acting like the dog and shit, but I kept pushing. But when I got to the part about the go hard midget, it was over for me." We both laughed.

"Moe, I got some Cash joints over here. Slim shit be proper. Send your line I'ma send you this. 'Till My Casket Drop' joint. And these two 'Killerz Ambition' joint by the homie Nate Welch. They official."

"I'm on my way." I sent the line for the books and laid back to read.

***

The next morning, I was awaken by a bag on my wall. It was Kilo. "Hey, Moe, I just got the Washington Post and the Times this morning, I got something that you need to read. Send your line."

A few minutes later, I had the Washington Post in my hand. Flipping through the paper, I pulled the Metro section out and the headline hit me right in the face...

THE MOST NOTORIOUS KILLER THE CITY HAS EVER SEEN BECOMES A GOVERNMENT INFORMANT!

THE MAN THAT AUTHORITIES BELIEVE IS THE MOST NOTORIOUS KILLER IN HISTORY OF THE DISTRICT OF CO-LUMBIA HAS NOW AGREED TO HELP THE CITY THAT HE HAS VICTIMIZED FOR YEARS. LUTHER FULLER, KNOWN BY POLICE AS KHADAFI HAS BEEN DETAINED AT A MARYLAND FACILITY SINCE ENGAGING IN A WILD WEST STYLE GUN BATTLE WITH A DECORATED DC DETECTIVE WHO POLICE SAY WENT ROGUE. LUTHER FULLER HAS AGREED TO CO-OPERATE WITH AUTHORITIES AND HELP THEM CLOSE OVER THIRTY UNSOLVED HOMICIDES, INCLUDING THE 2012 KILLINGS OF DC POLICE OFFICER EMILY PEREZ AND MOTHER OF TWO LATASHA ALLISON. TWO MURDERS THAT ROCKED THE NATION. LUTHER FULLER HAS TURNED ON ALL OF HIS PAST ACCOMPLICES, NAMELY ANOTHER SOUTHEAST MAN THAT AUTHORITIES ALSO BELIEVE IS A

PROLIFIC AND PSYCHOPATHIC KILLER. ANTONIO 'AMEEN' FELDER HAS BEEN ARRESTED AND HOUSED AT THE DC JAIL SINCE EARLY DECEMBER WHEN LUTHER FULLER IM-PLICATED HIM ON SIXTEEN COUNTS OF MURDER. INCLUD-ING THE HIGH PROFILE MURDERS OF SEVEN MEN ON ALA-BAMA AVENUE IN SOUTHEAST, BACK IN MARCH OF 2013. LUTHER FULLER STANDS NOW AS THE MOST NOTORIOUS CRIMINAL TO BECOME A GOVERNMENT INFORMANT SINCE RAYFUL EDMONDS.

"Aye, Moe." Kilo called out. "You got that?"

"Yeah, I got it." I replied knowing that my secret was now out of the bag. "I got it."

"Damn, Moe, kill my mother. You hot ass shit!" Kilo screamed on the tier. "Hot bitch ass nigga!"

I laid on the bed and read the article out loud in an attempt to drown out all the commotion on the tier. Every convict on the tier called me all kinds of 'rats' and 'hot niggas'. And as fucked up as I was, all I could do was lay there and take the abuse.

"That nigga Khadafi in 12 cell hot as shit!"

"Dick eating, hot rat, Khadafi!"

"You need a killing, you hot rat!"

"Get your hot ass off the tier! Hot bitch!"

"I'ma shit your ass down when you come out that cell!"

"You bet not go to rec no more. Cheese eating bitch!"

On and on it went, nonstop for the next two days.

***

"Come on, Fuller, pack all your shit." The CO at the door said. "Your leaving."

"Get the fuck off our tier, hot nigga!" a voice screamed out.

Quickly, I gathered all my stuff and wrapped it inside my blanket. As the CO cuffed my hands behind my back, I shouted. "Fuck y'all niggas! I'ma go home and fuck all y'all bitches! Then kill y'all mothers!"

"Fuck you, you rat bitch!" someone screamed.

"Ayo, Kilo!" I said and kicked the wall of my neighbor. "For all that shit you been saying, keep up with the news. Condon Terrace ain't never gon be the same when I finish with your family!"

"On the box." The CO called out. "Pop 12 cell, Let's go Fuller."

The screams and shouts started back up immediately once I was on the tier. But the only voice I didn't hear was Kilo's. Message delivered.

.

CHAPTER 24
MARNIE

"The healthcare industry, in other words, the people that accredits us and sign our paychecks have decided to slowly phase out the LPN positions." My supervisor, Toi Wiseman informed us at a meeting before our morning shift started. "So ladies if you wanna keep your jobs, you will have to go back to school and attain your certification to be paid as a RN. Going back to school is the bad news, but the good news is that Registered Nurses make more money than licensed practitioner nurses. About twenty dollars an hour more. I thought all those frowns would turn to smiles when I said that. Okay, let's go to work. Marnie, you got a cleanup on aisle nine."

"Damn, Ms. T, I just got back from maternity leave…"

"And what, Marnie. You thought that Mr. Watson stopped shitting on himself just because you left for a while. I don't think so, baby. Hurry up to room nine please, you're relieving Tomeka."

And just like that, I was back. Back at the nursing home taking care of elderly and terminally ill patients. The hours were long, my schedule unpredictable and the pay was okay, but I actually liked what I did. At one point, I thought about not coming back to work. I looked at my life after having my son and thought it looked pretty good. Having a house that was paid for, three luxury automobiles and a stash of money and drugs almost lulled me into a daydream of a 'set for life' chick. Almost. Then life happened and reality kicked in real quick. The money and the drugs were gone, the house was off limits to me by choice and all I really had left was two trucks and a new Benz. My future for me and my children was not as stable as it once was. Or that I believed it was. Now with Khadafi in prison facing a rack of time and us not communicating, I knew immediately that Forestville Health and Rehab Center was my final destination. I walked into room nine and whiffed at the smell.

Holding my nose, I looked at my 87 year old patient and said, "Mr. Watson, it's me Monica. I'm back!"

***

On my lunchbreak, I checked my phone and saw all the missed calls and text messages from Cree. I gave the gorgeous nigga one night of bomb sex and I couldn't get rid of the nigga now. Skipping all of his messages, I saw a missed call from Malachi Chu, Khadafi's attorney. Curiosity got the better of me and I called the lawyer to see what he wanted. It bet not be more money.

"Hello, I'm returning Malachi Chu's phone call to me earlier today." I told the female that answered his office phone.

Five minutes later, he came onto the line. "Ms. Curry? Hi listen, I'm kinda pressed, but since you brought me the money for Mr. Fuller, I want to return it to you. I am withdraw..."

"Return the money?" I asked confused. "But why?"

"I filed paperwork in both the D.C. courts and in Maryland to withdraw as the attorney on record for Luther Fuller. It appears that Luther contacted and entered into an agreement with the DC prosecutor's office. In fact, that story was one of topics in the Washington Post, and other convening newspapers. He's agreed to turn in state evidence on people known and unknown to the government in exchange for a lighter sentence. Morally, and professionally I do not work with people who do that.

"In other words, Ms. Curry, and please pardon my language, Luther has become a government whore who has to sell ass for the rest of his life. And that's a direct conflict of interest to me, between him and I. I am a defense attorney. I battle the prosecutors and district attorney's, not kowtow to them. So, please at your earliest convenience, stop by my office and pick up the money that you brought to my office weeks ago. Even if I'm not here, any staff has been instructed to give the money...in cash, back to you. Thank you and take care."

The line went dead on my phone and I had to close my mouth before something flew in it. I was flabbergasted, befuddled, astonished. It couldn't be true. Khadafi would never willingly agree to become a rat for the government. Leaving the cafeteria, I almost ran to the lobby of the nursing home. I searched all around until I found what I was looking for. The nursing home subscribed to the Washington Post yearly and I knew that the paper for today had to be down by the check in desk. I flipped through the front page and didn't see anything about Khadafi. Then I searched for the metro section and sure enough it was there...

THE MOST NOTORIOUS KILLER THE CITY HAS EVER SEEN BECOMES A GOVERNMENT INFORMANT!

I read the article and color drained from my face. I never thought I'd live to see the day that Khadafi Fuller became a broken and beaten man. He had now become the very sorta person that he hated. He killed rats wherever he found them. What could have happened in his life to make him stoop so low? To make him bend over and take dick from the U.S. Attorney's Office? To become exactly what Malachi Chu called him, a government whore.

Then it hit me. Like a strong gust of wind in a tornado, it hit me. I happened. Me, telling Khadafi that I had another man and that I was done with him had broken him. That and a desire to get back at the people that robbed me in our house. If I didn't know anybody else in the world, I knew Luther 'Khadafi' Fuller better than he knew himself. His unquenchable thirst, his insatiable hunger for revenge against me and whoever took his shit, became the most important thing in his life.

Khadafi wanted to do what he did best and that was to make the earth quake when he walked by. To instill fear in everybody that would test him. To kill all those that angered him. The only way to do that was to get out of prison. And by agreeing to tell on his friend Ameen, Khadafi planned to do just that. My head was so fucked up, that I knew I couldn't stay at work. I went immediately to my supervisor and forged sickness.

She told me to go home. I left the nursing home in lightning speed, but home was not my destination. Instead, I hit the Capitol beltway in route to Rte 70, then I'd take that to Clarksburg. My emotions changed in the car on the way to Seven Locks. I went from being shocked and incredulous, to being mad. How dare he become a rat and use me as the motivating factor? He got life fucked up. He was still the man I loved with all my heart, but his latest crime was unforgivable. And I'd forgiven a lot.

When his name was mentioned and he goes down in history as the Rayful Edmond of the 2000's, who am I supposed to be known as? The woman who stood beside him the whole time? Now. Not likely to happen. On the way to Seven Locks, I thought about our homeboy Worm from Capers, who the hood alienated after he was accused of becoming a rat. Then there was Creeko, the big homie who had sold everybody out by telling on a rack of murders. His whole street rep wipe away by one act of cowardness and dishonor. Khadafi knew about Worm and Creeko and purported to hate them both with a passion.

He promised to kill both men on sight to whoever listened and everybody knew he was serious. So, how could he let a moment of weakness and hurt make him sign a blood pact with the devil? I had to see him, to talk to him. I needed to see his face, look into Khadafi's eyes when he explained. I needed answers. I pulled into the parking lot and hopped out the Benz still dressed in nurses scrubs, and multicolored crocs.

At the visitors booth, I checked in and got the paperwork I needed to be able to visit Khadafi. But once I got back to the window, what the CO told me came as no real surprise.

"I'm sorry, ma'am but Luther Fuller is no longer here at the Seven Locks Facility. He was transferred to CTF in the District, this morning."

I walked out of there shaking my head. Khadafi was on CTF's notorious fourth floor. The place where the city had all of its rats until they were needed to tell on somebody. Even though the lawyer telling me, the newspaper proving it to me, and now the CO at Seven Locks verifying the truth for me, I still couldn't believe it. I pulled out of that lot with my phone in my hand. I knew exactly nothing about CTF and how their visits went, but I was about to find out. I called the one person who would know everything. I just hoped she answered her cell phone. The cell phone that she wasn't supposed to have.

The phone rang four times and just as I was about to end the call, Bay One picked up.

"Hello?"

"Bay, what's up, baby?"

"Marnie? Man, I was just about to call you."

"You saw the article in the paper, huh?" I asked.

"Did I? Me and the rest of the hundred bitches in here with me. Muthafuckas been talking me to deaf all morning. I didn't believe that shit, Marnie. I'm not gon believe it." Bay One stated emphatically.

"That's how I felt at first."

"See, you don't know how them people operate Marnie. They'll lie on you and try to sway public opinion either with your or against you. Then people know Khadafi is one of the thoroughest niggas this city ever produced. They know they can't keep him, so..."

"Bay." I interjected. "Khadafi ain't at Seven Locks no more."

"What? Not at Seven Locks? So, where is he?" Bay asked.

"Over there with you. Khadafi is on the fourth floor over there."

"Man...naw! Ain't...no way...get the fuck outta here. He trying something, Marnie. I know Khadafi. I raised him around the way. There's always a method to his madness. He always does shit for a reason. My nigga ain't no rat. He's making a play at something. Tryna catch one of them niggas on the fourth. That's it! Watch what I tell you. He's up to something and we just don't know what it is. I'm telling you, Marnie! I know it. I know I'm right."

"I wish that was true, Bay but it's not. We all know how wicked the government in D.C. can be, but boo, they don't do that. They don't authorize the post to publish shit like that and it ain't true. Muthafuckas'll get sued behind that type of shit. And believe me, the people at the Post verified that shit before they went to press with it. Plus there's some shit that you don't know. Two niggas caught me at my front door out Tacoma Park and made me go in the house..."

"What!"

"Yeah. They robbed Khadafi for the drugs and money he had in there. The thing is that whoever it was knew exactly what was in there. And even though he didn't say it, when I told him it was somebody we know, Khadafi knows that it was Pee-Wee's no good, snapping turtle lookin' ass. He wants to come home to catch Pee Wee and then kill him and whoever it was that came in the house..."

"I feel that, though, Marnie. If Pee-Wee did do some shit like that, then he needs ever bullet that Khadafi is gonna give him, in his life. You know how I feel about that snake shit."

"I know, but Bay after that happened, well before actually. I went out with a male friend and admitted it to Khadafi because I ran into one of his groupie bitches tryna visit him at Seven Locks. Girl, that nigga went off, threatening me and shit. I went right back off on his ass. So he's fucked up about both things. The home invasion and me messing with my friend. I'm telling you, Bay. That set him off. You know how unpredictable Khadafi is when he's mad. I think he made that deal with them people to get out quicker. Khadafi wants to kill people, me included."

"You think so?" Bay asked skeptically. "And you ain't scared. You know how that red, vindictive ass nigga get down. His murder is the meanest, I've ever seen."

"Am I scared? Naw. That nigga ain't crazy. Plus he loves me too much to hurt me. But we still need to talk. That's why I called. When would his visiting days be?"

"On Wednesdays. The fourth floor visits are on Wednesday. They shut this piece down when them niggas gotta visit their peoples. Visiting hours are from 8 am to 3 pm, then 4:30 pm to 8 pm."

"That's tomorrow. I can visit him tomorrow."

"Is that a good idea, though, Marnie. Given all that you've told me. The visits here are not like D.C. jail. They ain't behind no glass. The visits here are contact visits."

I thought about what Bay One had said. I would have to be cautious, but not deterred. "It's all good. I'll just bring my mother and the kids with me. He won't try anything in front of them."

CHAPTER 25
BAY ONE

"For your sake, I pray that you're right, Marnie."

"I know that man, Bay. I been with him for six years. Intimately. I know him."

"Okay. If you say so. I wish I could be there, though."

"I'ma call you after the visit and tell you all about it. Other than that, you good? Do you need anything? You know I'll get it to you?"

"Naw, I'm gucci, Marnie. If I need anything I'll let you know. especially since it looks like I might be here a while."

"Be there a while? Where at CTF? Why?" Marnie asked in rapid fire succession.

"Somebody got killed over here last year and this bitch that was my partner told the people that I did it. So, I gotta be here for a little longer to fight the body."

"Damn, Bay! When it rains it pours. You can't catch a break."

Exhaling, I replied. "I'm already hip. But I'll be a'ight. Let me get off this jack. I love you, girl. Call me tomorrow, okay?"

"I will, Bay. You take care and keep your head up."

"Always, Marnie. Always. A'ight bye."

I wrapped plastic around the phone after I powered if off. Once it was completely wrapped, I reached down into my panties and eased the phone into my pussy. There wasn't a better hiding spot in the building. Taking the towel down that covered my cell door's window, I walked out into the unit looking around for the CO. I found Sherita Fields shaking a cell down on the top tier. The CO, S. Fields was tall, about 6'3 and had big soup cooler lips, but she was pretty and young. And inexperienced. "Aye, CO. Fields?"

CO Fields stopped her search in stride as she gave me her full attention. "Listen, I need a favor."

"What is it, Lake? I don't be doing no favors and shit. That shit'll get a young bitch fired from her job. Know what I'm saying?"

167

I hear you, but that ain't what I'm on. I just need to get a message next door to CO Battle. She's working next door in one of the men's blocks."

"I fucks with Karen. That's my boo, right there. What you wanna tell her?"

"Tell her that my aunt Linda died and my uncle he's a message for her."

"Your aunt died and your uncle has a message for her?" CO Fields repeated.

"Yeah and can you please tell her I need to see her tonight."

"I take a break in an hour I'll do it then."

"Thank you. I appreciate it."

***

The lights in the unit had just went out when Karen Battle appeared at my door like a thief in the night. "What's up Lake? Got your message. I'm here. What's up?"

I was sitting on the bed in nothing but a tank top and some men's boxers, reading a Hip Hop Weekly magazine. I put the magazine on the desk and went to the door. "You know what's up, I miss you."

Karen glanced around furtively. "I miss you too, Bay but we gotta be discreet. You know these bitches be hating on you. Dropping notes and shit, talking 'bout you selling drugs and shit. They probably out they door right now, looking with their lookin' asses. That's why I had to creep over here like I did."

"Fuck that, look CO Fields told me earlier that she fuck with you. She's running the bubble right now, right?"

"Yeah but…"

"No, buts. Go back and holla at her and tell her you need to holla at me in the cell for a few minutes. Here, give her this." I said, producing a wad of money out of my sports bra. I peeled off two one hundred dollar bills and gave them to Karen. "Tell her it's from you."

The money seemed to do the trick. "Okay, Okay, I'll be right back."

***

"Take your boots and your pants off. And your panties." I whispered to Karen once my cell door was shut.

Karen did exactly as I told her to do. I reached under the bed and pulled out my strap on cunt rumption, just like the one I used on the rat bitch Tika. "Lay on the bed, flat on your stomach. As a matter of fact, take that pillow and lay it beneath your pelvis. I want to elevate that wet pussy."

"Bay." Karen said feebly as she laid down. "What are you about to do?"

"You're about to see and feel what I'm about to do."

Getting on the bed on all fours over Karen, I took the wrapper off a strawberry crème life savers candy and put it in my mouth. Then I got low and opened Karen's ass cheeks. I spit the candy out and used it to give some flavor to Karen's clit while I ate her ass. While the candy dissolved on the clit and in her wet pussy, my tongue positioned in and out of that phat ass. After a while, I ate what was left of the candy and dipped low to put my tongue game down on Karen's pussy. She had to grip the sheets on the bed and bite into them to keep quiet. After she came all over my face, I lifted up and slid my fake dick into her. Her deep intake of air let me know, that I was where I needed to be.

"This right here, they call the flat iron position." I whispered and laid on her back completely. Licking on Karen's ear, I fucked her until she came two more times.

***

"What did I do to deserve all that?" Karen Battle asked as soon as she was dressed.

"It's not what you did, but what I need you to do. It's really important, too, Karen."

"What do you need?"

"Today, you worked your regular shift. Tomorrow can you do some overtime and be on duty in the morning?"

"That's easy, why?"

"This is the hard part. My friend is upstairs on the fourth floor and I need …"

"Uh…uh, Bay. I can't take you to the fourth floor…"

"Let me finish. I'm not trying to go up there. I just need you to bring him to medical. It shouldn't be hard, he takes medication due to getting shot about nine or ten months ago. I'm not even trying to be near him like that. In medical they have adjoining holding cages. You can put me in one like I'm waiting for medical attention and put him in the other cage. I swear to God on my daughter's grave, ain't nothing crazy gon happen. I just need like five minutes to talk to him and that's it. Five minutes, Karen. If it wasn't super important, I wouldn't even ask you to do it and you know that."

Karen Battle bit her fingernails as she thought it over. "I can do it. It shouldn't be that difficult. I can go upstairs and get him myself. Bring him to medical and put him in a cage. That's doable. You got that, Bay. I got you."

***

I ended up in the first holding cage before anybody was in medical. No doctors, PA's, nobody. Since I knew that the Medical had to stay chilled at low temperatures despite the wintery mix of weather outside the jail, I was smart and wore thermal underwear under my uniform. I laid on the hard, cold, metal bench and waited. My thoughts raced and I wondered exactly what I'd say to Khadafi. There was so much to say and very little time.

My wait for Khadafi, didn't take very long. He was led into the cage next to me about fifteen minutes after I arrived. I caught a glimpse of him as he was put in the cage but that's it. The two cages were made of steel and fiberglass. The glass that separated the cages was painted black, so I couldn't see Khadafi, but I could hear him. Once the two CO's, Karen Battle included locked Khadafi's cage, they stepped off. Karen put up one hand and flashed the minutes to me. I nodded in understanding. Khadafi had no idea that I was in the cage next to him. My thoughts raced as I prepared for our confrontation. I walked up to the cage door and called out to him.

"Khadafi!"

"Who is that?" I heard him respond.

"Come to the back of the cage by the crack. You can hear me better and we ain't gotta talk loud."

"Bay One?"

"Yeah, it's me."

"But how did you..."

"Don't trip on all that, just come to the back by the crack."

A minute late, I heard Khadafi say, "I'm at the crack. What's up, Bay?"

"Fuck you mean, what's up, Bay? What the fuck is up with you?"

"What you mean, what's up with me? Ain't shit up with me."

"Nigga, I can't tell. The Washington Post says otherwise. Tell me it ain't true."

Khadafi's silence spoke loudly to me. My heart was broken. "So you gon' go out like that, huh? No tricks, no gimmicks, straight like that?"

More silence.

"And here I was thinking that it's somebody on the fourth floor that you're tryna get to to kill. Here I was thinking that it's a trick to what you're doing. I didn't know what it was, but I convinced myself of that because nothing or nobody could ever make me believe that Margaret Henderson's son..."

"Leave my mother out of this, Bay."

"How the fuck I'ma do that when I know that she's turning over in her grave right now. I'm glad that she's not here to see this shit. Your mother was one of the thoroughest bit...chicks that Capers ever raised. Them muthafuckin' drugs just did her bad. But she didn't raise no punk. I didn't raise no punk. You are the realest nigga ever to come out of our neighborhood. Nobody has held it down like you. How are you gonna do this to us? To me? Huh? How?"

"I ain't got no answer for that, Bay. Nothing that you are gonna understand. So, I'ma be quiet and let you talk."

"You gon let me talk, huh? You gon' talk to the government and tell on that dude Ameen, but you can't talk to me?" No answer. "Slim, the dude Ameen took a murder beef for you. If it wasn't for him, you'd be in the feds with a million years. You can't fuck him over like that."

"He also tried to me kill twice."

"And he saved your life twice. Your mind is fucked up right now, Khadafi. It's playing tricks on you. You tryna give yourself reasons to justify what you doing. You fooling yourself if you think what you doing is the right thing to do. And you gotta be careful because you are the easiest person to fool. Don't try and use what Ameen did to you to make yourself feel better about telling on him. See him in the streets. You know how that this goes. You fucked the man's woman and got her pregnant. He was supposed to see you about that. You killed Bean and Omar about the same shit."

"That was different."

"How? If anything, what you did to him was worse. He gave his life for you and you started fucking his woman. Your betrayal was worse. You killed Tee behind his betrayal of Damien. Creeko, too. Remember that? Remember the tattoo…"

"How can I forget it. It's tattooed across my chest in big bold letters. Every time I look in the mirror, I see it."

"You can't see it. How can you see it and read it and know it's there and still do what you're about to do? You killed people just because you believed they did shit…"

"Cause in my eyes, everyone of 'em was guilty. Tee, Creeko, Devan, Omar, Bean, guilty. They were all guilty."

"I'll give you that, but in whose eyes are you guilty in? You deserve a killing, too, then right?"

"You and I both know the answer to that. But who's gonna be my executioner?"

"Somebody will. Karma is a muthafucka and you can't keep escaping death. It's gon' find you somewhere Khadafi, especially now that you're on this sucka shit."

"Sucka shit? That's what it is because I wanna kill the muthafucaks that have crossed me?"

"Oh? So, that's why you're doing this? Because what you think Pee Wee did?"

"You've been talking to Marnie, huh?" Khadafi asked.

"You need to talk to Marnie. She loves you, but she ain't feeling this hot shit either."

"Bay, I done already told you that you ain't gon' understand my mean for doing what I'm doing. Marnie knows why I'm doing it. She's partly to blame, too. But fuck it, y'all know how I get down. I'm still the same nigga."

"You the same nigga? What they feeding y'all up on that hot floor? You ain't the same nigga that I knew. That I watched grow up. The young nigga that was fucking my daughter and I didn't give a fuck because something in me wanted y'all to be together. It didn't work out that way, but up until Esha's death, all she talked about was you and how gangsta and real you were. She was a fan, Khadafi. And now, just like your mother, she's turning over in the grave. The Khadafi that me, your mother, and Esha knew, would never eat government cheese. Never fold, never bow down, never get on his knees and eat prosecution dick. You ain't the same nigga, so stop saying that shit. And you right about me not understanding your reasons for eating cheese. I'll never understand it. I could've ratted on TJ and got him a rack of time. But that ain't how I'm built. And that ain't how you built. I crushed TJ and nailed his ass to the pavement. Just like you've done to countless muthafuckas. And that was what we were built to do. That's how we right our wrongs. Not by getting on no stand and selling out no good man who helped us. If you wanna get back at Pee Wee, do it the right way. The Capers way."

"These people ain;'t gon let me do it like that. I can't beat 'em this time. They mad about the cop dying. If I back out the deal I made, I'm facing thirty or forty years. I can't wait that long to kill Pee Wee. I'ma do whatever I gotta do to kill his ass this year. And he ain't the only person on my list."

"So, no matter what I say or what I've already said, you gon' still get on the witness stand and cook that man like that?"

"I don't have no choice. It ain't personal. Ameen is just a pawn on the chess board right now. I gotta move the pieces, Bay. I gotta win the game. Make muthafuckas feel my pain."

"And what about Ameen's pain? He don't deserve that shit. He lost everything in the world, but his freedom. Don't take that away from him."

"If he was in my positon, I believe he'd do the same thing. I gotta mission to complete, Bay. I know what I'm doing is fucked up, but I don't have another way out. My way out is through Ameen and I gotta do what I gotta do."

"Nobody has ever hurt me like you're hurting me right now. I'm crying over here. My heart is fucked up, Khadafi. I love you so much. But if you don't tell me right now that you ain't gon do this rat shit, I…you will be dead to me. Do you hear me? Dead! I will never speak to you again. Never. Do you care at all about our love, Khadafi?"

"I do, Bay. But you gotta do what's best for you. And I gotta do what's best for me. What you eat don't make me shit. I'm sorry that I hurt you, but I'm not going back on what I've done. I'ma finish what I started. And when I get home, I'ma still send you a rack of money. Whether you accept it or not. I might be dead to you, but you will always live within me. You, Esha, Quette, my mother, Kemie. All of y'all. One day, you might even understand…"

"I'll never understand. Aye CO! I'm ready to go! Lake is ready to go!" I yelled out the cage.

"I'ma always love you, Bay. Irregardless of what you said here today."

"Nigga, fuck you! You rat. All you love is cheese! CO! I'm ready!"

CHAPTER 26
KHADAFI

"Nigga fuck you! You a rat. All you love is cheese! CO! I'm ready!"
I sat down on the metal bench in the cage and wiped my eyes. I couldn't tell Bay One, but her words penetrated my head and heart. She said that she was crying. Why couldn't she understand that I was crying too. Her hearts broken. My is heart is broken. Being a rat ain't no easy shit to do. At least not for me. But what other choice did I have? The deck was stacked against me and I could no longer play it with my poker face. I had to cheat. I heard the CO's the cage next to me and then footsteps recede.

"What the fuck am I doing?" I asked myself.

"You're trying to get home to your children." My conscience answered. "And get back at the people who've done you wrong."

"Come on, Fuller." The female CO said as she opened the holding cage. "Medical has been cancelled for this morning."

I walked back into my unit on the 4th floor and stared all around the block. There were dudes everywhere. The unit functioned just like any other unit I'd ever been in. At tables spread throughout the unit, dudes played cards, dominoes, scrabble, and chess. The TV rooms were semi full, the news on all the TVs. Dudes congregated on the tiers talking, reading.

You had the Christian brothers who fellowshipped and prayed and sang all day. You had a whole community of Muslims in the block. The adhere was called for every prayer and the brothers assembled and prayed five times a day. The Imam was a dude named Keith McGill, but he went by his Muslim name of Homza. Everything was the same, felt the same. But only the people in the unit knew the difference.

Everybody housed in the unit was rats. I leaned on the wall next to myself and shook my head. I felt like I was in an episode of the Twilight Zone. I leaned on the wall and felt sick to my stomach. I rushed into my cell and heaved everything out of my stomach. I threw up and I cried. Laying my arms on the metal bowl, I layed my head down and wept like a baby. I kept thinking about what Bay One had said about my mother, about Esha. I wondered if they were really somewhere looking down on me in disapproval.

I thought about Damien Lucas and what he would think of me now. I thought about Mousey. He would be destroyed by my actions. I was now going against everything that I ever said, every principle that I had ever stood for. Just to save myself and avenge my wrongs. Nobody would understand my situation, especially after all I'd done. All the people I'd killed for the exact same reasons.

"…in whose eyes are you guilty in?"

"Mine! I'm guilty in my own eyes!" I said aloud, suddenly. "And I gotta live with this guilt for the rest of my life. Be tortured by it forever. Isn't that enough?"

As soon as the words left my mouth, I knew the answer to the question. It was No. My guilt would never be enough to undo all that I was about to do, had done already."

"The first law of nature is self-preservation." I told myself.

"…be true to the game, respect the code, and remember the death before dishonor." Ameen had said to me once.

"A rat anywhere is a threat to the game everywhere." Buddy Love had told me.

"Rats die a thousand deaths, but good men die only once." I had heard before.

I got up from the toilet and drunk some water out of the sink. Then I brushed my teeth and washed my face. I looked in the mirror and couldn't believe what stared back at me. Right before my eyes, my head morphed into a large rat's head. "What the fuck?" I shook my head real hard and looked in the mirror again. The reflection was me.

"I'm losing my mind in this joint."

***

Luther Fuller in 42 cell. You gotta visit." The CO called out in the unit.

I looked up from my Scrabble game and heard the CO. "I gotta visit, cuz." I told Moe Brown from 15th Place. "We can finish this when I get back or start a new one. Either way, you gon' lose."

"I'm only down fifty points. One seven letter word'll put me right back in the game. I'ma leave this one right here. Ain't nobody gon' fuck with it."

***

I walked into the visiting area and expected there to be fiber-glass and phone receivers, but there were none. The visits were contact visits. I bent the corner and saw Marnie. My emotions were mixed, but my dick got hard at the sight of her. Her skirt, her blouse, her heels. In her arms was a wrapped up bundle. A smile crossed my face then because I knew that the bundle was my son. My daughter looked up and saw me. She jumped off of her grand-mother's leg and bolted straight to me.

"Daddy! Daddy! Daddy!" my daughter screamed as she latched onto my leg and wouldn't let go.

I reached down and picked her up. She hugged my neck so tight. Tears came to my eyes and wet my daughter's hair as I stood there and hugged her. Then Dada started kissing me all over my face, oblivious to my tears. "Hey, baby girl! Daddy misses you!"

"I miss you too, Daddy!"

"I love you, Dada!" I told her.

"I love you too, Daddy!" my daughter said.

"Hello? We are over here, too. Can we get some love, too, brotha?" Marnie asked.

"My bad, cuz." I said and handed Dada back to Ms. Tawana. "How you doing, Ms. Tawana?"

"I'm good, Khadafi. How about yourself?"

"Just tryna make it." I told her and then hugged Marnie. We kissed. Then I grabbed my son from her before sitting down across from them. I pulled the tiny blanket back from his face and stared at Khamani. A tiny pacifier in his mouth was his only concern as a baby. His eyes were closed, but it didn't matter. I already knew that his eyes were mine and my eyes his. My heart swelled and filled me with emotion. I lifted Khamani to my face and kissed his.

"He's beautiful cuz. No bullshit."

"Uh… I don't know if you can refer to a boy as beautiful, brotha. But I feel you, though. Calling him handsome doesn't seem like it's enough, does it? I get the same way when I hold him."

I held my son and my daughter sat beside me throughout most of the visit. I talked to Marnie and her mother. Kicked it with my daughter and fed my son his bottle. After about an hour, Marnie told her mother to take the kids to the car. I kissed them both goodbye. As soon as Marnie and I was alone, I asked her, "Now what was all that shit you was talking, cuz? Tell me that shit to my face."

"Khadafi, I didn't come here to fight you or fight with you, but you know what's up with me. If you act up in here, we are gonna tear these people shit up. So, you decide your next move."

"You talked real slick on that phone. Said whole lotta tough shit. Repeat it now."

"So, now you wanna act tough again, huh? You wanna beat me up about what I said to you on the phone? Would that make you feel better and more manly? Because if it will, I'd rather you do that, than do what you're doing now."

"What I'm doing now? What talkin' to you?"

"Naw, talking to them people. About Ameen. Listen, I know how you feel. I…"

"You can't possibly know how I feel, cuz. Nobody knows what I feel. Because you ain't never been in this position." I interjected.

Marnie leaned forward and looked me straight in the eyes. "You right about that. I ain't never been in this position, but let me tell you something. I've been in a worse position than you. I thought you were dead when you last got shot. My grief was so bad that I put the barrel of the gun you gave me in my mouth. I know I told you about the first time, but this time it was different. I went through with it, Khadafi. I put the gun in my mouth and pulled the trigger. And continued to pull it until I realized that something was wrong.

180

I checked the gun and saw that it was empty. It was fuckin' empty. You..."

"...took the bullets out of the clip." I said remembering. "I did that after you told me about the first time you tried to kill yourself. I thought that would give you time to think if you ever got that sad again."

"Well, you thought right and you know what else? You saved my life and the life of our son without even knowing it. I went to find the bullets and reload, but by then my mother was there to talk to me, to stop me. I wanted to die to be with you. I didn't care about either of our children. All I cared about was you. Finding you in the afterlife. You ain't never been in that position, so don't preach to me about nobody knows how you feel and I ain't in your position. I have to be in your position, though, because you are my heart and as long as you're in here, a part of me is in here with you. I told you on the phone that I have another man. I don't. I was hurt and stressed out about bumping into Erykah and I wanted to hurt you. That's all. About the money and shit that them niggas took out the house, fuck all that shit. None of that ever meant anything to me. I know you, Khadafi. We been together a long time. I know what you're saying even when you don't say shit. I know you wanna get at Pee Wee because he's the likely suspect in what happened at the house. I didn't think about it then, but now I know that I made you mad and that you wanted to get back at me, too. I know that's how you feel and I know that that's what made you cooperate with them people. Your emotions got the best of you and I understand. But, baby I love you and would never leave you for another man. Never. I'd rather die first. You, me, and our two kids are bonded together for this life and the next. Do you remember what I told you the day you came in and told me that you had to leave because the cops thought you did something?"

"What? When you told me that I didn't have to make excuses if I wanted to leave?"

"Naw," Marnie laughed, "Not that part. I'm talking about what I said right before we made love for the last time. I told you that whatever the situation was with cops that we, you and I would deal with it. The same way we always deal with shit. I told you that I was with you, ride or die, whether it was a year or life in the pen. You remember I told you that?"

"Yeah, I remember."

"Well, that hasn't changed, Khadafi and like I said, fuck Pee Wee, he'll get what's coming to him. This shit you're dog, telling on Ameen, you can't do it, baby. You can't. That's not who I fell in love with. I didn't fall in love with Rayful Edmonds, I fell in love with Wayne Perry, and Kevin Grey and Sean Branch and Antone White. I fell in love with Tony Lewis and Michael Frey. All the gangstas in D.C. live within you.

"That's who I fell in love with. Not Alpo and Moe Brown and Ginguis big tall ass. Them niggas ain't you. Do you see what I'm trying to say to you? Do you understand where I'm coming from? You can't testify against Ameen. You can't help the prosecutor's office solve no murders. That ain't us baby. That ain't us. Whatever situation you're facing, in DC and or Maryland, we gon' deal with it. Like real street muthafuckas. With our heads held high and our dignity intact."

I dropped my head for a minute and when I looked back up, there were tears in my eyes again. "I heard what you said, cuz, but I already did it. In my anger, I told them everything. Everything I stood for, I threw it away already. The damage is already done. I crossed over. Ain't nothing I can do to take back what I already did. The deal has been signed. Everything is already done. I'm sorry, Marnie. Please forgive me.

"You gotta understand that I wasn't in the right frame of mind. I wasn't me. But they don't wanna hear that shit. So, I gotta do what I promised. What's already been done. I'm in too deep, Marnie! They got me by the balls. If I back out of the deal, I'm screwed all the way. Life sentence shit. I'm not going to do that, cuz. I'm almost home.

"After Ameen's trial, I'll be there. So, please understand me when I tell you that I wanna be with Khadajah, Khamani, and you.

Not in prison doing no hundred years. I need you. I need our children. I'm a different man now."

"Yeah, you are a different man now," Marnie said as she stood to leave. "And I don't know if I can continue to love the one you've become."

***

"Pull yourself together." A voice inside my head said.

"How can I do that?" I asked. "I'm a rat now. And I hate rats."

"Do you hate yourself?"

"Of course, I hate myself. I should've never did that shit. I can't be no rat."

"Yes, you can." The voice stated. "You told already, so that makes you a rat already. It's a done deal like you told your woman. Now you gotta live with it."

"Now I gotta live with it." I repeated to myself. "This shit is crazy."

I walked out the cell looking for my Scrabble partner. I had to do something to get my mind off of my situation. I looked around for Moe Brown. Then I found him. He was at the back of the tier with James Montgomery, Yusef Summons, Ratbo from the farms and Isaac "Zeke" Burgess. I called his name but he didn't hear me. I walked down the tier towards him. I could hear their conversation as I got closer.

"Nigga, you hot as shit, James. Everybody know your shit wicked." Moe told James Montgomery. "You telling on all the niggas you grew up with down the West. You hot as shit."

James Montgomery's face balled up immediately. "Moe, you hotter than me."

"How you figure that?" Moe Brown asked.

"Because, nigga, y'all case is bigger and more high profiled. And it's more niggas on y'all case than mine."

"That don't mean shit. The niggas I'm telling on didn't grow up with me."

183

"Man, stop lying. Lying ass nigga. The jury ain't even gon' believe your lying ass. Kevin grew up with you. Rodney grew up with you. Keith grew…"

"You can't count Keith McGill, he telling too. That ain't but two niggas that I grew up with that I'ma bake, you got like ten. Let me see…Vito, Bill, Chen, Pimp, Poo Poo, Draper, Sean Birdy, Erick Birk, Meechie…"

"That's only nine, nigga. You said ten. See, you lying again. Hot ass nigga. That's why you got that shit anyway. So you hot in more ways than one. Way hotter than me, ass nigga."

"Who do you think is the hottest one between us, Yusef?" Moe asked.

The tall, brownskinned dude, shrugged his shoulders and said, "I don't know. Both of y'all on fire. Hot ass shit. Is there degrees to this hot shit? Like can one nigga really be hotter than another one if we all hot?"

"How many people you told on?" James asked Yusef.

"Nothing but fire. It would've been more, but tiny cupped." Yusef replied. "Both of y'all told on more niggas than me."

"And me." Ratbo added. "All I got was one nigga. Big Nate Welch. I got him real good, though. Got him forty years in the feds."

"You scorched him, slim?" Zeke asked amused.

"Did I? Got on that stand and burnt his ass to a crisp." Ratbo said and laughed.

Then all the dudes in the circle laughed. I just shook my head and turned around.

"What the fuck have I done to myself. This shit's crazy."

CHAPTER 27
AMEEN & NICOLE

"Allahu Akbar. Allahu Akbar. Allahu Akbar. Allahu Akbar. Allahu Akbar…Ash hadu an la waha llaha…Ash hadu anal waha wahal…"
"The muzzin is calling the adhen, ock." Saifullah Ackasith told me.
"I see him and I can hear him." I replied still reading the papers in my hand.
"You ain't gon come to the prayer?"
"Naw, ocki, y'all go 'head. I'm good."
"How you gon' be good, Ameen and you ain't offering the prayer?"
"I don't really feel like I gotta explain myself to another man." I said aggressively.
"You, right ock. My bad. But I gotta tell you that Allah gon punish you, ock. You hear the call to prayer and you see the brothers getting in the ranks. And you still ain't joining the ranks. That's pure disobedience and arrogance. Like the Shaitan. Allah's gonna punish you." Saifullah said and then walked away.
"I'm already being punished." I mumbled, but kept reading.
I couldn't believe it. In the back of my mind, I never really believed that Khadafi would snitch. But according to the papers in my hand, he had done exactly that. He'd told on Lil Cee and that man was dead. Killed by me to protect Khadafi. The irony in the situation was unbelievable. The turn of events, the drama. Everything, that had happened in the last year was unbelievable, but it was real, it had happened. First Kenya getting killed, then Shawnay leaving, and now Khadafi is telling on me about the murders I committed to avenge my daughter.
I thought back to the days I spent with Khadafi in Beaumont. I thought about him killing Keith Barnett for the same reason. I looked down the tier at the Muslims assembled for prayer. I listened to the melodic sounds of the Quran being recited in every rakah. The scene and the sounds tugged at my heart. I had been Muslim

185

for eighteen years and now I was disregarding everything that made me who I was. But in my mind, I had nothing to be thankful for and nothing to repent from.

So, I had nothing to say to Allah. I hadn't spoken to or prayed to him in a year. But that didn't mean that I didn't feel Islam tugging at my heart strings every now and then. And right now was one of those times. So, I turned my back to the brothers and went to my cell. What I needed was a visit from Nicole. Not prayer. I pulled the cell phone out and covered up my cell door, after getting it closed. But before I called Nicole, I decided to try Shawnay's phone again.

"The subscriber that you are trying to reach is unavailable."

I ended the call and dialed Asia's cell phone number. Same results. I called Nicole.

"Hey, boo, what's up?" Nicole asked.

"Have you talked to your friend at Quantico lately?"

"Uh...naw. Not lately. As soon as I do, I'ma let you know. How are you doing?"

"As good as can be expected. I been reading Khadafi's statements and still can't believe that he's actually a rat. I can't believe it. I saved his life twice. And this is how he repays me. I didn't tell his ass to get into no gunfight with no cops. He's trying to take what little bit of life I have left. I can't catch a break."

"Don't talk like that, Antonio. You sound defeated."

"I am defeated. The government has the best possible witness against me. How can I get out from under the weight of that. Khadafi's gonna crush my ass in court."

"No, he's not. You have the best lawyer in the city and a confessed killer as a witness. You haven't lost yet. I don't wanna hear you talk like that. Have you talked to Rudy?"

"Yeah I did. This morning. He said the judge granted the speedy trial motion. So it looks like I go to trial in May. The faster the better. If I lose, I can appeal quicker."

"I just told you that you're not gonna lose, didn't I?"

"How can you be so sure, Nic. Are you gonna be on my jury?"

"I might, baby, I might. Do you need to see me?"

186

"Does a bear shit in the woods?"

"I'll take that as a yes. I'll be there later on. Bye."

Once I was called for the legal visit and was about to leave out the block, the CO passed me two pieces of mail with my visiting pass. I stopped and read the return addresses. I didn't recognize either name. Marquis Venable and Bayona Lake.

"Pop one grill, CO." I called out as I ripped opened the first letter from the dude Marquis. As I walked, I read...

Ameen,

You don't know me, Moe, but I have heard a lot about you from my brothers, James and Clarence. They both speak very highly of you. I guess y'all was in the feds somewhere together. Anyway, I read the article in the paper and got your name out of it. The dude that's about to roc the mic in your demo was recently in the cell right next to me. He told me some stuff that might help you in court. Send somebody at me and let me help you out. It's the least I could do for another good man.

Death Before Dishonor,

Kilo Venable

By the time I reached the visiting hall, I had read both letter. A smile crossed my face. Maybe things were starting to look up for me. Maybe. I walked into the lawyer room in the back and saw Nicole sitting at the table writing. She stopped and stood up as soon as I walked in. She came around the table and embraced me, kissed me, and grabbed me.

"When you called, I was getting my toes done." Nicole said and stepped out of one of her heels. "You like."

Nicole's toes were painted red, but the big toe had a multicolored design and small black letters on it. Just two A.F. "I love 'em. As a matter of fact, sit down so that I can lick them."

"Damn, you a freak, boy." Nicole sat down and I pulled my chair up close to hers. "Hurry up, though, because you know I wanna taste that dick before they count."

"You just watch out for the cops." I told her and went to work on her feet. I sucked on Nicole's toes and envisioned all the times that I had done the same thing to Shawnay. And only Shawnay. Every time I tasted Nicole's pussy and every time I had sex with her, I felt like I was betraying my marriage vows. I felt like I was cheating. On a wife that was nowhere to be found. Then I wondered if she was doing the same things. If another man had her toes in his mouth, too. That thought made my stomach flip, but I kept doing what I was doing. I moved up Nicole's leg licking and kissing everything that I passed on the way to her pussy. She wasn't wearing any panties.

"That's my girl." I whispered before tasting her clit, her wetness, the phat lips of her pussy. She tasted so damn good.

"Ooooh…oooh…oh my gawd…Antonio…it's your tongue…is in me…so deep…it feels…hold up, stop…stop…they coming!"

I quickly sat back in my seat and acted like I was reading the envelopes that I brought with me. Nicole did the same. Seconds later, two CO's walked by and counted me. There were dudes in other rooms, but none by us.

"Damn, boy, that was close." Nicole said and laughed. "That shit was feeling so good that I almost didn't hear them coming. That was too close. They gon fuck around and kick my geekin' ass outta here for good. Then what I'ma do?"

"I can't answer that, but I know what I'ma bout to do." I said.

"And what's that?"

"I'm about to eat that pussy some more."

"Naw, brother, it's my turn." Nicole said and got on her knees and crawled towards me. She pulled my dick out of my jumper. Then put it in her mouth.

"Look at your ass. I thought you was worried about getting caught and kicked out of the DC Jail."

Nicole tried to say something, but I held her head so that she couldn't get off the dick. "Don't talk with your mouth full. You can answer me later."

188

I threw my head back and zoned out. I was somewhere else. I pulled Nicole up off her knees and positioned her up on the table where she was laid back on the table. Her skirt was at her waist. I stood between her legs and eased into her wetness. I held both feet in my hands and beat that pussy up, remembering the times I had done Shawnay the same way.

"This pussy is so good! Damn, baby! Shawnay, your pussy is so good!"

***

"Listen, Nic. I need you to go and see these two people." I said and pushed both letters across the table to Nicole.

"Who are they?"

"A dude named Marquis and a broad named Bay One. Read the letters right quick." I waited until Nicole had read both letters. "What do you think about that?"

"From where I sit, it's definitely a good look. Although, lately in court, prisoners testifying for the defense hasn't been necessarily helping them out. I'ma go and talk to both of them and take their statements. I'll get them to Rudy and he can decide whether or not he can use them. I'ma do that asap. CTF is right across the street, I can see...uh...what's her name? Bayona Lake. I can see Bayona Lake today. Tomorrow, I'll go to Seven Locks and see Marquis. Anything else, sir?"

"Naw, but Nic, listen I just want you to know how much I appreciate everything that you've done for me. And that's been way too much. Please let me pay you some..."

"Now you're disrespecting me, Antonio. Making me feel cheap. Like a whore..."

"Nic, stop that bullshit. I been knowing you all my life. We from the hood. We don't do all that extra sensitive shit."

"Yeah. You're right. I was just messing with you. But on a serious note, you know that you don't owe me anything. I told you when we started this thing that I would do anything for you and that's what I meant. It hurts me to see you back in here, so I'm dedicated to making you comfortable and helping you beat this shit by any means necessary."

"Thank you, Nic. I appreciate you."

"Hey, I already told you ten times. I'd do anything for you."

***

I opened the driver's side door of my Audi and tossed my purse and briefcase into the passenger seat. My cellphone vibrated. It was a text from Antonio.

I can still taste you on my lips. Thanks again.

Leaning back in my seat, I kicked off my heels. Tears came to my eyes immediately. The feelings that I felt for Antonio had basically popped up out of nowhere. In my mind, I told myself that I was just having fun in between relationships. I told myself that Antonio was a childhood crush and that having sex with him was purely selfish on my part. I knew all about his wife, his family, his life outside of me. But somewhere along the way I lost my way. I forgot what my position was.

I allowed my heart to get involved. And I never even realized it until I lay on the table in that small room, with Antonio in between my legs. My eyes were on the initials A.F. for Antonio Felder, that was on my toes. I was caught up in the passion of a forbidden act. An investigator, empowered by the city, getting fucked in a room at the DC jail by one of its inmates. A man charged with a double digit counts of murder. I never realized that I had let my feeling get involved until Antonio called me his wife's name. My euphoria turned into mortification immediately.

I couldn't believe it, but I kept quiet. Antonio never said a word, so neither did I. I wiped my eyes and got myself together, but when I put a foot up onto the seat, I could see the initials on my toes again. A.F. Then my tears started again. I was in love with a man who loved someone else. The pain in my chest was a dull ache. A dull yearning. I wanted Antonio to be mine. I needed him to be mine.

But it wasn't meant to be. His wife came to mind. His need and desire for her. For his kids.

Guilt started to eat at me. I knew where his wife and kids were and had kept that information to myself. He'd asked me and I'd lied to Antonio. All because I wanted him for myself. But now, as the hurt in my heart subsided, I knew that I was wrong to withhold the info that Antonio so desperately needed. Then suddenly, a thought hit me. I thought about something that Khadafi had told the prosecutor. And I remembered what Antonio had told me about that incident.

If I could persuade his wife to come back to D.C. she could help Antonio in trial. As bad as I wanted Antonio in my life, I accepted that he couldn't be mine. And no matter who he belonged to, he didn't deserve to be in prison for the rest of his life. I pulled myself together and skipped my feet back into my Guiseppes. I got out of the car and walked over to E Street and CTF.

In the lobby, I encountered a CO at the front desk. "How may I help you?"

"I'm an investigator with the Public Defense Service and I need to see an inmate of yours." I passed her my credentials.

"What inmate would that be, ma'am?" the CO asked.

"Bayona Lake." I replied.

***

Wrapping the cellphone up good, I stuffed it into my powder bottle and put it on the desk. I thought about the text message that I had just sent Nicole.

Anthony Fields

CHAPTER 28
AMEEN

MAY 2014 THE TRIAL...

"Ladies and gentlemen of the jury, the defendant in this case is a very dangerous man..."

"Objection, your honor, government counsel is characterizing the defendant. That's highly prejudicial to the defense."

"Sustained." Judge Reena Raymond said. "Mrs. Sloan, please refrain from any characterization of the defendant. You can argue your case when the official proceedings begin. These are just opening arguments."

"Sorry, your honor, I'll rephrase." Ann Sloan said to the judge and then walked over to the jury panel. "One act of violence in this case, lead to another and another. The defendant Antonio Felder lost his sixteen year old daughter to a senseless act of violence. But as a civilized society, we cannot allow parents to become vigilantes. And in this case that's exactly what happened. Antonio Felder, after learning that his daughter was dead, armed himself with an assault rifle and a handgun.

"He went to the 4300 of Alabama Avenue in Southeast and he surprised a crowd of innocent people. Antonio Felder, unleashed a barrage of bullets into that crowd of people. After several of the victims fell to the ground suffering from gunshot wounds, the defendant walked around to every victim and issued the cap disgrace. A bullet to the head to ensure that they were dead. Seven people ladies and gentlemen. Seven innocent people, killed because the defendant suspected that the man who killed his daughter whom he didn't know at the time was outside. The defendant Antonio Felder..."

I sat in my seat at the defendant table dressed in a black Armani suit and Armani loafers. My head was shaved clean and so was my face. Black Armani personality glasses sat atop of my nose. Fear of the unknown tugged at me, but I was like "Fuck it, bring it on."

For the next thirty minutes we sat there and listened to the US Attorney outline her case to the jury. Then when she finally finished, it was Rudy's turn. And Rudy loved the center stage.

"Good morning, ladies and gentlemen. You have just heard an elaborate and detailed opening from government counsel, where she took you all on a wonderful ride. Well, that's what this trial is, ladies and gentlemen. A ride. One that's purely made up and circumstancial. Maybe I'm a little more realistic. I'm not the glitz and glamour and made for TV movies type. I enjoy simple and concise litigation. The defendant lost his daughter. And what a tragic experience that was, any parent on this jury can empathize on what that must have been like for Antonio Felder. His sixteen year old daughter was gunned down at a local gas station. Sixteen years old. She'll never have children, get married, nothing, because she's gone. Now nobody knows who killed Kenya Dickerson. No one was ever arrested for her murder. The government can only speculate on who her killer was. Speculate and conjecture. That's it. They want you to believe that Antonio Felder killed seven people for absolutely nothing, when he had no clue as to how killed his daughter. There's no evidence, no DNA, nothing physical to prove that Antonio Felder was on Alabama Avenue that night, let alone firing two weapons…physical evidence is tangible evidence, fingerprints, hair follicles, fibers, DNA, something that we can all see and touch. In this entire case, there is none. NONE, ladies and gentlemen, that links Antonio Felder to any murders or any crime period. What the government is going to give you is a witness, who says… "Uh…Antonio Felder told me this…he told me that." Here say, speculation and conjecture is all you'll get in this trial. The government has to do better than that. Make them do better, force them to uphold the law here and prove to you beyond reasonable doubt that Antonio Felder committed any of the crimes with which he is charged. They say…"

Rudy spent the next fifteen minutes trying to unravel the story that the government had just spun to the jury. All I could was sit back and enjoy the two lawyers going at it like adversies in a death match in a cage.

"Counselor, are you ready to call your first witness?" the judge asked.

"I am, your honor, the government calls detective Corey Winslow to the stand."

The black detective that tried to interview me at the Homicide building walked up to the stand and sat down.

"Please state your name and position for the record." Ann Sloan instructed.

"Corey Winslow. I'm a homicide detective for the Metropolitan Police Department, assigned to the 1st District Precinct."

"Detective did you investigate the murder of Kenya Dickerson?"

"Yes. I did."

"Did there come a time when you encountered the defendant?"

"Yes, it did. After Kenya Dickerson was killed and we were able to identify her, I was able to ascertain information about who her parents were. I called Antonio Felder and asked him to come down to identify his daughter's body."

"Did he I.D. the body?"

"He did. He showed up about fifty minutes later and Id'ed his daughter."

"How would describe his demeanor at that time?"

"I would say that he was very distraught. He took one look at his daughter and turned away. He dropped his head into his hands and wept openly. Then suddenly, he left in a hurry. In a purposeful…"

"Objection." Rudy stood up and said. "The witness is attempting to describe the defendant's state of mind at that time. He couldn't know his intentions or his state of mind."

"Overruled. The witness can make an observation of what the scene was. He described the scene. He can do that. He never said he knew what was on the defendants mind. Overruled. Continue counselor."

"Detective, can you tell us what your investigation into the murder of Kenya Dickerson uncovered?"

"I only investigated the case for a few days, before I was reassigned and another detective took over her case. But my preliminary investigation revealed that Kenya Dickerson's boyfriend Tyjuan Glover had an altercation with another man, as Kenya watched. Three days later, Tyjuan Glover was killed as he left his home. Kenya Dickerson witnessed that murder. She was then targeted and killed by the same man who killed Tyjuan Glover."

"Let me stop you right there, detective. Was the identity of that man ever revealed?"

"Yes, it was. The man's identity was known to police immediately after Kenya's death."

"Did the police tell Antonio Felder who the suspected killer of his daughter was?"

"I'm not sure, ma'am. I didn't tell him. As I stated earlier, I was reassigned and I can't say for sure if Maurice Tolliver, the detective who took over the case, told Antonio Felder the man's name."

"Okay, detective, do any other murders happen the day Antonio Felder ID'ed his daughter?"

"Yes. Somebody went to the 4300 block of Alabama Avenue and killed seven people. As a matter of fact, the murders were committed not even two hours later."

The detective stayed on the stand for a whole hour. He told the jury about Tashia Parker's murder, the eight murders on the basketball court, and the link to the first seven murders. He painted a picture of countless murders happening for no reason other than the fact that my daughter had been killed.

"Your cross, Mr. Sabino." The judge announced.

"Thank you, your honor." Rudy approached the witness stand. "Detective earlier you alluded to Antonio Felder identifying his daughter and then weeping, correct?"

"That's correct."

"Then you went on to say he just left, right? He walked out?"

"Yes."

"According to you, he left in a hurry and with a purpose correct?"

"That's what I saw."

"That's what you saw. Could you please leave the stand and show us, the jury what a purposeful hurried leave is?"

The detective looked first at the US Attorney, and then at the judge.

"Your honor if the court will allow it. The detective claims that my client left in a hurry with a purpose. As if to imply to the jury that he was on the way to kill seven people on Alabama Avenue. And I'd like the jury to see what a hurried, purposeful leave is because I don't have a clue as to what one looks like. That reference to my client would leave the jury to speculate and we don't want that. Please instruct the witness to demonstrate what he saw."

"I'll allow it. Please demonstrate what you saw, detective."

"Uh...I...I...I can't do it exactly. I don't..." the detective stammered.

"Okay, that's what I thought. Is it fair to just say that my client, the defendant just left after ID'ing his daughter?"

"That's fair to say."

"Did you go to the scene of the seven murders on Alabama Avenue?"

"No, I did not."

"Did you interview witnesses?"

"No."

"Did you investigate the triple homicide that happened on Burns Place?"

"I was one of the many detectives who investigated it, yes."

"Did you interview witnesses?"

"I did."

"Did any witness mention Antonio Felder?" Rudy asked.

"No."

"Did anybody pick Antonio Felder out of a photo array?"

"Don't think so."

"Did you or any of the other detectives who investigated the triple homicide, find any evidence that links Antonio Felder to that crime?"

"No."

"To save time detective, let me ask you this, in all the crimes that you just testified about to this jury, was Antonio Felder a suspect?"

"Yes, he was."

"How so?"

"Because all the murders were link to one another and it started after Kenya Dickerson was killed."

"Did you ever arrest Antonio Felder for any of these crimes prior to December 16th?"

"No."

"And why not, detective? He was a suspect, right?"

"We had no evidence to prove that he was involved in anyway."

"Thank you, detective. No further questions."

The next government witness was a dude named Jeremy 'J Pack' Jenkins. He testified about the shooting on Alabama Avenue and how the shooter went down killing his friends. He was there on the scene, he said and he saw the shooter.

"Mr. Jenkins, what did the shooter look like?"

"He was dressed in all black clothes, he was brown-skinned, he was bald headed, and he had a beard, a long beard."

"You saw the shooter's face right?"

"Yeah, I saw him."

"Do you see that man in this courtroom today?" the US Attorney asked.

"I think so, yeah."

"Mr. Jenkins it's either yes or no. Not you think, so. Which is it?"

"Yeah, I see him. He's sitting right there." The dude pointed.

"Your honor, let the record reflect that the witness is pointing at the defendant."

"Noted for the record. Proceed."

"Nothing, further."

***

198

"Mr. Jenkins, were you interviews by detectives about this case the night of the shooting?"

"Yeah."

"Did you tell the detectives that the shooter was, brown-skinned, baldheaded, and wearing a beard?"

"Naw, I didn't."

"And why not?"

"Because I didn't want to be hot. I wanted to find the dude."

"You didn't want to be hot. And you wanted to find the shooter on your own? And do what to him?"

"Kill him for killing my homies."

"Okay, Mr. Jenkins weren't you in fact arrested on December 3rd for trying to kill someone?"

"Objection, your honor. The witness is not on trial here."

"Under the 6th amendment's confrontation Clause, your honor." Rudy stated.

"Objection overruled. When you put this man on the stand, counselor you knew that his motive for testifying could come into question. Well, it's happening. Continue, Counselor Sabino."

"Answer the question, please Mr. Jenkins."

"Yeah, that's true." The witness said.

"And isn't it true that you told the police about this bearded brown-skinned man for the first time on January 20th, when detectives came to DC Jail to speak with you?"

"That's right."

"And isn't it true that you were shown a twelve prison photo array that day?"

"Yes."

"Your honor, I'd like to introduce the photo array into evidence as exhibit 1 A."

"It's been noted." The judge said.

"Mr. Jenkins, is this the photo array that you were shown that day?"

The witness looked at the photo array. "Yes. That's is it."

"Did you that day pick anyone off that photo array as being the man you saw?"

"Yes, I picked one."

"The faces are all numbered under the photo, correct?"

"Yeah."

"Please tell the jury which number or face did you pick out."

"I...I...I...picked out number six."

Rudy got the photo array from the witness and looked at it. "Number six, huh? Your honor, please let the record reflect that the witness on January 20th of this year, picked a man who is not the defendant. In fact number six on this array happens to be a detective at the 5th District Precinct that is known to the court."

"Let me see that," the judge ordered. Rudy handed her the array. "The record will reflect that the witness identified a DC police officer."

"No further questions."

***

Did you say something to the judge about this shock belt they got me wearing?" I asked Rudy as soon as I was in the cage behind the courtroom.

"Of course. Judge Raymond says that the US Marshal's Office asked for the belt, due to the high profile nature of your charges. She won't budge. The belt stays."

"Damn. I keep sitting there at the table waiting for one of the Marshal's to accidentally hit the button and shock the shit out of me."

"What do you think about the first half of the trial?" Rudy asked.

I smiled. "As always you handled business. It's in our favor so far."

"Those were just the prelims, kid. Watch what I do to their star witness."

The rest of the afternoon, the government put on medical examiners, crimes scene search officers for two different crime scenes. Then they rested for the day. Judge Raymond called an end to the day at 3:40 pm. Before leaving, I looked into the gallery to see if anyone I knew was there. I spotted Furquan, Angenic, and Nicole. Nicole waved at me and smiled. I smiled back.

***

The next day was pretty much the same as the afternoon from yesterday. The government paraded ballistic experts, doctors, detectives, and CSI technicians on and off the stand to illustrate for the jury how brutal and vicious all the crimes scenes were. At the end of each person's testimony, Rudy asked the same questions.

"Sir, did any of the evidence that you gathered tell you who committed the murders?"

And with each question of each witness, the answer was the same. NO!

"Is there anything that you collected, guns, shell casings, bullets recovered from the victims, prints, a cell phone, a brush, comb, anything that connects the defendant to a crime?"

The answers were always. No! The judge called a halt to the trial at 3:30 pm. And just like that the 2nd day of my trial was in the books.

Anthony Fields

CHAPTER 29
AMEEN

"...you've tuned into the Donnie Simpson morning show. That's right, I'm back by popular demand. We got a new one by Tank that I want you to hear. So everybody listen up..."

Every now and then/ I think of all the times we shared/ you're the only one who let me know you really cared/ I miss you more and more/ and day by day it's hard to see/ just how you loved me so/ and everything you gave to me/ I still believe, I believe in you and me/ and that one day we will be/ together, and I know it sounds strange to you/ but I never moved on/ because my heart wouldn't let it go/ still I let you know/ I gotta let you know/ that I still believe...

Listening to Tank's song and staring out the window of the court bus as I was transported to court, made me nostalgic. I had only been home two years, but I had experienced a lot in those two years. Good and bad. So no matter how things turned out for me, I could live with it. It wasn't like I was innocent anyway. I had killed all the people that I was accused of killing. And if everything was to rewind and go the way it went, I'd do the same things over again. This was the life I chose. This was the hand I was dealt in life and I would continue to play it with a poker face.

At the Superior Court building, I got dressed into my street clothes and shock belt. About thirty minutes later, court was in session. The government's first witness of the day consisted of people who were on the basketball court never Alabama Avenue and had survived the massacre out there the day eight people were killed. In vivid detail, they each described the carnage, the mayhem, bullets flying, bodies dropping, blood splattering, bones breaking, the aftermath, the clean-up, rehab, the nightmares. And again, with each witness, Rudy kept his cross examination brief and concise.

"That day on the basketball court was a painful time I know, but did you see who was doing the shooting that day?"

"Yes, I did."

"Can you tell us who you saw with the guns doing the shooting?"

"Yes. It was two people wearing Muslim clothes..."

"When you say Muslim clothes sir, what does that mean?"

"The way people that you see on the news that live in Muslim countries like Cron...the clothes they wear? The women, I mean. In the long dresses that come to their feet and the veils. The head covering things that they wear were only their eyes can be seen. That's what I'm talking about when I say Muslim clothes."

"So the people who were firing guns onto the court that day were dressed in long dresses and a head covering that only showed their eyes?"

"Yeah."

"Okay. Did you see the defendant, Antonio Felder out there that day?"

"No."

"No further questions."

And so it went with each person the government put on the stand. Their last witness of the day was Donna Jasper, who calmly and methodically detailed her kidnapping and being held hostage. She spoke of being forced to call her son. She talked of being in the van later and how she escaped. Rudy's cross examination of her mirrored the others.

"Ms. Jasper do you recognize the defendant in this case?"

"Um...just from being in court and pictures I was shown."

"Okay. Pictures you were shown and court, I got you. Is the defendant that's sitting there at that table, the man that kidnapped you?"

"I don't know. He could be yes."

"I'm sorry, Ms. Jasper, you lost me. You said three different things in one sentence."

"You said and correct me if I'm wrong. I don't think so..."

"I said I don't know."

"Excuse me, you're right. You don't know. He could be. And yes. Which answer are you giving to my question? Do you need me to repeat it?"

"No, I don't need you to repeat anything. I know what you asked me."

"And your answer is what?"

"My answer is, I don't know for sure. The two men who kidnapped me were wearing disguises."

"How do you know this, Ms. Jasper. That they were wearing disguises? Could you see the disguise plainly?"

"Of course I couldn't see that they were disguised. The police told me that they probably were disguising themselves."

"Now we're getting somewhere. The police told you that the man who kidnapped you were wearing disguises. And before being told that by the police did you know for sure that the kidnappers were wearing disguises?"

"No, I did not."

"For the record could you please tell this court how you described your kidnappers?"

"I described what I saw. One man was wearing a Department of Public Works Uniform with the hat to match. And the other wore regular clothes, jeans, I believe, boots, a sweatshirt, and all black jacket. The man in the regular clothes wore a multicolored hat on his head and he had dreads. Dreads and glasses."

"Okay, were you shown a photo array of the men after you were interviewed by the police?"

"Yes, I was."

"And what happened?" Rudy asked.

"I couldn't pick anyone out because I didn't see anyone that I recognized."

"

"Your honor let the record reflect that the witness was shown the same photo array that already entered as exhibit 1A, and that the defendant's pictures is included in the array and the witness could not, did not positively Id him."

"Duly noted, counselor." The judge said.

"Ms. Jasper, have you ever seen the defendant, Antonio Felder before today?"

"Not that I know of, but he could've been…"

"There are over two hundred thousand black men in the District of Columbia, Ms. Jasper isn't it true that any number of them could have kidnapped you?"

The witness did not speak.

"Your honor, would you please instruct the witness to answer the question."

"You have to answer the question, Ms. Jasper." The judge told her.

"What was the question again?" the witness asked.

"Isn't it true that you have no clue as to who kidnapped you, because according to the police, your kidnappers were wearing disguises?"

"I don't know if they were wearing disguises or not. And if I saw the two men in here today, I could pick them out."

"So, you don't see one of the men in this courtroom that kidnapped you?"

"No, I don't. I already said that, didn't I?"

"No further questions."

Rudy walked back to the defendant table and leaned towards me. "The US Attorney is getting her ass handed to her on a plate. Don't look now, but she's livid. I watched her turn three shades pink in five minutes. I believe that's it for today. Tomorrow we get Fuller. So, lace your shoestrings up tight. Things will heat up tomorrow."

"Court is adjourned until tomorrow morning at 8:30 am. Counselors Sabino and Sloan, I need to have a word with you both at the bench. Now!"

CHAPTER 30
KHADAFI

"Your honor, the government calls Luther Fuller to the stand." US Attorney Ann Sloan announced to the court. From the cage behind the courtroom, I heard the prosecutor say my name. Then I knew it was my time to take the stand. I imagined if the butterflies I felt were because of stage fright or the fact that I had to face Ameen. The Marshalls came and got me out the back. I was led to the witness stand.

"Please state your name for the record, please."

"Luther Antwan Fuller."

"Mr. Fuller, do you recognize anybody in this courtroom?"

"Yeah."

"Who do you recognize?"

"Him right there." I said and pointed at Ameen.

"And who is that man right there?"

"Antonio Felder. But I call him Ameen. Everybody in prison calls him Ameen."

"Your honor, please let the record reflect that the witness has positively identified the defendant by his government and street name." Ann Sloan stated.

"It's reflected. Proceed."

"Mr. Fuller take us to February of 2012, when you were getting released from the DC jail."

I ran the whole story down and ended it at the part where Ameen killed Lil Cee.

"Are you sure that it was Ameen who killed Charles Gooding?"

"I'm positive that it was him. Although, I was surprised that he shot Lil' Cee and not me, I watched him kill Lil Cee. Later he told me that he did to save me."

"Was Ameen wearing a mask?"

"Naw."

"Describe the way he looked that night."

"The same way he always looked. Bald head and long beard."

"You say the way he always looked. Does the defendant look that way now?"

"Naw. He cut his beard. He's had a beard ever since I met in 2005."

"Okay, did you see Ameen again after that night?"

"Naw, not until he showed up at my car lot out the blue one day."

"And what happened, then?" the prosecutor asked me.

"He told me that his daughter had been killed and he broke down crying."

"Where were you and Ameen when all this took place?"

"In the office of my trailer that sits on my car lot."

"And Ameen told you that his daughter was killed and that he..."

"Objection, your honor, the government attorney is leading the witness."

"Sustained. You can't lead him, counselor."

"I'm sorry, your honor. Mr. Fuller, what happened after Ameen told you his daughter had been killed?"

"He told me that she had told him about a situation that happened at a movie theatre that involved his daughter's boyfriend and a dude with green eyes. After the movie incident, the green eyed dude killed his daughter's boyfriend while she watched. He told me that he told his daughter not to attend her boyfriend's funeral, but she went anyway. After the funeral, she was killed. Ameen told me that he believed the green-eyed dude was his daughter's killer and that the dude hung on Alabama Avenue."

"Go on Mr. Fuller, and then what did Ameen tell you?"

"He told me that he went to Alabama Avenue in search of the green-eyed dude, his daughter had told him that the dude's name was Tyger, he killed seven people who were out there. He told me that he walked around to each person because he wanted to see their eyes. He said Tyger wasn't out there and that he going to kill everybody that be out there until he catches Tyger. Then he asked me to join up with him."

"Antonio Felder, told you that he killed seven people on Alabama Avenue, then asked you to join him? To do what?"

"To kill people. He asked me to kill with him."

"And did you kill with him?"

"Yes, I did."

"Let me stop you right there. Mr. Fuller, did you want to be here today?"

"Naw."

"Did you want to take the stand and testify against Antonio Fuller?"

"No, I didn't."

"And why is that?"

"Because he was a good friend of mines. Still is."

"So why are you here today testifying against your friend?"

"Because what we did was wrong. All the people that we killed. It was wrong. My conscious been bothering me and I decided to come clean. For the families we hurt. To show that I'm sorry."

"Okay, Mr. Fuller, once you teamed up with Ameen, who did you kill first?"

"I killed a friend of mine named Tashia Parker."

"And why did you kill Ms. Parker?"

"Because Ameen needed answers about dudes from here neighborhood. She was from the same neighborhood as Tyger. He asked me to talk to her. I did, but she wouldn't talk. I called Ameen and told him the situation. He came to the hotel where we were and tortured information out of her. Once he did that, I feared that she would tell the police what happened and I'd go to jail for it. So, I killed her to silence her."

"Then what happened?"

"A day or two later, we went…me and Ameen went to an address that Tashia gave us looking for Tyger and his cousin Choppa, who we learned drove the getaway car the day Ameen's daughter was killed."

"And what address was that, that you went to?"

"2213 Burns Place, Southeast."

"When you and Ameen went to the address, who did you find there?"

"Three people, two women and a man that we knew was Choppa."

"What happened next?" the US Attorney asked me.

"We bogarted our way in and Ameen killed everybody in the house."

A loud gasp escaped the mouth of the jurors. Then there was a clamor in the gallery that got the judge's attention.

"I will clear the gallery if I hear one more sound. Continue with your direct."

"Thank you, your honor. Mr. Fuller, did you learn who the victims were that Antonio Felder killed?"

"Yeah. Choppa, his mother, and Choppa's girlfriend."

"And you say that Antonio Felder killed all three of them?"

"Yeah, that's what I'm saying. And he didn't stop there." I said, my rat juices were flowing.

"He didn't stop there? What did Antonio do next?"

"He cut off Choppa's finger and wrote a message in his blood."

"Antonio chopped off someone's finger and wrote a message in who's blood?"

"He cut off Choppa's finger and used it to write a message in Choppa's blood."

"And what did that message say?"

"Now, we're hunting Tygers."

"Meaning?"

"It was a message to the green eyed duded named Tyger that we were coming for him."

"Your honor, I'd like to request a short recess, so that the witness can get a drink of water."

"We'll take a short break here. We will resume court in fifteen minutes."

I left the witness stand and went to the back of the courtroom, to an empty cage. The prosecutor came in the back as soon as I was in the cage. Her smile radiant.

"You're doing great, Khadafi. The jurors love you."

"How long is all of this gonna take? I'm getting tired."

"It's gonna take as long as I need it to take to convince these jurors that Antonio Felder killed sixteen people." To her assistant, she said, "Go and get Khadafi an energy drink."

***

Mr. Fuller, whose idea was it to shoot up the basketball court?"

"Ameen's. The burqa and nigabs we wore were all his idea."

"Why did he decide to have y'all dress up in Muslim attire?"

"Both of us are Muslims, so we are familiar with the Islamic attire that the women are required to wear. We...well, he knew that the women's burqa, which is the long dress and the nigab, the vieled head wrap would be perfect for shooting up the basketball court. So that's what we wore when we did it."

"And then what happened after that?"

"After, we kidnapped Donna Jasper and made her call her son Fellano Jasper. Her son agreed to bring Tyger to the prearranged location."

"And what location was that?"

"Firth Sterling Road at the bottom of Barry Farms projects."

"Did Fellano Jasper come to Firth Sterling?"

"Yeah."

"And did he bring the green eyed dude Tyger?"

"Yeah, he came and brought Tyger."

"What happened next?"

"Ameen killed Tyger, the dude who killed his daughter and I killed Fellano Jasper."

"And then what?"

"And then nothing. It was over. Ameen was satisfied that he'd avenged his daughter."

"I have nothing further for this witness, your honor."

"Your cross, counselor."

"Thank you, your honor. If the court would just let me go over some notes. Court's indulgence...okay, I'm ready. Now, Mr. Fuller, you told this jury that you came forward because what you did was wrong and that your conscious bothered you, correct?"

"Yeah."

"But that's a lie isn't it, Mr. Fuller?"

"Huh?"

"What you said while sitting on the stand is a lie, isn't it? Just like all the other lies you've told isn't that right?"

"Objection, your honor, defense counsel is badgering the witness. And being argumentative."

"Sustained. Cut it out, counselor. Proceed in a different fashion."

"Sorry, your honor. Mr. Fuller, isn't true that you were involved in the shootout with a police officer?"

"Yes."

Once I answered that question, they came rapid fire, hard and brutal. Things became an all-out slugfest between me and Ameen's lawyer.

CHAPTER 31
DETECTIVE COREY WINSLOW

Everything looked pretty good for the government at first. Then Rudolph Sabino happened from my seat in the gallery, I watched what seemed like a lion eating a gazelle.

"Once you realized what type of time you were facing out in Maryland, you decided that you wanted to go home, ain't that the truth?"

"Naw."

"Oh, you don't want to go home?"

"Yeah, I meant…"

"I know what you meant, but what I'm asking you is this, didn't you know that you were facing a lot of time in Maryland for shooting the D.C. cop?"

"He shot me, too. We shot each other."

"That's not what I asked you sir. Please answer only the questions that I ask. Didn't you know that you were looking at, at least twenty years in Maryland?"

"Yeah, I knew that."

"And isn't it true that you knew that you were about to be charged in D.C. with kidnapping?"

"The detective told me that…"

"So, all this stuff you told the jury about feeling bad and your conscious bothering you was all lies wasn't it?"

"Naw."

"It wasn't? Well, did you come forward to the cops before the shootout where you were injured and subsequently charged with assault on a police officer?"

"Naw. I didn't come forward before that, naw."

"And then you learned that the officer died, didn't you? You learned that he died and figured that you'd face more time, right?"

"Wrong, my lawyer told me that the cop died of some natural stuff and not the bullets, I fired."

"Do you lie Mr. Fuller?"

"Naw."

"You don't lie at all?"

"Yeah, I've lied before, but I don't lie no more."

"You don't lie anymore? You're lying right now, aren't you?"

"Naw."

"Okay…okay. How many people have you killed, Mr. Fuller?"

"A lot."

"A lot, huh? Can you put that into numbers for us, please?"

"A lot. That's all I know. I don't know no numbers."

"Okay. In 2007, in a prison in Texas, didn't you kill Keith Barnette?"

"Yeah."

"And didn't Antonio Felder tell the authorities that he did it to free you?"

"Yeah, he did that."

"Then you came home in 2008 and killed several people."

"Yeah."

"Was one of those people a woman named Charlene Gooding?"

"Yes."

"And another one of those people was a three year old toddler named Charity Gooding?"

"Uh huh."

"Yes or No, Mr. Fuller?"

"Yes."

"Now, the man that you have sworn under oath that Antonio Felder killed, Charles Gooding weren't Charlene Gooding and Charity related to him?"

"It was his mother and sister."

"His mother and little sister. And you executed them, didn't you, Mr. Fuller?"

"Objection, your honor." Ann Sloan shot to her feet and said. "On two points. First asked and answered. Defense Counselor has already asked that question and had it answered by the witness and need I remind the court that the witness is not the one on trial here. Mr. Sabino is trying the witness."

214

"Sustained on both parts. Tread light, Mr. Sabino, but continue." The judge stated.

"Okay, you were arrested for a double homicide in 2011, correct?"

"Yeah."

"Accused of killing Gregory Strong and Devan Harris?"

"Yeah, that's right."

"You were acquitted at trial, right?"

"Yes."

"Because the witness, the main eye witness was killed right outside this courthouse wasn't she?"

"That's what I heard."

"Do you know who committed those murders, Mr. Fuller?"

"Ameen told me that Lil Cee killed them. Right after he killed Lil Cee."

"Good answer, Khadafi." I whispered to myself and scored on point for the government.

"Glad you came back to that. Was anyone else there at the scene when Ameen killed Lil Cee outside of the jail?"

"Yeah, my girl. She was inside the truck waiting for me."

"And she saw Antonio Felder kill Charles Gooding?"

"Yeah."

"And her name is?"

"Monica Curry."

He never told us that? We could've subpoena Monica Curry. I made a note to do just that in my note pad.

"Let me direct your attention, Mr. Fuller to the day at your car lot, when as you Ameen came to you for help, to join him in killing people. He told you that he killed seven people?"

"That's what he said."

"Was anybody else around when he said that?"

"Naw, just me and him."

"Are you aware that there's no evidence that he was ever there on Alabama Avenue that night?"

"I was told that, yeah."

"So, you want us to believe Antonio confessed to seven murders to you, because you wouldn't lie?"

"You can believe what y'all wanna believe. I know what he told me."

"And all the murders that you've testified to, that you say that you and Antonio Felder committed, since there's no evidence to link Antonio to any of it, you want this court to believe you, why?"

"Because I'm telling the truth."

"And you don't lie, righ?"

"Right."

"No further questions, your honor." Rudy Sabino said and walked over to the defense table.

***

"You got to them." I exulted to Ann Sloan once we were out in the hallway.

"You think so, huh?"

"Yeah, in the beginning it looked bad, but then Sabino looked like he was just arguing with the witness and then he just stupped. Totally, captivated. I think that's a good sign."

"It better be because we just rested our case and hung the conviction of Antonio Felder on Luther Fuller. And judging by the looks on the jurors faces, I don't think they liked Khadafi too much."

"That's what you got? I didn't get that. We'll see, I guess. What's on your agenda for the rest of the evening?" I asked.

"I need to regroup and figure out how much damage may have been done today and if I decided it was a lot, how I can possibly remedy it. But that can come later. After say, one of the foot massages you are so good at."

"A foot massage sounds great. When and where?"

"My office in one hour." Ann gathered her things and walked away.

"Damn…shit. Fuck this pussy! Fuck this pussy! I want you to cum in this pussy. Cum in me you black muthafucka. You making my pussy sore and you have to cum in me to cool it off."

I stopped mid stroke and pulled off the Magnum condom. I slammed my dick back into Ann Sloan and a few minutes later, I did as she requested. Again and again.

***

Hours later fully dressed and exhausted. I leaned back in one of the chairs in Ann's office. My eyes closed, I remembered something from the trial. "Earlier in court, did you catch the part where Khadafi told Sabino that his girlfriend, Monica Curry witnessed the Charles Gooding murder?"

"I caught that, Corey." Ann said and shuffled some papers on her desk. She pushed one sheet across her desk.

"What's that?" I asked as I rose to get the sheet of paper.

"His witness list, Sabino's witness list. He knew what Fuller would say, so he preempted us. At the bottom, you'll find Monica Curry's name. He might put her on the stand tomorrow. Who knows? He beat us to that punch though."

"Maybe not. Curry is Fuller's girlfriend. She has to be on his side. So, she won't go against Fuller."

"Have you seen her anywhere near him since he turned? I haven't. And I'd be willing to bet you that if she's on that list, Sabino has already talked to her. Her name wouldn't be on that list if he hadn't. Monica Curry is gonna contradict Fuller and say he committed the Gooding murder or that Antonio Felder did not. Rudy Sabino is a strategist. He baited us in. He baited Khadafi in. Once Monica Curry contradicts Fuller's story on that account, his credibility will be in the sewer. None of the jurors will believe him, ever again. That's if they ever did."

"What about Felder? Do you think Sabino will put Felder on the stand?"

Ann rose from her seat and paced the floor. She stopped and turned to face me. "Remains to be seen! But he could. Antonio Felder's murder conviction was overturned and can't be brought out on cross examination. He beat the Texas murder beef. Can't bring that up. He has a clean slate. So Sabino might put him up there. We'll have to wait and see."

CHAPTER 32
AMEEN

"Mr. Sabino, it's your turn. Is the defense ready to put on its case?"

"The defense is ready, Your Honor." Rudy responded.

"Call your first witness to the stand."

"The defense calls to the stand…Marquis Venable."

The whole courtroom watched as a brown-skinned young dude with dreads that hung down to the small of his back. His solid green jumpsuit was crisp and fresh. He wore retro-colored Jordan's XX on his feet and glasses on his face. He was also handcuffed to a belly chain that encircled his waist.

"Do you promise to tell the truth so help you God?"

"I do." Kilo responded.

"Okay. Please state you name for the record and your age."

"Marquis Venable. I'm twenty nine years old."

"Mr. Venable why are you wearing a belly chain and hand-cuffs?"

"Because I'm incarcerated. At least until I go to trial."

"And what are you incarcerated for? Awaiting trial for?"

"For murder. First degree murder while armed."

"Mr. Venable are you housed at the DC Jail or CTF?"

"Neither. I am being housed at Seven Locks Detention Center."

"And while housed at the Seven Locks Detention Center, did you have the opportunity to encounted a man named Luther Fuller? Well first, let me established this…the defendant in this case…Antonio Felder, do you know him."

"Naw. I never met him before in my life."

"Okay. Did you have the chance to encounter Luther Fuller?"

"Yeah. The pigs…I mean police put him next door to me in the hole after he almost beat a dude to death in his population unit."

"Is that righ? Okay did you know Luther Fuller?"

"Not before that day, but I'd heard about him before. His street rep was legendary."

"His street rep?"

"Yeah, his…well, I'm not comfortable saying all that, you dig."

"Okay, Mr. Venable. I'm…well, did you ever converse with Luther Fuller?"

"Yeah, all the time. He slept right next door."

"And did there come a time when he mentioned his case to you?"

"Yeah, he told me all about the gunfight with him and the cop, and the time he would be facing if Maryland convicted him. Then he said he had some charges coming in D.C., too."

"Did he mention a man named Antonio Felder to you?"

"Naw. He kept talking about a dude named Ameen, though. I saw the article in the paper and figured out that Ameen was Antonio Felder."

"And what did he say about Ameen?"

"That that was his man and he was a good dude, but he was gonna tell the prosecutors in D.C. that Ameen killed all the people he killed…"

"The people who killed Marquis, just to be clear?"

"Luther Fuller told me that he killed a lot of people, but was going to lie and say that Ameen killed the people."

"And why would he do that?"

"To get out of prison. He said that he had two kids and he didn't want them to grow up without him. He said that he was gonna put everything on Ameen."

"And Marquis, how did you become known to the defense?"

"I read the article in the Post about Khada…Luther Fuller making a deal with the government to testify against Ameen…Antonio Fuller and I felt that I had to let somebody know about what Khad…Luther Fuller told me. I had my family to find him and I wrote to him."

"No further questions, your honor."

"Ms. Sloan, your cross."

Ann Sloan's skirt was a little tight, but she moved with alacrity and grace. I watched her move across the courtroom as if it was hers. She commanded everyone's attention.

220

"Mr. Venable, how long was Luther Fuller in the cell next to you?"

"For about two weeks or so, I guess."

"And according to you, y'all didn't know each other, right?"

"Right."

"And you mean to tell me that a man you don't know confesses his sins to you and he didn't even know you?"

"That's what he did. Straight up."

"But why would he do that?" Ann Sloan asked.

The dreaded youngsta on the stand shrugged his shoulders. "I don't know. Maybe he felt that I'd be a good listener."

One of the jurors snickered. That made me smile.

"And you want us to believe that this man that didn't know you. Just confided all of his personal business to you? Just because he was housed in a cell next to you?"

"It's not about what you believe. It's about the truth and that's what I just said. If you wanna know why Luther Fuller decided to tell me what he told me, you gotta ask him."

"Your Honor, I have no more questions for this witness."

"Sir, you may step down."

After Kilo was taken in the back of the courtroom, Ann Sloan, spoke to the judge.

"Your Honor, if Mr. Sabino plans to parade every criminal that's ever been in a cell next to Luther Fuller into this court, I'd like to concede..."

"Enough, both of you. Your oral motion is denied, Counselor Sloan, Mr. Sabino, please continue with your defense." Judge Raymond commanded.

"I'd like to call Bayona Lake to the stand."

The door to the courtroom opened and Marshal's lead a short, stocky woman with a man's hair cut to the stand. She was dressed in a two piece dark blue uniform. A belly chain around her waist, her wrists cuffed to the chain.

Once she was seated on the stand, Rudy said, "Please state your name?"

"Bayona Lake. But everybody calls me Bay One."

"Okay, Bayona, why are you wearing a belly chain and cuffs?"

"I'm locked up over CTF. Fighting a body."

"Right. Do you know the defendant in this case?"

"Outside of what Khadafi told me about him, Naw."

"Well, let's establish one thing. Who's Khadafi?" Rudy asked.

"Khadafi is Luther Fuller. We used to call him Dirty Redds, but he came home from doing ten years for killing Tee and he changed his name to Khadafi."

"And how did you come to be here today?"

"I had some information that...I read about what Khadafi was doing to his man Ameen...Antonio Felder and thought it was messed up what he was doing. Especially, since he had already told me some stuff. I got my counselor at CTF to send a letter to Antonio Felder and he sent his investigator to see me. I told her everything that I'm about to tell y'all."

"And what do you want to tell this court, Bayona?"

"That Khadafi is lying on that man. And he's doing it for reasons that I know about."

"Bayona, did Khadafi ever visit you, while at the CTF?"

"Yes. Several times. He was my youngin'."

"By that you mean, he was your younger friend?"

"Yeah. I raised him in the hood. I've been knowing him since he was a baby. I grew up with his mother and their family."

Rudy pulled a couple papers out of his brief case. "Your honor, I'd like to enter these into the record as exhibit 2A, 2B, and 2C."

"Let me see those, Mr. Sabino."

Rudy walked up and handed the judge the exhibits.

"Explain to the court exactly, what these are counselor." The judge said.

"On one page, exhibit 2A, that's copy of a fake ID that Luther Fuller used every time he went to the CTF to visit Bayona Lake. Below that is a copy of the form he filled out and signed. The next two exhibits are enlarged photos of Mr. Fuller inside a visiting room at CTF, visiting Bayona Lake."

"The court recognizes the exhibits and enters them to the record. Proceed."

"Ms. Lake did there come a time when Khadafi, mentioned his friend Ameen?"

"Yeah, he told me that somebody killed Ameen's daughter and that he was about to go ham."

"He was about to go ham?"

"Yeah, that's slang talk for hard as a muthafucka."

"Okay. He told you he was about to go ham?"

"Yeah. He was upset. Said he was gonna kill a lot of people."

"Okay. Bayona was there a time when you came to see Khadafi since he's been incarcerated?"

"Yes. He's now housed at the CTF, too. In January, we ended up in the medical department together, but in different holding cages."

"Did y'all have the chance to talk?"

"We did talk, yes."

"And what did you and Khadafi talk about?"

"His girlfriend, his kids and some other stuff."

"Other stuff like what?"

"We talked about his house being robbed and his girlfriend messing with another man."

"Just so we're clear, do you know Monica Curry?"

"Yes. She's Khadafi's girlfriend. The mother of his two kids."

"Are you and her friends?"

"Of course. I raised her, too. She was best friends with my daughter, Esha."

"Okay, tell us about your last conversation with Monica."

"She told me that she admitted to Khadafi that she had another man and that their house had been robbed. She said that he didn't take that info well. After that is when I saw Khadafi at CTF in medical. He told me that he had to get out to kill the dudes who went into his house and he wanted to kill the dude that his baby mother was messing with. I confronted him about the newspaper article and he told me that he had to put the murders on Ameen in order to get out of prison. He told me that he had to lie on his friend so that the prosecutor's would let him go."

"No further questions."

"Your witness Counselor Sloan."

"Thank you, your honor. Ms. Lake is it customary for inmates on the fourth floor at CTF to be around the rest of the CTF population?"

"Naw. That almost never happens."

"Almost never happens, but it happened in your case, right?"

"Yeah, it did."

"And if it never happens, why do you think it happened in this case?"

"Divine intervention, I guess."

"Yea, I bet. Ms. Lake what are you charged with, that has you incarcerated at the CTF?"

"Murder. I'm charged with killing a dude who killed my daughter."

"So you feel a common bond with the defendant?"

"Huh?"

"You're here because you and the defendant both had a child murdered?"

"No, that's not why I came here today."

"Isn't it true, Ms. Lake that you were recently indicted and charged with strangling a woman at the CTF?"

"That's what they say I did, yeah…"

"And isn't it true that that woman was killed because she was believed to have been a rat? An institutional rat that told CO's you sold drugs at the CTF?"

"I have no clue as to why she was killed."

"And isn't it true that you hate rats?"

"They had the biggest in the world in my hood. I been around them all my life."

224

"I'm referring to human rats, Ms. Lake? Isn't it true that you hate people who snitch on others?"

"Nobody likes a snitch, do they?"

"I happened to love snitches, Ms. Lake. But you hate them, correct?"

"Yeah, I hate them."

"And isn't that the real reason you're here today, to get back at Khadafi because he's snitched on his friend?"

"Naw. I'm here to let the court know that Khadafi is a liar and he'll do anything to get out of prison. He'd tell on his mother to get out. They need to know that before they convict an innocent man."

"No further questions."

"Let's take a recess for lunch and continue at 12:15 pm. Court's adjourned."

***

"How are you doing, big guy?" Rudy asked me. "Having fun yet?"

"I'm good, Rudy. I'm good. You did your thing out there and I think the jurors were receptive to two things. One that Khadafi is a liar and two that he wants to go home."

"And that's exactly what we need them to know. I think we got them, kid. Trust me, after these next two witnesses…"

"Who's up next?" I asked.

"We got the girlfriend, Monica Curry and a surprise witness. I can't tell you who it is until I make sure that they are here at the courthouse. Just fall back and let me handle this. Let me earn this money."

"Earn your money, then champ, earn your money."

***

"My next witness that I'd like to call is Monica Curry."

Khadafi's baby mother was beautiful. Petite, caramel complexed and classy.

"State your name for the record please." Rudy told her once she was seated.

"Monica Curry."

"Ms. Curry, are you a mother?"

"Yes, I have two beautiful children."

"And how old are your children?"

"Khadajah is almost four and my son Khamani is six months old."

"Can you please tell the court who the father of your children is?"

"Yes. His name is Luther Fuller."

"Do you know the defendant in this case?"

"Not personally, no. But I've heard his name mentioned for years. Him and Khadafi that's Luther's nickname...they were locked up together. A murder happened at the prison. A murder that Khadafi did, but Ameen, his friend took the beef so that Khadafi could go home."

"Is that all you heard about Ameen?"

"No, what happened was, when Khadafi went home, he started messing with Ameen's baby mother. Ameen found out. When Khadafi went back to prison, Ameen stabbed him. Then for the next three years they were bitter enemies. They ended up at the DC jail together in 2011 and they stabbed each other there. That I know for sure, but the rest is what Khadafi told me."

"Okay. Speaking of Khadafi being at the DC jail in 2011, did there come a time when he was released from there?"

"Yes, in February of 2012."

"Was Khadafi picked up from the jail or did he walk home?"

"He got picked up. I waited outside for an hour to pick him up."

"So you were at the DC jail when Khadafi walked out of the gate?"

"Yes."

"Ms. Curry did something happen at the DC jail that night?"

226

"Yes. A man was killed. I saw it."

"Okay, good. Was that man named Charles Gooding?"

"The news said that was his name, yes."

"Did you talk to the police about what you say? The murder, Ameen?"

"No. The police never came to me and asked me anything."

"Okay. Did you see the person who killed Charles Gooding?"

"Yes, I did. I saw him good."

"Do you see that man in the courtroom today?"

Marnie looked around the courtroom then replied, "No, he's not here."

"Did Antonio Felder kill anybody that you know or didn't know that night?"

"No he wasn't even there. The dude that killed the other dude...Charles Gooding, he was tall, about 6'12 and skinny. He had long cornrow braids and a tattoo on his face. And that man ain't in this courtroom."

"Did you a few months ago, experience something dangerous, traumatic?"

"Yes."

"What happened, Ms. Curry?"

"I was ambushed by two masked men while going into my home. They robbed the house at gun point and took a lot of money."

"Did you tell Khadafi about this incident?"

"Of course, I did. He was very upset. He wanted to kill people, he said."

"Is that all Khadafi said?"

"No."

"What else did he say?" Rudy asked her.

"That he was gonna do whatever it took to get, home and when he got home, that everybody was going to pay."

"Thank you, Ms. Curry no further questions."

"Your cross, Counselor Sloan."

United States Attorney Ann Sloan stood and said something that nobody expected.

"Your honor I don't have any questions for this witness."

CHAPTER 33
NICOLE

"Your honor the defense calls to the stand Luther Fuller."

Marshalls went into the back somewhere and came back with the dude Khadafi. He was a feared killer according to everybody that know him, but to me he didn't look so menacing, the expression on his face was one of pure disdain and he acted perturbed at being called back to the stand.

"Mr. Fuller, have you been charged with any murders?" Rudy asked him.

"No."

"But you've admitted to committing several, right?"

"Yeah."

"And how is that you haven't been charged with murder when you sat right on that stand and admitted to killing Tashia Parker, Fellan Jasper, and some people on the basketball court?"

"I took a deal that the government offered me. They gave me immunity from all crimes if I told the truth about all the other murders that Ameen did."

"Is that right? So, you get to go home, right?"

"I guess."

"You don't guess anything, it's either you go home or you don't."

"Yeah, they said I can go home."

"What about your charges in Maryland?"

"They've been dropped."

"That was some deal you got from the government, wouldn't you agree, Mr. Fuller?"

"Yeah, I guess it was."

"No further questions."

"Any cross, Counselor Sloan?"

"None your honor."

"Defense Counselor, how many more witnesses do you plan to call?" the judge asked.

"Just one your honor. The defense calls to the stand…Shawnay Felder."

A small smile crossed my face as I watched the doors to the courtroom open and Antonio's wife walked in. She as breathtaking. Her appearance had changed a little since I'd seen her last in her home in Texas, but she was here and I was glad. I watched Antonio almost break his neck to watch his wife, his kids mother walk down that aisle to the witness stand. His eyes were glued to her every step.

"Please state your name for the record, please."

"My name is Shawnay Felder."

"Mrs. Felder, are you any relation to the defendant?" Rudy queried.

"Yes. He's my husband." Shawnay replied.

Every juror in the box leaned forward to hear whatever the woman had to say.

"Mrs. Felder, have you been living in Washington DC, lately?"

"No, I haven't. I've been living in Texas."

"And why have you been living in Texas?"

"I wanted to get away from the memories of my slain daughter."

"And your husband, why wasn't he with you?"

"Antonio wanted to remain here to be near her grave. He didn't want to leave her by herself. So, we separated and I went to Texas."

"Mrs. Felder do you have a son named Kashon?"

"Yes, I do. He's almost five years old."

"And could you please tell us his father's name?"

"His father's name is Luther Fuller."

Another clamor arose in the courtroom and the judge was livid.

"Marshal could you please clear my courtroom gallery. Thank you."

Seconds later, I was ushered out of the courtroom door.

CHAPTER 34
AMEEN

"How did that happen, Mrs. Felder, if you're married to Antonio Felder?"

"In 2008, Antonio was still in prison and Luther was always stopping by to bring money for me and the kids because Antonio told him to. I was young, I was vulnerable, I gave into the desires that I felt. In 2009, I gave birth to a son and knew immediately who his father was, but I kept that info from both Antonio and Luther. I ended the situation with Luther months after it started and hadn't seen him in years. In 2011, Antonio came home from prison and I confessed everything to him. He forgave me and we got married in February of last year. On Valentine's Day."

"Was Khadafi… Luther Fuller upset about your wedding?"

"I believe so."

"Do you believe that he would lie on Antonio to get him out the way, just to be with you again?"

"I believe that without a doubt."

"Okay, let me direct your attention to…excuse me," Rudy has to consult his notes. "to the 30th of March 2013. Did there ever come a time when you learned of a heinous crime happening on the 30th of March?"

"Yes, it was weeks after my daughter's death, three people were shoot to death in a house on Burns Place. I remember it vividly, because the house I grew up in is nearby."

"And where were you that night on the 30th of March?"

"At the grand opening of Antonio's store."

"Was Antonio Felder at that grand opening that day?"

"Yes, he was."

"And did there come a time when he left for any reason?"

"No, he never left. We served customers until the store closed and then we…me, my husband, and my two children left and went home."

"Did Antonio Felder leave your sight at all that night?"

231

"No, he did not."

"No further questions for the witness."

"Any cross examination Counselor Sloan?"

"No, your honor."

"Does the defense rest in this case?"

"Yes." Rudy Sabino said. "the defense rests."

I couldn't believe my eyes or my ears. My heart swelled with pride and love as I watched Shawnay get off the witness stand. I could smell her scent as she walked by. She looked at me and winked. She was back. And that in itself was a good sign. Had she returned just to help me? Was she about to disappear again? I couldn't let that happen. "Rudy." I called out.

"Yeah, kid?"

"Get some contact info on my wife. Tell her I love her. Tell her I need to talk to her. Tell her…"

Rudy smiled. "You can tell her yourself, big guy. I have her info already and besides she says that she's staying. Your children are outside with her. They want to see you, but not like this. I have to get back to the trial. I'll be back."

"Mr. Sabino, Ms. Sloan can we squeeze in both closing arguments, today or do you think we should wait until tomorrow?

Both lawyers conferred for a minute and then said, "We can do them now. They won't be that long."

"Okay, let's do that then." The judge decided.

I didn't hear a word of either closing argument, all I kept hearing was what Rudy told me earlier. Shawnay was back and my kids were outside the courtroom. And they wanted to see me. I had to fight back tears, I was so excited. I kept looking behind to see if I could catch another glimpse of Shawnay. I couldn't. The next thing I know I was being led out of the courtroom. My jury was in deliberations.

CHAPTER 35
KHADAFI

"Cuz, put me down with the lick on the weed."

"Slim, them people let me go down to District Court and fuck my girl. I got the weed from her. I be eating street food and all that shit." Stanley Currie bragged.

"Damn, cuz, they ain't fuckin' with a nigga like that with me." I said.

"That's because the muthafuckas they got you tellin' on ain't no big fish nigga. I'm about to get a nigga the real live death penalty out Virginia. I just burnt up a rack of niggas from up the forty. Me and Red Ray bitch ass. I'm about to go out Alexandria and do this nigga Tommy Hager in. I cooked his ass once, but he got back on appeal, so I gotta go and cook his ass again."

"Hold on, hold on...they call you Wali, right?"

"Yeah that's me."

"I'm hip to you, cuz, the homies out Pollock chased you around the yard, Moe Styles, Buckey Fields, Merwin, Youngboy Lee, and Devon. They say you jacked everybody at that joint. And they say you fast as shit and light on your feet. We heard about that down Beaumont. That shit happened in like 2007, right?"

"Yeah, them bitch niggas tried to get me, but I'm too smart for that shit. I got hit one time." Stanley Currie pulled his shirt back to reveal his shoulder, "Right here. The knife got stuck in me. I'ma kill all them bitch niggas when I catch them especially the lil red nigga that stabbed me. I ain't even know they knew Lil Tommy. Fuck them niggas, though, slim. This is the part of the game that the youngstas don't like. But I don't give a fuck."

I watched the big 300 pound hot nigga talk that gangsta shit like he wasn't a real rat as he fired up a fat ass blunt of Kush. He hit the weed a few times and then passed it to me.

"You know what's some wild shit, though, slim?" Stanley said as he coughed smoke out of his lungs.

"What?" I asked, inhaling the smoke of the weed.

"You. They say you killed a nigga out the feds for being a rat. Cut the nigga up in a rack of pieces and everything. Then you turned around and became the same thing that you killed the dude for being. That's wild as shit."

I passed the blunt back to Stanley. "Here you go, cuz, I'm good. Thank you." I left the cell and walked back to mine. I felt like I was caught in the Matrix or something. I was on a labyrinth wandering around aimlessly.

***

It was two days after Ameen's acquittal that Ann Sloan and Detective Winslow came to see me at the CTF.

"We got good news and bad news." Ann Sloan offered. "Which one do want first?"

My spirits tanked. I knew that the people who sat in front of me wasn't going to hold up their end of the bargain. "C'mon cuz, I did everything y'all asked me to do. I told you everything I knew. I cooperated completely and here y'all come with the bullshit. I signed a deal with you to do what I did and in exchange for my cooperation, my charges would be dropped, here and in Maryland. That's what I signed up for."

"Listen to me, you piece of shit. I know what the fuck I told you. I know what you signed. I know our agreement. Did I say anything about not honoring our agreement? No. So, shut the fuck up and listen to what I have to say. The good news is that I'm working to get another shot at Antonio Felder and some other people and you'll be able to help me. So, I'm not upset about Felder's acquittal. I rushed to judgement and should've fought harder to have the trial delayed.

"The speedy trial killed us, not you. We didn't have time to cover all of our bases. The agreement that we made is gonna be executed upon. But… the bad news is…when I made the deal with the District Attorney Delores Monroe, it was a deal with her. Unfortunately, since then she has been demoted and another person is in her office. A man named Tom Dexter. At the time when DA Monroe agreed to drop your charges you were only charged with the crimes involving Maurice Tolliver.

"Last week and we just this found this out, that guy you beat up with the phone at Seven Locks has been clinically declared as 'brain dead'. He's been transferred to hospice care and his family is suing the State of Maryland. That in conjunction with all of the tax payer's money that will be spent to care for the guy who you damn near killed has the new DA pissed off. He's charging you with assault and malicious wounding. There's no way we can get around it. I'm sorry."

"Y'all tricked me. I can't believe it. I let y'all trick me like that."

"We didn't trick you, Khadafi. You tricked yourself. Since we still need you, I'm gonna keep talking to the new DA and see if we can get you to a diversion program or something. All is not lost. Give me some time and I'ma make it work out. Trust me."

I stood up and headed for the door. "I already did that once and look what that got me."

***

Four Months Later...

"Mr. Fuller in light of your cooperation with the government in DC and your acceptance of responsibility in this case. I accept your plea. I hereby sentence you to three years to be served in the Maryland Department of Corrections.

To Be Continued...
The Ultimate Sacrifice 6
Coming Soon

Submission Guideline

Submit the first three chapters of your completed manuscript to ldpsubmissions@gmail.com, subject line: Your book's title. The manuscript must be in a .doc file and sent as an attachment. Document should be in Times New Roman, double spaced and in size 12 font. Also, provide your synopsis and full contact information. If sending multiple submissions, they must each be in a separate email.

Have a story but no way to send it electronically? You can still submit to LDP/Ca$h Presents. Send in the first three chapters, written or typed, of your completed manuscript to:

LDP: Submissions Dept
Po Box 944
Stockbridge, Ga 30281

DO NOT send original manuscript. Must be a duplicate.

Provide your synopsis and a cover letter containing your full contact information.

Thanks for considering LDP and Ca$h Presents.

BOW DOWN TO MY GANGSTA

By **Ca$h**

TORN BETWEEN TWO

By **Coffee**

THE STREETS STAINED MY SOUL **II**

By **Marcellus Allen**

BLOOD OF A BOSS **VI**

SHADOWS OF THE GAME II

By **Askari**

LOYAL TO THE GAME **IV**

By **T.J. & Jelissa**

A DOPEBOY'S PRAYER **II**

By **Eddie "Wolf" Lee**

IF LOVING YOU IS WRONG… **III**

By **Jelissa**

TRUE SAVAGE **VII**

MIDNIGHT CARTEL III

DOPE BOY MAGIC III

By **Chris Green**

BLAST FOR ME **III**

A SAVAGE DOPEBOY III

CUTTHROAT MAFIA II

By **Ghost**

A HUSTLER'S DECEIT III

KILL ZONE **II**

BAE BELONGS TO ME III

By **Aryanna**

CHAINED TO THE STREETS III

By **J-Blunt**

KING OF NEW YORK V

COKE KINGS IV

BORN HEARTLESS IV

By **T.J. Edwards**

GORILLAZ IN THE BAY V

TEARS OF A GANGSTA II

De'Kari

THE STREETS ARE CALLING II

Duquie Wilson

KINGPIN KILLAZ IV

STREET KINGS III

PAID IN BLOOD III

CARTEL KILLAZ IV

DOPE GODS II

Hood Rich

SINS OF A HUSTLA II

ASAD

TRIGGADALE III

Elijah R. Freeman

KINGZ OF THE GAME V

Playa Ray

SLAUGHTER GANG IV

RUTHLESS HEART IV

By **Willie Slaughter**

THE HEART OF A SAVAGE III

By **Jibril Williams**

FUK SHYT II

By Blakk Diamond

THE DOPEMAN'S BODYGAURD II

By Tranay Adams

TRAP GOD II

By Troublesome

YAYO III

A SHOOTER'S AMBITION III

By S. Allen

GHOST MOB

Stilloan Robinson

KINGPIN DREAMS II

By Paper Boi Rari

CREAM

By Yolanda Moore

SON OF A DOPE FIEND II

By Renta

FOREVER GANGSTA II

GLOCKS ON SATIN SHEETS II

By Adrian Dulan

LOYALTY AIN'T PROMISED II

By Keith Williams

THE PRICE YOU PAY FOR LOVE II

DOPE GIRL MAGIC II

By Destiny Skai

TOE TAGZ III

By Ah'Million

CONFESSIONS OF A GANGSTA II

By Nicholas Lock

PAID IN KARMA III

By **Meesha**
I'M NOTHING WITHOUT HIS LOVE II
By Monet Dragun
CAUGHT UP IN THE LIFE II
By Robert Baptiste
NEW TO THE GAME III
By **Malik D. Rice**
LIFE OF A SAVAGE III
By Romell Tukes
QUIET MONEY II
By **Trai'Quan**
THE STREETS MADE ME II
By **Larry D. Wright**
THE ULTIMATE SACRIFICE VI
By **Anthony Fields**
THE LIFE OF A HOOD STAR
By Rashia Wilson

Available Now

RESTRAINING ORDER **I & II**
By **CA$H & Coffee**
LOVE KNOWS NO BOUNDARIES **I II & III**
By **Coffee**
RAISED AS A GOON I, II, III & IV
BRED BY THE SLUMS I, II, III
BLAST FOR ME I & II

ROTTEN TO THE CORE I II III

A BRONX TALE I, II, III

DUFFEL BAG CARTEL I II III IV

HEARTLESS GOON I II III IV

A SAVAGE DOPEBOY I II

HEARTLESS GOON I II III

DRUG LORDS I II III

CUTTHROAT MAFIA

By **Ghost**

LAY IT DOWN **I & II**

LAST OF A DYING BREED

BLOOD STAINS OF A SHOTTA I & II III

By **Jamaica**

LOYAL TO THE GAME I II III

LIFE OF SIN I, II III

By **TJ & Jelissa**

BLOODY COMMAS I & II

SKI MASK CARTEL I II & III

KING OF NEW YORK I II,III IV

RISE TO POWER I II III

COKE KINGS I II III

BORN HEARTLESS I II III

By **T.J. Edwards**

IF LOVING HIM IS WRONG…I & II

LOVE ME EVEN WHEN IT HURTS I II III

By **Jelissa**

WHEN THE STREETS CLAP BACK I & II III

THE HEART OF A SAVAGE I II

By **Jibril Williams**

Anthony Fields

A DISTINGUISHED THUG STOLE MY HEART I II & III
LOVE SHOULDN'T HURT I II III IV
RENEGADE BOYS I II III IV
PAID IN KARMA I II
By **Meesha**
A GANGSTER'S CODE I &, II III
A GANGSTER'S SYN I II III
THE SAVAGE LIFE I II III
CHAINED TO THE STREETS I II
By J-Blunt
PUSH IT TO THE LIMIT
By **Bre' Hayes**
BLOOD OF A BOSS **I, II, III, IV, V**
SHADOWS OF THE GAME
By **Askari**
THE STREETS BLEED MURDER **I, II & III**
THE HEART OF A GANGSTA I II& III
By **Jerry Jackson**
CUM FOR ME I II III IV V
An **LDP Erotica Collaboration**
BRIDE OF A HUSTLA **I II & II**
THE FETTI GIRLS **I, II& III**
CORRUPTED BY A GANGSTA I, II III, IV
BLINDED BY HIS LOVE
THE PRICE YOU PAY FOR LOVE
DOPE GIRL MAGIC
By **Destiny Skai**
WHEN A GOOD GIRL GOES BAD
By **Adrienne**

THE COST OF LOYALTY I II III
By Kweli
A GANGSTER'S REVENGE **I II III & IV**
THE BOSS MAN'S DAUGHTERS I II III IV V
A SAVAGE LOVE **I & II**
BAE BELONGS TO ME I II
A HUSTLER'S DECEIT I, II, III
WHAT BAD BITCHES DO I, II, III
SOUL OF A MONSTER I II III
KILL ZONE
By **Aryanna**
A KINGPIN'S AMBITON
A KINGPIN'S AMBITION **II**
I MURDER FOR THE DOUGH
By **Ambitious**
TRUE SAVAGE I II III IV V VI
DOPE BOY MAGIC I, II
MIDNIGHT CARTEL I II
By **Chris Green**
A DOPEBOY'S PRAYER
By **Eddie "Wolf" Lee**
THE KING CARTEL **I, II & III**
By **Frank Gresham**
THESE NIGGAS AIN'T LOYAL **I, II & III**
By **Nikki Tee**
GANGSTA SHYT **I II &III**
By **CATO**
THE ULTIMATE BETRAYAL
By **Phoenix**

243

BOSS'N UP **I , II & III**

By **Royal Nicole**

I LOVE YOU TO DEATH

By Destiny J

I RIDE FOR MY HITTA

I STILL RIDE FOR MY HITTA

By **Misty Holt**

LOVE & CHASIN' PAPER

By **Qay Crockett**

TO DIE IN VAIN

SINS OF A HUSTLA

By **ASAD**

BROOKLYN HUSTLAZ

By **Boogsy Morina**

BROOKLYN ON LOCK I & II

By **Sonovia**

GANGSTA CITY

By **Teddy Duke**

A DRUG KING AND HIS DIAMOND I & II III

A DOPEMAN'S RICHES

HER MAN, MINE'S TOO I, II

CASH MONEY HO'S

By Nicole Goosby

TRAPHOUSE KING **I II & III**

KINGPIN KILLAZ I II III

STREET KINGS I II

PAID IN BLOOD **I II**

CARTEL KILLAZ I II III

DOPE GODS

By **Hood Rich**

LIPSTICK KILLAH **I, II, III**

CRIME OF PASSION I II & III

By **Mimi**

STEADY MOBBN' **I, II, III**

THE STREETS STAINED MY SOUL

By **Marcellus Allen**

WHO SHOT YA **I, II, III**

SON OF A DOPE FIEND

Renta

GORILLAZ IN THE BAY **I II III IV**

TEARS OF A GANGSTA

DE'KARI

TRIGGADALE I II

Elijah R. Freeman

GOD BLESS THE TRAPPERS I, II, III

THESE SCANDALOUS STREETS I, II, III

FEAR MY GANGSTA I, II, III

THESE STREETS DON'T LOVE NOBODY I, II

BURY ME A G I, II, III, IV, V

A GANGSTA'S EMPIRE I, II, III, IV

THE DOPEMAN'S BODYGAURD

Tranay Adams

THE STREETS ARE CALLING

Duquie Wilson

MARRIED TO A BOSS… I II III

By Destiny Skai & Chris Green

KINGZ OF THE GAME I II III IV

Playa Ray

SLAUGHTER GANG I II III
RUTHLESS HEART I II III
By Willie Slaughter
FUK SHYT
By Blakk Diamond
DON'T F#CK WITH MY HEART I II
By Linnea
ADDICTED TO THE DRAMA I II III
By Jamila
YAYO I II
A SHOOTER'S AMBITION I II
By S. Allen
TRAP GOD
By Troublesome
FOREVER GANGSTA
GLOCKS ON SATIN SHEETS
By Adrian Dulan
TOE TAGZ I II
By Ah'Million
KINGPIN DREAMS
By Paper Boi Rari
CONFESSIONS OF A GANGSTA
By Nicholas Lock
I'M NOTHING WITHOUT HIS LOVE
By Monet Dragun
CAUGHT UP IN THE LIFE
By Robert Baptiste
NEW TO THE GAME I II
By **Malik D. Rice**

Life of a Savage I II

By **Romell Tukes**

LOYALTY AIN'T PROMISED

By Keith Williams

Quiet Money

By **Trai'Quan**

THE STREETS MADE ME

By **Larry D. Wright**

THE ULTIMATE SACRIFICE I, II, III, IV, V

By **Anthony Fields**

THE LIFE OF A HOOD STAR

By Rashia Wilson

Anthony Fields

BOOKS BY LDP'S CEO, CA$H

TRUST IN NO MAN

TRUST IN NO MAN 2

TRUST IN NO MAN 3

BONDED BY BLOOD

SHORTY GOT A THUG

THUGS CRY

THUGS CRY 2

THUGS CRY 3

TRUST NO BITCH

TRUST NO BITCH 2

TRUST NO BITCH 3

TIL MY CASKET DROPS

RESTRAINING ORDER

RESTRAINING ORDER 2

IN LOVE WITH A CONVICT

Coming Soon

BONDED BY BLOOD 2

BOW DOWN TO MY GANGSTA

Anthony Fields

CPSIA information can be obtained
at www.ICGtesting.com
Printed in the USA
BVHW061729250122
627124BV00014B/526